Town in a Strawberry Swirl

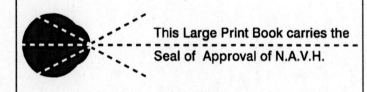

TOWN IN A STRAWBERRY SWIRL

B.B. HAYWOOD

WHEELER PUBLISHING
A part of Gale, Cengage Learning

GALE
CENGAGE Learning®

Farmington Hills, Mich • San Francisco • New York • Waterville, Maine
Meriden, Conn • Mason, Ohio • Chicago

LIBRARY OF CONGRESS CATALOGING-IN-PUBLICATION DATA

Haywood, B. B.
  Town in a strawberry swirl / by B. B. Haywood. — Large print edition.
    pages ; cm. — (A Candy Holliday murder mystery) (Wheeler Publishing large print cozy mystery)
  ISBN 978-1-4104-6898-7 (softcover) — ISBN 1-4104-6898-4 (softcover)
  1. Holliday, Candy (Fictitious character)—Fiction. 2. Missing persons—Fiction. 3. Murder—Investigation—Fiction. 4. Maine—Fiction. 5. Large type books. I. Title.
PS3608.A9874T73 2014
813'.6—dc23   2014016554

Published in 2014 by arrangement with The Berkley Publishing Group, a member of Penguin Group (USA) LLC, a Penguin Random House Company

For Freda

AUTHOR'S NOTE

Those of you who have read more than one book in the Candy Holliday Murder Mystery series will notice an interconnected storyline that runs through all the novels. It's not necessary to have read any prior books in the series to enjoy the one you now hold in your hands. In fact, if you haven't read any of the previous books, this is a good place to start. However, if you *have* read other books in the series, you'll find within these pages a few additional clues to the wider story taking place in Cape Willington, Maine. Many thanks to Mary A. Cook for speed-proofreading and commenting on the manuscript at the last minute, to Teresa Fasolino for once again perfectly capturing the essence of Cape Willington in her cover art, and to family, friends, and fans for continued support. For more information about the Candy Holliday Mysteries

and Holliday's Blueberry Acres, visit holli
daysblueberryacres.com.

PROLOGUE

She felt like a fly suddenly caught in a spider's web.

She backed away, putting some distance between herself and the body, and froze there. She had to take a moment to think, to consider her options — though with all the thoughts racing through her brain, it was difficult to make sense of any of them.

Her first instinct was to flee, to extricate herself from this situation as quickly as possible. She could leave the body where it was at and simply walk away. Drive back to her office, go about her business as usual, pretend none of this had happened. And try to forget what she'd just seen.

She hesitated, though. That was the most attractive choice, but was it the right one?

She could approach the body, put a finger to its wrist and neck, check for a pulse and breathing. But she knew there was no need. From where she stood, the damage looked fairly severe. She wasn't a doctor but she didn't have to be. She averted her eyes, not wanting to look too long, lest it give her nightmares for the rest of the week.

She shifted, maintaining tight control of her emotions. This wasn't the time to panic.

Her eyes fell on the probable murder weapon lying not too far away on the dirt floor of the hoophouse. She dwelt on it for a long moment as her gaze narrowed. Something about it scratched at her senses, making her feel uneasy, but she couldn't determine what it was. She was tempted to take a few steps closer for a better look, but she remained firmly planted to the spot upon which she stood. She was afraid to move a muscle.

The proper thing to do, of course, would be to call the police and report what she'd found. But she dismissed that idea almost instantly. Warning bells were going off inside her brain, almost physically ringing in her ears. Something about this whole scene was wrong. It looked set up — manipulated. How and in what way, she could not tell. But there were too many unknowns, too much to absorb right now.

She knew somehow, instinctively, that if she called the police right now, she'd wind up in jail before lunch.

She had no idea how she'd reached that conclusion but she felt the truth of it in her bones. If the police started asking questions, she'd have no answers for them — at least, none that she wanted to share right now. They'd ask why she'd come out to the berry farm this morning, and why she'd wandered specifically out to the hoophouse. She'd have to tell them about the e-mail, and how she'd been instructed to delete it to avoid leaving a paper trail. They'd grill her about the secret arrangement she'd had with the victim, and the rumors flying around town, which would pull her in even deeper.

It was all too messy to explain. It would make her an immediate suspect.

No, the best course of action, she decided, was to follow her first instinct. Leave this place as quickly as possible. Get in her car, drive out of the parking lot, hurry back to town, lock herself in her office, and wait for someone else to find the body.

She might even want to think about an alibi. Maybe she should take an early lunch, get a salad and a glass of iced tea someplace where she'd be noticed and could be seen reacting to the news in surprise like everyone else when the inevitable discovery happened.

But first she wanted to make sure she

didn't leave any traces of her presence behind. Forensics teams could find evidence in just about anything these days — a clump of dirt, a speck of fabric, a fingernail, the tiniest hair follicle. She had to make it appear as if she'd never been here.

She scoured the area visually, but she hadn't touched anything that she could remember. And she couldn't see any hairs or fibers that might have fallen off her. There wasn't much she could do about that anyway. But there *was* something else she needed to address.

She looked down at her feet. Before she left the car, she'd had the good sense to switch out her new Manolo Blahnik silver sandals for the calf-high black rubber boots she kept in the trunk, in anticipation of situations just like this. Most of her listings were residential homes in nice neighborhoods with paved driveways and concrete walkways, but she handled plenty of farms and rural properties as well. Who knew where a typical day might take her? This little unexpected side trip out to Crawford's Berry Farm was a perfect example. Every day was different. It paid to be prepared.

She'd bought the Manolo Blahniks at the Neiman Marcus store in Copley Square just a few weekends ago, on a two-day shopping spree in Boston to celebrate a big sale. They'd cost her seven hundred dollars. No sense ruining them tromping around a berry farm. It had been a wise decision to make the switch to the rubber boots, given the farm's dirt pathways and occasional muddy patches, like the one she'd encountered just outside.

But the boots left distinctive footprints. She'd have to erase them. How to do that?

Turning, searching for an idea, she spotted an old broom that had somehow made its way out here, leaned up against one corner of the hoophouse. It looked like it had been used to clear out spiderwebs and brush dirt off walls and framework.

Just what she needed.

Forcing herself to move, she crossed to the broom and in short order swept away all her own footprints. She used the broom lightly, brushing loose dirt around, doing her best to disguise the fact that she was tampering with evidence at a crime scene. But it couldn't be helped. It was pure self-preservation at this point.

Once she'd finished her task, she headed outside, down the gentle slope toward the barn, doing her best to keep a low profile as she retraced her steps across the strawberry fields, dashing the broom at the footprints

13

behind her as she went.

Back at the car, she pulled off the rubber boots and tossed them onto the floor behind the driver's seat. After erasing any trace of the final few footprints, she tossed the broom onto the back floor as well, making a mental note to dispose of it as quickly as possible. Still in her stocking feet, she plopped into the driver's seat, closed the door, and started the engine.

In a few moments she'd be free and clear, but these were the tensest ones of all, with a clean escape so close and yet so far. As she closed her fingers around the leather-wrapped steering wheel, she noticed her hands were shaking. She was breathing heavily. For the first time a wave of anxiety threatened to overwhelm her and she began to feel lightheaded, but she fought it down. She swept pale blonde hair back from her thin face and turned to look out the side and rearview windows as she backed up and started off.

So far, so good. The place still looked deserted. But as she gunned the engine and started out the dirt lane toward the main road, she noticed in the distance another vehicle turning in toward the berry farm — an old pickup truck, it looked like.

Doc Holliday's truck, she thought, her

heartbeat spiking at the realization.

She cursed and slammed on the brakes, fighting down her panic. She looked to either side, seeking an escape route, and spotted a farm lane on her right. It led off along a line of low trees, cutting past the berry fields that ran down the slope toward the sea.

Without hesitation, she yanked the steering wheel to the right, gunned the engine, and tore across the fields.

From the *Cape Crier*
Cape Willington, Maine
June 20th Edition

THE CAPE CRUSADER

by Wanda Boyle
Special Correspondent

Flash! The Tale Ripens!
Rumors of the impending sale of Crawford's Berry Farm, located west of Cape Willington out past Blueberry Acres, continue to swirl, with talk of a sweetened deal and juicy backroom glad-handing. We've heard it on good authority that a formal offer has been made for the charming coastal property, and owner Miles Crawford continues to mull his options. However, despite repeated efforts by this reporter to obtain a statement, Miles refuses to confirm or deny any details. Should he sell or shouldn't he? We want to hear your voice, Capers! Sound off!

Strawberry Fair Takes the Cake
With strawberries ripening all around us, red is the official color of the month here in our village, and the juicy berries will take center stage when the first annual Strawberry Fair kicks off in Town Park on

Saturday, June 21st, from ten to four. Sponsored by the newly formed Cape Willington Heritage Protection League as a way to promote the positive aspects of our community, this family event will include booths, activities, live music, and performances, as well as one of our favorite foods — strawberry shortcake! Crawford's Berry Farm will supply all of the strawberries for the event, so you know they'll be the plumpest and juiciest in New England! League co-chairs Cotton Colby and Elvira Tremble promise their Fair will be the fairest of them all, so don't miss this fun-filled event, rain or shine!

(Ahem!) A Pat on Our Own Backs!

The outpouring of support and good wishes we've received since we merged my popular *Cape Crusader* blog with the print and online editions of the *Cape Crier* has been TRE-MEN-DOUS! *Thank you* so much for all the kind comments and suggestions, and keep them coming! By merging Cape Willington's two most popular news and information sources, we're creating one local super-source guaranteed to provide you with all the latest updates, details on community events, and neighborhood profiles on a daily basis! And we're working on a mobile app too, so with all our other social media outlets, you'll have no excuse for not taking us with you wherever you go! There are no flies on us — we're moving too fast!

Time for Tea

Four P.M.? It must be time for tea! We're thrilled to announce the opening of a new tea shop in Cape Willington! The Red Clover, owned and operated by Kate and Paul Ashley, opened its doors for business at the end of May. They specialize in herbal teas, and make many of their own blends. I have personally taste-tested several myself, and they're scrumptious! The Ashleys also offer black, red, green, and white teas (how colorful!), along with homemade baked goods. There's even Wi-Fi in the shop, so your gadgets can come along with you. Drink tea! Show your support! We want this shop to stay!

For the Birds — and Bird Lovers!

Who hasn't seen Doris Oaks around town with Roy? They are partners for life . . . Roy being Doris's pet parrot! Doris tells us she bought Roy on eBay a few months ago as a way to relieve her winter boredom, and it worked! No more boredom!

Doris and Roy are now one of our favorite new couples! They regularly volunteer at the Cape Willington Historical Society and Museum out at the English Point Lighthouse, and you also might spot them at yard sales around town. It seems Roy has an insatiable appetite for small hard plastic toys, so Doris's new full-time job is finding an endless supply for him. At least she's getting them at bargain prices! They say couples begin to look alike after a while. Maybe that's why Doris can be easily spotted these days in her bright green and orange plumage! It's nice to see birds of a feather flocking together!

Another Happy Couple Takes a Spin
This romantic "I do" will send you spinning. Kate Birch and Pete Barkely (of snowplow fame), both from Cape Willington, wed on June 10th at the Cape Laundromat over in Fowler's Corner. Pete thought Kate was nice because she found him an empty dryer for his wet clothes, and then he only had eyes for her the whole time his clothes were in the dryer. He finally got up the nerve to ask for her phone number, and the rest is romantic history. Kate says Pete is her green-eyed dream come true — and he knows how to

do his own laundry! He's a keeper!

Tasty Tidbits

If you love the Strawberry Fair and want to try growing your own strawberries, Finch's Garden Center has an abundance of berry plants for sale. Plus, they're offering an ongoing session on how to plant, grow, and harvest the berries. So what are you waiting for? Get yourself over there! It's well worth the time and effort. . . . The library knitting group will be knitting with *what*? That's right — plastic grocery bags! They'll teach you how to transform your plastic bags (the kind we're not supposed to use anymore) into yarn-like strips, which you can then use to knit a great-looking tote bag. Now that's recycling at its prettiest! The knitting group meets every Thursday evening at 7:00 at the Pruitt Public Library. Everyone is welcome, and beginner knitters are encouraged to attend. . . . July will be Decorate Cape Willington Month, so get out your best lawn ornaments and start decorating the great outdoors! Anything goes, from Margaritte Jordan's giant wooden blueberry pie (which a tourist offered to buy from her last summer!) to Walter Gruther's hundreds of plastic

21

smiley-face clams and lobsters. Let's decorate the town like nothing ever seen before!

Official Judicious F. P. Bosworth sightings for the first two weeks of June:

Visible: 7 days
Invisible: 7 days

We'd sure love to see you more than half the time, Judicious!

ONE

As Henry "Doc" Holliday pulled his old pickup truck to a stop in the makeshift parking lot near the barn and farmhouse, he wondered where everyone was at.

The berry farm looked suspiciously deserted, especially on this sunny Thursday morning in late June, when the brief but bountiful strawberry-picking season was in full swing along Maine's Downeast coast.

Where were all the people?

Where was Miles?

Doc squinted out through the windshield at the fields in front of him — six or eight of them all told, including two strawberry patches about an acre and a half each in size, a large vegetable garden with separate plots for pumpkins and squash, and separate raspberry and blueberry patches, as well as a small apple orchard and even a few cherry trees, all artfully arranged along a prime piece of fertile coastline that had been farmland for as long as anyone could remember — then he shifted his gaze off to his left.

From where he sat, Doc had a magnificent view past the farmhouse, through a stand of trees, and down a long, gradual slope to an expanse of sea that stretched all the way to the horizon, shimmering like pale blue diamonds in the morning light.

He turned back toward the barn and fields with a frown. *It sure is a pretty piece of land,* Doc thought, and he wondered, not for the first time, if all the rumors about an impending sale of the berry farm were true. He had difficulty believing it himself. Why would Miles Crawford want to give up this small slice of paradise, especially with that stunning ocean view?

Given the time of year, Doc had expected the parking lot to be full. But a handwritten sign nearby, nailed to a stake stuck into the ground at the front edge of the nearest field, explained the lack of patrons:

NO BERRY PICKING TODAY, it read.

Doc tilted his head thoughtfully as he shut off the engine. He supposed the fields were closed today to give the berries a little more time to ripen, and the warm, sunny morning would certainly help. They'd had a snowy March and a cool, rainy spring, and everyone in the village was hoping this was the beginning of a warming trend.

Doc climbed out of the cab and stood for a few moments beside the truck, hands stuck in the back pockets of his chinos. He stretched dramatically as he surveyed the property with a discerning gaze. The place was as neat as ever. Miles obviously took great pride in it. The tractor was in its shed. A glance inside the barn revealed neatly arranged tools, a well-organized workbench, tidy stacks of supplies. The patch of grass around the house had been mowed recently. Nary a stray leaf spotted the graveled driveway.

The fields were equally well tended, and some were already beginning to yield. Rhubarb had come first, a couple of weeks earlier, followed by strawberries, which would be available into early July. After that would come raspberries, blueberries, tomatoes, and corn, before they headed deep into harvest and apple-picking season, ending with pumpkins and squash.

It was the circle of life here in coastal Maine, Doc thought as he ambled toward the barn.

Just the way he liked it.

"Hey, Miles!" he called out. "You around?"

He received no answer.

Miles Crawford wasn't necessarily the most sociable type. He'd been out here at Crawford's Berry Farm for the better part of thirty years, at least as far as Doc knew. The place was only a few miles west of Blueberry Acres, where Doc lived with his daughter, Candy. They were all part of the same small agricultural community. Naturally Doc and Miles had run into each other at the same farm stores and supply centers, nodded to each other at meetings and events, waved a finger or two when they'd driven past each other on the road. But for some reason they'd never taken the time to strike up a conversation and get know each other better. Miles just seemed to prefer to be off on his own. Some Mainers were like that.

But they also could be helpful and informative when asked. A few weeks earlier, when Doc had been talking to Candy about the possibility of making some upgrades to Blueberry Acres, he'd mentioned some of the things Miles had done over the years out here at the berry farm — such as putting in the cherry trees, and building commercial-grade hoophouses. Miles had two of them. Hoophouses were Quonset hut–style greenhouses made from hoop-shaped steel tubing covered with double plastic sheeting instead of glass or corrugated steel. The endwalls usually consisted of wood frames, also covered with plastic sheeting, with a door at each end. Typically hoophouses were sixteen feet wide, eight feet high at the central point, and twenty or twenty-five feet in length. A mechanical heating and ventilating system kept the temperature inside to around seventy degrees. There were a few design variations, with some of the hoophouses peaked along the roof. But no matter their size or style, they could greatly extend the growing season here in Maine — even make it a year-round activity.

A couple of years earlier, Doc had read in an organic agricultural journal that a single hoophouse could bring in an additional income of ten thousand dollars a year. That got him to thinking. One or two of those, he realized, and they could greatly diversify their crops to supplement their annual blueberry yield. They could start seeds while it was still cold outside, have crops earlier, and get their revenue streams going quicker. They could branch out to things like early tomatoes, peppers, lettuce, cucumbers, herbs, even flowers. And they could work with the local co-op, which would distribute their products to other wholesale and retail outlets across the region.

It was, Doc thought, a very appealing idea.

He had planned on calling Miles to ask about his hoophouses, to get some idea of what was involved in putting one up, but by chance they'd run into each other at Gumm's Hardware Store in town a week earlier. They'd started talking, Doc had asked a few questions, and Miles had extended an invitation to visit on this Thursday morning for a walkthrough of both hoophouses.

So here was Doc. But no Miles in sight.

Doc surveyed his surroundings a few more moments, then ambled tentatively to the open barn door. He peered inside, just to make sure Miles wasn't working away quietly and obliviously in some dark back corner of the building. But the place was empty and silent. Not a stray scrap of paper. Not a bale of hay or a bag of topsoil out of place. Not a mouse or a barn cat. Strangely untouched, like a carefully preserved museum. And a little unsettling.

Doc scratched his head. Surely Miles had to be around here somewhere. Had Doc mixed up the date or time?

He turned back toward the house and squinted against the reflecting sunlight off the windows. A white late-model truck and an older green station wagon were parked to one side of the building. Doc had seen both vehicles many times before, while passing Miles on the road.

His vehicles were here. So where was Miles?

Probably in one of the back fields, Doc guessed, so he moved on, circling around the side of the barn and heading back along the vegetable garden, which occupied a fairly large plot between the barn and the house. He moved with his usual lopsided gait, the result of an injury while bicycling many years ago. But he'd never let it slow him down.

He followed a path that led out past the barn to the edge of the first strawberry patch, where he stopped and studied the landscape again. A breeze blew down from the northwest, tousling his gray hair, but he barely noticed. From here he could see the small maple sugaring house, off in the woods behind the house, and he had a better view of the second strawberry patch, toward the west, and the two hoophouses that bracketed it.

Perhaps that's where Miles is, in one of the hoophouses, Doc thought, and he started off again toward the closest one. When he

29

reached it, he peered inside and then entered hesitantly.

Less than a minute later he emerged, his face white, covered in a sheen of sweat. He was moving quickly now, hopping along as best he could, heading toward the house, until he remembered he was carrying a cell phone with him.

He cursed himself for his forgetfulness as he stopped and fished it out of his pocket. He fumbled it a bit, out of breath, as he flipped it open. He'd never upgraded to one of those fancy smart phones like his daughter had. He preferred the old tried-and-true technology of five years ago. It worked just fine for his purposes.

With fumbling fingers, he pressed out the keys 9-1-1 on the phone, then hit the send button. He held the phone to his ear and waited while it rang at the other end of the line, his mind racing.

Miles Crawford, he thought. *It can't be possible. . . .*

When a voice answered the call, asking the nature of his emergency, Doc said, in as clear a tone as he could manage, "You'd better connect me with the police. This is Henry Holliday. I'm out at Crawford's Berry Farm. I think there's been a murder."

TWO

"Wait until you see what Herr Georg has cooked up this time!" Maggie Tremont said as she came breezing through the doorway that led to the bakery shop's kitchen in the back. Her hair was up in a net and her arms were lightly dusted with flour. "He's outdone himself! You'll be amazed."

Candy Holliday dropped into a vacant chair at a small oak table by the front window, set her tote bag down at her feet, and tilted her head upward, sniffing the aromas. "Let me guess. Something with strawberries?"

"Fresh from the berry farm," Maggie confirmed happily. "Miles Crawford dropped them off first thing this morning. You should see how plump and juicy they are. I don't know what he does out at that farm of his, but whatever it is, it's working. He grows the biggest, tastiest berries in the region."

"I bet Herr Georg had a field day with those."

"He's had the ovens fired up all morning. And the place has been hopping ever since we opened. We had lines out the door an hour ago. This is the first lull today. Tea?"

Without waiting for an answer, Maggie scooted behind the counter just as several more customers entered the shop, setting off a tingling bell over the door. She greeted them with a smile and a wave as she busied herself with cups, saucers, and teapots. "Welcome to the Black Forest Bakery," she said lightly as she worked. "If this is your first time here, we have pastries, cakes, and other fresh-baked goods in the glass display cases, and imported packaged items on the shelves and counters around the shop. We can also ship just about anywhere in the country. Are you folks from around here?"

As is turned out, the customers were from New York, which led to a discussion about home states, local destinations, cars, hotels, traveling with kids, strawberry-picking season, the weather, the latest meet-up of the Yankees and the Red Sox, the new sports shop down the street, several other new businesses in town, some of the places up and down the street where Maggie had worked previously, like the dry cleaner's and the old Stone & Milbury insurance agency, and finally her own current situation.

"I've only been working here for three weeks, and I love it!" Maggie exclaimed as she brought out a tea tray for Candy. She set down the teapot, two delicate cups, silverware, a sugar bowl, and a small plate of baked goodies, but left Candy to pour as she hurried back to her duties behind the counter. "I've learned so much!" she continued, barely taking a moment to breathe. "And Herr Georg, our baker, has just been wonderful to work with. Perhaps you've heard of him? He's very passionate about what he does. He's such a sweetheart too. And so talented! He made these strawberry tarts this morning. You really should try one. They're guaranteed to melt in your mouth. Here, I'll get you a sample. . . ."

Five minutes later, with the customers happily settled at a nearby table, Maggie dropped into the chair opposite Candy. "I hate to sit in front of customers but I just need a minute off my feet," she said, raising her legs and wiggling her toes inside her sneakers. "I've been up since six A.M.! I'm not used to these baker's hours."

"They rise before the sun, I know," Candy said, the voice of experience. She had worked part-time at Herr Georg's bakery for the past few years, until she'd had to give it up because of time constraints. "So you seem pretty happy here. I assume everything's working out okay with the new job?"

"It's the best thing that's ever happened to me," Maggie said, suddenly earnest as she leaned in close to her friend and spoke in low tones. "I feel like I have a new lease on life. And Herr Georg has been so helpful! He's taught me all sorts of things. And I'm getting pretty good at it. I'm thinking of making a career out of this — if I can get used to the hours!"

Candy patted her hand. "You'll be fine. I'm just glad everything worked out the way it did."

"Well, if it hadn't been for you, I wouldn't be here now."

"I hated to leave, but I had no choice," Candy admitted, a bit wistfully as she looked around the shop. "I couldn't do both jobs — well, three jobs, if you count the farm. I loved working for Herr Georg, but things just got too crazy over at the newspaper. You know what it's like. It's been that way ever since Ben left town."

She paused, and for a moment her heart skipped a beat at the mention of his name. She hadn't thought about Ben Clayton in a while — well, at least in a day or two.

Could she still be missing him after all this time?

Ben was the former editor of the *Cape Crier,* the village's local paper. He had held the job for several years, and he'd hired Candy as the publication's community correspondent. But a little more than eighteen months ago he had resigned abruptly and moved out West. Since then, there'd been two other editors at the *Crier.* One had lasted five months, the other seven. Owing to the frequent personnel changes and resulting confusion in the office, the paper lost its focus and some of its steam. Sales dropped, and there were rumors they'd be shut down. But right after the beginning of the year a regional media conglomerate based in Portland had unexpectedly purchased the *Crier* and given it new breath. They'd also asked Candy to take over temporarily as interim editor until they brought in a new full-time editor and publisher.

After giving it a lot of thought, she'd agreed to step into Ben's old shoes, though somewhat reluctantly — she still had a blueberry farm to run, she frequently reminded herself — but her father had insisted she grab the opportunity, and she had come to enjoy her job at the paper. It was more work than she'd expected, no doubt, but it also had its exciting moments, and its rewarding ones as well. And fortunately, thanks to a few editorial changes she'd made, she'd managed to stabilize sales and even increase circulation, which gained the attention of the head office.

She'd been the paper's interim editor for more than five months now, with no idea of how much longer she'd be doing the job. So for the time being, she was sitting in Ben's old chair, working at his computer, just trying to get the paper out on schedule. She'd had some trepidation about the job at first, wondering if she might be getting in over her head, but she soon found that she'd learned a lot from Ben while working with him. She'd located some of his old schedules and editorial planners, which helped her get things back on track. She'd also managed to resolve some budget issues, and found that she could hire a few extra freelance writers to help her create copy for the now-biweekly publication.

Still, it was a lot of work, and took her away from the farm, which worried her. She knew there were other things she should be doing instead of sitting in an office all day typing away at a computer — things like yanking weeds out of the vegetable garden or walking the blueberry fields with a sweep net, checking for spanworms and flea beetles. Or clearing out that thin patch of woods at the top of the ridge west of the farmhouse, so they could expand their fields — or leveling out the spot behind the barn where they planned to build a hoophouse, possibly this fall, right after harvest, if they could put the money together. . . .

"Well," Maggie said, bringing her back to the moment, "if you hadn't recommended me for this job, I probably wouldn't be here."

"Then it all worked out for the best. This is a perfect match for you," Candy said, "and Herr Georg obviously loves having you around. Besides, he needs someone who can work here more than two days a week, like I did. And with the paper and the farm, I just didn't have the extra time."

"I know!" Maggie said, brightening. "I'm up to almost twenty-five hours a week now, and I'm learning a trade. All thanks to you." She raised her teacup, gently clinked it against Candy's, and together they sipped.

"So," Candy said after a few moments as her nose caught some disparate scents, causing her to crane her head around, "what exactly *is* Herr Georg cooking up back there?"

Maggie gave her a look of mock surprise. "You mean the Great Detective hasn't figured it out yet?" She smiled slyly at her friend. "You used to work for him, so you're familiar with a lot of his recipes, right? And you used to be a pretty good detective. Why don't you take a guess?"

"*Used* to be?" Candy's arched an eyebrow at the challenge. "Think I need help sharpening my detecting skills?"

Maggie gave her an innocent look. "Well, it *has* been a while since we've had any excitement around here, hasn't it? Not since . . . well, not since your fortieth birthday party, if I remember correctly — right around the time Ben left town. So yes, you probably could use the practice. Consider it professional training." She placed her feet firmly on the ground, planted an elbow on the table before her, placed her chin in an upturned palm, and said in a challenging tone, "So, what do *you* think he's making?"

"I think," Candy said as her cornflower blue eyes twinkled devilishly, "that I detect a hint of cinnamon."

Maggie scrunched up her nose. "You have to be more specific. What else?"

"Well, let me see." Candy closed her eyes, crossed her arms, leaned back in her chair, and inhaled deeply. After a moment, with her eyes still shut, she said, "The most obvious possibility is a strawberry shortcake, but that seems too simple for Herr Georg. So is a traditional strawberry pie — although I'm sure he'll make both of those before the week is out. But I'd expect something a little fancier from him." She paused a moment, still sniffing the air. "He could be making a strawberry Black Forest cake, which is scrumptious, but I don't think he uses cinnamon in that. So my guess is it's some type of *obstkuchen* — a torte or multilayered cake, using some type of fruit — in this case strawberries, of course. And maybe with a few tablespoons of cinnamon sugar added in?" She opened her eyes and raised an eyebrow. "So how'd I do?"

Maggie looked impressed. "I guess you haven't lost your detecting skills at all."

"And there's something else too. Home-made whipped cream?"

"Key lime strawberry whipped cream," Maggie admitted, letting out a breath, as if she'd been deflated. "You must have peeked!"

"Actually," Candy said with a sly smile, "he made it two years ago when I worked here. And if I remember correctly, it was fantastic. I can't wait to taste it again."

As if on cue, Herr Georg Wolfsburger, the mustachioed proprietor of the Black Forest Bakery, emerged from the back kitchen carrying a glass platter high in the air, held up by his splayed fingers. On it was the strawberry *obstkuchen.*

"Ah, Candy, *meine liebchen,* here you are," the baker said to her with a toothy grin. "I thought I heard your voice. You are here just in time to taste my latest creation!"

It was almost too pretty to eat, still warm from the oven and topped by a circle of small, perfectly ripened berries set delicately into the whipped cream.

Maggie was right. Miles Crawford grew the most beautiful berries this side of the Mississippi.

Herr Georg cut a delicate slice for her, topped it with a dollop of whipped cream and a strawberry, and set it down in front of her. She was just about to dig in when she was distracted by the sound of a siren. A moment later, her cell phone rang in her back pocket.

It was her father.

She listened to his latest news in shock, her face turning pale. When she finally lowered the phone and keyed off the call, she stared out the window into the distance for a few moments, shaking her head. "I can't believe it. We were just talking about him."

"Talking about who, honey?" Maggie asked, concern evident in her tone.

Candy looked over at her friend, and then up at Herr Georg. She could hardly find the words to tell them what she'd just learned.

"That was my dad on the phone. He found a dead body in the hoophouse out at the berry farm."

Her mouth had gone completely dry. She had to stop for a moment before she continued. "It's Miles Crawford."

THREE

Maggie's hand went to her mouth in an involuntary gesture. Disbelief showed in her wide brown eyes. "Oh no, that can't be true. Not Miles. He's too good a person."

Herr Georg looked equally stunned. "But how can this be possible? What you're saying is inconceivable. It's preposterous. It's . . . it's . . ." He sputtered, unable to find more words to express his feelings. But his face turned a blustery red, evidence of his sudden distress. It made his white mustache and eyebrows stand out more prominently on his face. "Surely there must be some mistake," he said after a few moments. "Perhaps it was an inaccurate report, or a case of mistaken identity, or a hideous prank. . . ."

Again his voice trailed off as another thought came to him. "But if this is true, and Miles really is gone, what does that mean for his customers? What will happen to the farm? Who will take care of the strawberries?" The baker shook his head, unable to absorb all the ramifications of this shocking bit of news. "Oh my, I hope it's not true. For his sake, and for ours."

"I agree with you on that," Candy said, sharing his concerns, "but Dad sounded pretty definite about what he saw in that hoophouse."

"And what exactly did he see?" Maggie asked, still holding on to a faint hope. "Could he have been mistaken, like Herr Georg said? Maybe a false report?"

Candy took a few moments to think back over her conversation with her father, but before she could respond, they heard a second siren, closer than the first but headed in the same direction — away from them, out of town.

Candy knew exactly what it meant. "The police are responding to the call," she said softly, as if that settled the matter.

And it did. The sound of the sirens suddenly made it real for them.

"Dad must have been right. There's been another murder."

Falling into silence, all three of them leaned closer to the front window and looked out, turning their gazes northward, up along the gentle curve of Main Street,

43

though they couldn't see the police station from their vantage point. It was located just outside of town, up on Route 1, also known as the Coastal Loop. But they could see much of the rest of the village. The place had a festive feel today, probably due in part to the warmer weather. Flags and streamers flew from posts and lights, and signs in shop windows announced early-season sales and special summer deals. It was a colorful scene.

The summer season wouldn't kick into high gear until after the Fourth of July, but late June always brought an early wave of tourists and travelers from places such as New York and New Jersey, Pennsylvania and Massachusetts and Connecticut, who spent a few days or perhaps a week unwinding here along Maine's rugged Downeast coastline. They soaked in the smells of the sea, the sights and sounds of the busy working village, and the warmth of the intensifying sunshine as they peered into shop windows, licked at ice cream cones, chewed on warm fudge or freshly baked pastries, and chatted with family, friends, and strangers.

Not surprisingly, no one seemed at all distracted by the sirens fading into the distance. The normal sounds of the village returned. Life went on as usual.

But not for Miles Crawford.

Candy felt a rising intensity in her chest, a signal that she was needed elsewhere. She leaned over, picked up her tote bag, and rose. "I have to go. Dad might need my help. Besides, I'm the editor of the paper now. I guess I have a new front page story to write. Time to get back to work."

Maggie offered to go with her, and Herr Georg as well, for moral support. "We'll close down the shop if we have to," the baker told her, meaning every word.

But Candy shook her head. "I'm not sure what will happen when I get out there. I'm not even sure they'll let me get close to the place. You're better off staying here. I'll drop by a little later on and fill you in on all the details."

Moments later she was out the door and headed up the street to her old Jeep Cherokee, which she'd parked near the diner. As she went, she brushed back her honey-colored hair and glanced at her watch. It was almost ten thirty. The streets were busy with traffic and pedestrians. But she hardly noticed any of it.

Her mind was a swirl of thoughts and emotions. Her first concern was for her father. If what he had told her on the phone was true, and he had indeed found a body in the hoophouse out at Crawford's Berry Farm, then the police would be involved, and Doc would be tied up for hours. There would be questions and statements, reports and documentation, photographs and fingerprints. She didn't want him to go through that alone. He had turned seventy earlier in the year. He wasn't a young man anymore. Who knew how something like this might affect him?

But she also knew he wasn't easily rattled. Henry Holliday was good old Maine stock. He could take care of himself. He knew how to handle these types of situations, since he'd been indirectly involved with a few of them over the years. If he really had found a body, he'd approach it the same way he approached everything else in life — with common sense, professionalism, and toughness.

Her thoughts turned to the town next, and how it might be affected by another death, this time of a fairly prominent and well-established local citizen. Herr Georg was right, she knew, as much as she hated to think that way right now — what would happen to the berry farm and strawberry crop if Miles was gone? Would the berry-picking operations continue? Would his relatives take over? He'd been divorced and living alone for a while, Candy knew. She thought he had a couple of kids, though she had never met them and didn't know their names. What would they do with the place? Would they put it up for sale, fulfilling the rumors swirling around town? And what would happen to it after that? Would the berry farm still be there in a year or two?

According to the rumors — which were completely unsubstantiated at this point, as far as Candy knew, and despite what Wanda Boyle had written in her column in the latest issue of the paper — some sort of real estate conglomerate had designs on the farm. Whispers around town said they planned to do away with the farmhouse, barn, and fields, and turn the property into some sort of upscale resort. It made sense, given the location and magnificent ocean views, but Candy had a hard time believing Miles Crawford would ever sell the place. He seemed entrenched out there.

But could there be a shred of truth to the rumors? Something that led to his apparent death?

Candy had to admit she didn't know the answers to any of those questions, for she didn't know much about Miles himself. He'd had a family out there once, she knew, but they'd all left. He ran the place pretty much by himself now. Maybe it had just become too much for him.

She'd occasionally seen Miles around town, and had always thought of him as a solitary person, though he seemed relatively content. And he'd done wonders with his farm, working primarily alone. She was struck by the thought that if Doc hadn't come along when he had and found the body, Miles might have lain there for days before someone stumbled across him.

There were other questions and concerns in her mind, including the obvious one:

If Miles really had been murdered, who could have done it?

She shivered at the thought that it might well have been someone local. That made the most sense, she knew. Everyone around town was talking about the rumored sale. Maybe someone didn't want that to happen.

But who?

She could think of several people.

Which brought her to today, and the two meetings she had scheduled for this afternoon: one with Mason Flint, the chairman of the town council, and the other with members of a newly formed civic group, the Cape Willington Heritage Protection League. The meetings were an hour apart, starting at one o'clock. She'd scheduled them that way on purpose, in an effort to keep them to a manageable length of no more than forty-five minutes each. She needed to be back on her computer by mid-afternoon, so she could finish up a couple hours of work before heading home to Blueberry Acres to do a few chores and make dinner with her father.

But the day had become suddenly complicated, and she wasn't sure what the rest of the morning or the afternoon would bring.

As she hurried along Main Street, weaving around strolling couples and families, those two meetings began to weigh heavily on her thoughts, especially the one with the members of the Cape Willington Heritage Protection League. Currently the league consisted of five women, who were very vocal about their concern not only for village's heritage, but also for its reputation. They believed a number of unfortunate events over the past few years had cast a bad light on the community. Cape Willington's image as a quintessential New England coastal village was threatened, they'd concluded. Somebody had to do something about it or risk permanent damage to the village's character and reputation. So the ladies had started appearing at town council meetings, where they'd made their opinions heard. They wrote letters to the editor and hung up signs in shop windows and on bulletin boards at public buildings. They held meetings in a conference room at the library and requested audiences with prominent individuals around town, including members of the wealthy Pruitt family, requesting everyone's support.

Over the past six months or so, they'd gone a step further, sponsoring events that promoted a positive image. The largest and most recent was the upcoming Strawberry Fair, a community get-together they'd planned for the upcoming Saturday afternoon in Town Park. It would be a relatively low-key affair, unlike some of the town's bigger events, such as the Blueberry Festival, the Lobster Stew Cook-off, the Memorial Day Parade, and the Pumpkin Bash. There would be booths and activities, food tables, a strawberry pie baking contest, pony rides, and a farm animal petting area, as well as music and performances. They promised a fun, colorful event for all ages, one that celebrated the town's history and heritage — and they wanted to make sure it was properly covered by the newspaper. They were campaigning for a front page story in the *Crier.*

That was the alleged purpose of this afternoon's meeting. But Candy suspected there was more to it. She sensed the ladies of the league wanted something else from her — perhaps an editorial coming out against the sale of the berry farm, or something like that.

At least she knew what Mason Flint wanted. The chairman of the town council had made no bones about his reason for wanting to meet with her: He wanted her help in quashing any rumors swirling around town about the sale of the berry farm. He'd already told her as much over the phone yesterday morning, when he'd called her himself to schedule the face-to-face in his office.

"As far as I can tell, there's absolutely no truth to these rumors," he'd said. "It's bad for business. Those ladies of this so-called 'protection league' are just stirring things up for the sake of stirring things up. I need your help in calming them down. We need to smooth this whole thing over before the tourists arrive in full force for the Fourth of July. We don't need any trouble in town right now."

So Candy found herself being pulled in both directions, while fighting deadlines and doing her best to get ready for the harvest out at Blueberry Acres, which would start in earnest in about a month. That's why she'd stopped in at the Black Forest Bakery for a cup of tea and a quick sit-down with Maggie. She'd needed a few moment's respite from the hectic pace of the busy season.

Unfortunately, those moments had been fleeting.

Her thoughts angled back to the meetings. They were certainly important. But by the time she reached the Jeep and climbed inside, she'd decided to cancel both.

She dropped her tote bag onto the passenger seat and pulled her phone out of the back pocket of her jeans. She swiped and poked at the screen, calling up her contacts, searching for Mason Flint's number. But before she made the call, she hesitated.

Was she overreacting? Maybe Maggie and Herr Georg were right about the alleged death of Miles Crawford. Maybe it really was just a false report, or a case of mistaken identity, or simply a hoax or a prank of some sort. Maybe Doc was being misled. Or maybe, if Miles really was dead, it hadn't been murder at all, but a farm accident of some sort. Maybe he'd even died of natural causes. He couldn't be more than sixty years old, but unfortunately those things happened all the time. It would be tragic, yes, but it wouldn't be as earth-shattering as a murder.

Perhaps she should wait, and find out what really happened before she stirred things up more than they already were. Better to learn the facts first, rather than jumping to conclusions.

She reconsidered her decision about the meetings. She'd already delayed the meeting with the league members once, last week, citing deadline issues. If she called off the meeting today, she knew it would cause trouble. Same thing with Mason Flint. Although genteel on the surface, he could be tenacious when he wanted something. He wouldn't let her easily escape a meeting about something that mattered to him, especially if the town was involved.

Without making any calls, she keyed off her phone, dropped it onto the seat beside her, and started the engine. Glancing over her shoulder, she backed out of her parking spot and headed south on Main Street. Traffic was congested in Cape Willington's small downtown, and it took her a few minutes to reach the red light at the southern end of the street. She waited in line with other vehicles before making a right-hand turn onto the Coastal Loop, hoping for the best

but prepared for the worst as she headed
out toward Crawford's Berry Farm.

FOUR

Leaving the village behind, Candy joined a stream of cars that followed the narrow two-lane road as it meandered along the coastline, winding past beach cabins, gray-sided bungalows, an occasional barn, and a few old open-mouthed garages that stored ancient lawn furniture and unused croquet sets, garden hoses, and old car parts. The road curved around a shallow inlet and dipped through a low spot beside the ocean before rising through a stand of thin pines and coastal shrubbery, still showing some of its spring green, though the color would wash out to a dull gray-green by mid-summer.

In short order most of the cars in front of her slowed and pulled into dusty dirt driveways, or angled off onto side lanes, so that by the time she reached the turnoff on the right that led to Blueberry Acres, she had the road mostly to herself. Rather than head toward home, she continued straight ahead, along the coast, as she checked her watch again and nudged up the needle on the speedometer, though it was hard to get any vehicle much above forty or fifty miles an hour on these back rural roads.

The morning was surprisingly bright and clear. Spring in Maine was a tenuous thing, or so Doc had told her on numerous occasions. At times it played havoc with the crops. April could often be warm — into the seventies or even eighties — causing plants to send out early shoots and buds, cautiously testing the weather. But May could easily turn cold and rainy, and the overcast days could carry on for weeks without a break. The sun would disappear from the sky and the crops would become dormant, caught mid-bud, awaiting the return of spring warmth, which never quite seemed to arrive. Cabin fever often set in. If they were lucky, spring would finally show up around Memorial Day, when they'd dip their toes into the cold ocean water for a few moments to officially welcome the season.

Weather like that made her appreciate days like this even more. For the past week or two they'd had mostly warm sunny days, cool nights, and a reasonable amount of rain, often at night — good for growing berries. The fields out at Blueberry Acres were ripening nicely, and they'd have a good crop this year, which they needed.

Miles had obviously had a similar good year out at the berry farm, from reports she'd heard. She'd been so busy over the past few weeks, she hadn't had a chance to stop by to chat with him yet, though it had been on her agenda for a while. She'd just never managed to get around to it. Now she regretted not taking the time to visit him.

But she also knew the real reason she'd continually postponed her visits. Miles was a true, no-nonsense Mainer, and could be a tough nut to crack when he wanted to be. Under the bill of a faded orange ball cap with an agricultural logo on it, his weathered face was usually placid and unreadable, and he excelled at using short sentences that consisted primarily of words such as *yup* and *nope* and an occasional *ayuh* thrown in just for the fun of it. You had to patiently tap at that crusty Maine veneer and phrase your questions properly to communicate with him in any real way.

Candy was used to dealing with stoic farmers like Miles. She ran into a lot of them, being a farmer herself, though she was still relatively new to the vocation. The best way to deal with them, she'd discovered, was simply to match her own cadence to theirs, give them some space, and wait them out. Eventually they'd reward you with a few golden nuggets of information. It just took time and patience.

But those two commodities had been in short supply lately, as her life grew increasingly busy owing to her work at the paper, so she'd never managed to swing by the berry farm to exchange pleasantries with Miles. Now she was finally visiting him — but not under the conditions she ever thought possible. . . .

Shocked back to the moment, she saw the oncoming car seconds before it was about to hit her. It came screeching out of a turnoff just ahead on the right, its tail end spinning around as it twisted in her direction. It came right at her, straddling the center of the road, rocking back and forth a little on its springs as it settled into the road. Gaining speed, it hurtled toward her with no signs of slowing.

Candy felt every nerve and cell erupt inside her. Her survival instincts took over as she yanked the steering wheel to the right and jammed both feet onto the brake pedal.

The Jeep rattled and the brakes squealed as the tires bit and the right side dropped off the asphalt. The Jeep bounced up and then thumped down viciously before coming back up again, tossing her hard against the seat belt. She tightened her grip on the steering wheel as the tires jounced around and the vehicle fully left the road, dropping down onto the narrow shoulder. The front wheels caught a rut and tried to pull her into the trees on her right, but she instinctively turned the steering wheel in the other direction. The back tires would have slid out from underneath her had it not been for the vehicle's four-wheel-drive system, which gave her the grip she needed. It kept her going in the right direction as the oncoming car — a low-slung silver sports car with a black convertible top, which was up and in place — shot past her in a blur and a swoosh of sound.

Candy had the driver's side window open halfway and could feel the cone of air pushed aside by the speeding vehicle. It rushed through the opening and tossed around her hair. She might have made some sort of sound, a yelp maybe, but she wasn't quite sure. Maybe the sound had come from somewhere else — the Jeep or the other vehicle as it roared past.

Candy kept her gaze focused straight ahead as the Jeep slowed, but from the corner of her eye she caught a glimpse of the person behind the wheel of the silver sports car. An image flashed in Candy's mind and seemed to freeze there for a few moments: a wraith-thin woman with bleach-blonde hair, dressed all in black, bejeweled fingers gripping the black leather-wrapped steering wheel, bright red lipstick against a smooth, pale face, partially hidden behind huge silver-rimmed sunglasses.

Then the image was gone in a wisp of colors, and the silver convertible was gone too, disappearing behind her in a ricochet of sound. A moment later the vehicle re-appeared in a smaller version in Candy's rearview mirror, but it quickly shrank into the gray distance.

With a spray of dirt and pebbles, the Jeep came to an abrupt stop on the rough shoul-der of the road. Candy allowed herself to be thrown forward a little in the seat belt before pulling herself back. She started breathing again, not realizing she had stopped.

She shook her head in disbelief. Her ears were ringing from the shock of the close call. She took a few more breaths to calm herself, fingers still clutched tightly on the steering wheel. She noticed that her knuck-les had turned bone white.

She forced herself to loosen her grip and, after a few more moments, put one hand on her chest. She could feel her strongly beating heart.

Finally she turned around and looked back over her shoulder.

There was no sign of the silver convertible that had literally run her off the road. Just empty asphalt and a dissipating cloud of dust caught in the sunlight, drifting off with the sea breeze.

Candy turned back in the other direction, forward again, focusing in the side lane just ahead, from which the silver sports car had burst seconds earlier.

A small red-and-white sign stood out amid the foliage by the side of the road. It was attached to a stake planted deeply into the ground. A red arrow pointed to the right. Above the arrow she read the words, CRAWFORD'S BERRY FARM — TURN HERE.

Candy's brow tightened as her gaze angled to the right, in the direction of the berry farm. She shook her head.

Why would someone come speeding out of that road?

But there was more. She had not only recognized the driver, but glimpsed the license plate, a Maine personalized plate that read *LSG1*.

Candy had seen it before — and she'd seen the silver sports car before too. It was a BMW. The black cloth convertible top had been up and the windows slightly tinted, but there was no mistaking the wraithlike woman behind the steering wheel. She was a well-known local businesswoman, a real estate agent rumored to be involved in the secret real estate deal involving Crawford's Berry Farm.

"Lydia St. Graves," Candy heard herself mutter into the sudden silence.

FIVE

She found Doc sitting inside a police cruiser, talking to Officer Molly Prospect of the Cape Willington Police Department, who was taking his statement. The passenger side door was open, so Candy went to her father, leaned over, and gave him a quick hug.

"Dad, are you okay?" she asked, crouching beside the car so she could get a better look at him.

He turned toward her with watery eyes and a weak smile. "Hello, pumpkin. And yup, I'm fine." He reached up and patted her hand. His smile disappeared quickly. "Miles isn't doing so well, though. I seem to have stumbled across his body, much to my surprise — and his as well, I imagine. Never had anything like that happen to me before — or him either, I guess."

Candy's jaw tightened. "So it's true, then?"

Doc nodded sadly. "It's true, all right. Miles is gone. Saw it with my own two eyes." To emphasize his point, he jerked a thumb out the windshield of the police cruiser, toward the fields and the hoophouse in the distance.

Candy turned in the direction he indicated. She saw a small group of police officers and a few men in ties and jackets arrayed around one end of the hoophouse, which stood off on one side of a strawberry patch, fifty or sixty yards away. An ambulance was parked nearby.

"They haven't brought out the body yet," Doc said with a frown. "I think they're waiting for the medical examiner, and maybe a forensics team. Not sure. They're not saying much."

Candy watched the activity around the hoophouse for a few moments, then turned back to her father. "What happened to him?"

Doc was about to answer, but Officer Prospect spoke up before he did. "I'm still taking his statement," she told Candy, leaning forward a little and looking over at her from the driver's seat. She gave Candy a pleasant smile. "I just need him for a little while longer, okay?"

Candy hesitated and blinked a time or

two. It took her a few moments to realize she was being politely dismissed. "Oh, okay, I . . . I guess I'll let you two talk then. I'll just wait over here until you're finished."

She started to back away but Officer Prospect spoke up again. "Actually, if you wouldn't mind, Ms. Holliday," she said, pointing out through the windshield toward the hoophouse with her pen, "I think the chief would like a few words with you."

Surprised, Candy looked off across the fields again. "Chief Durr? With me?"

The officer nodded. "He said to send you up when you arrived."

"He did? So . . . he's expecting me?" She gave them both a questioning look.

"He'll explain up at the hoophouse." Officer Prospect pointed out the windshield again as Doc sat silently in the passenger seat. He looked like he wanted to say something to her but had been instructed not to. An odd moment passed between father and daughter, and Candy's alert sensors went up. "Dad, what's going on?"

His face turned grim and he shook his head. "That's what we're trying to figure out, pumpkin." He met her gaze. "They'll show you up at the hoophouse. You should probably go on up. Talk to the chief yourself. See what you think."

65

Candy was silent for a moment as she felt a tinge of trepidation. "What's this about? Are you in trouble?"

Doc shook his head. "No, nothing like but . . . But, well, there's some evidence you need to take a look at."

"Evidence? What kind of evidence?"

When she received no answers, Candy let out a breath, and her shoulders slumped forward a little. "Okay, I get it. There's only one way I'm going to find out, right?"

She straightened, patted her father on the shoulder, and turned to face the fields. "I'll be right back. Don't you go anywhere."

"I won't, pumpkin. I'll be right here."

As the wind picked up, she started off across the makeshift parking lot, past Doc's old pickup truck, still sitting where he'd left it, and angled around the barn. On the far side she passed a vegetable garden that looked like something you'd see on a TV show, with green tomatoes plumping up, bright green cucumbers on thickening vines, artfully arranged bean teepees, neat rows of carrots and radishes and lettuce, and a back row of sunflowers still a few weeks from full bloom. Beyond that was a small herb garden with a thick hedge of lavender. Farther on, the strawberry plants in straight rows were thick and heavy with fruit, ripening in the sun.

She couldn't help but notice how green everything looked, and how well tended. The path that led up toward the hoophouse was weedless. The soil looked dark and rich. Miles had planned and worked the farm meticulously for years, getting the most from the fertile land.

Why on earth would he want to sell this? she wondered.

It was a prime piece of property, oblong-shaped, with woods on the right beyond the fields and the sea to the left at the bottom of a long, gentle slope. Now that she saw it again for herself, she could understand why so many rumors about the place were floating around town.

And she was beginning to think there was more truth behind the rumors than she'd previously believed.

As she approached the hoophouse, one of the uniformed police officers standing just outside the doorway spotted her and frowned. He looked like he was about to chase her away, but after a moment he seemed to recognize her and called to someone inside.

A few moments later Chief Darryl Durr emerged from the hoophouse, looking grim-faced and preoccupied. Absently his gaze shifted back and forth across the fields before finally alighting on her. His expression relaxed slightly and he gave her a thin smile and a nod in acknowledgement. She nodded back as she crossed the distance between them.

"Hello, Ms. Holliday," he said as she reached him. "Thanks for coming on up. I suppose you heard we've had a little trouble around here this morning."

"Yes, Chief, I heard."

"And you've talked to your father and Officer Prospect?"

Candy dipped her head. "I did. But they didn't tell me much. What's this all about?"

The chief crooked a finger and turned. "Come on, I'll show you."

He turned back toward the hoophouse, pointing to a cardboard box lying on the ground outside the doorway. "I'll need you to put on some booties first. Once we get inside, follow instructions and stay in the designated areas. Don't touch anything. We have ourselves a live crime scene here. We've done a preliminary sweep of the area, but we have a full forensics team coming in from the state. They'll be arriving shortly."

Candy hesitated, and felt a chill. She wasn't sure she was ready for this, and she had no idea what to expect. But she did as he asked, and steeled herself before following him inside.

The place was like a mausoleum. It had an almost spiritual presence to it, a reverence usually reserved for centuries-old European cathedrals, though it was nothing more than a plastic-sided, semitransparent, steel-tube-framed structure designed to serve as a makeshift greenhouse. It was several degrees warmer inside than out, and more humid. The earthy smell of soil and vegetation mingled with the scents of the officers around her, and something else that lingered in the air, something unpleasant.

Chief Durr was several steps ahead of her, following a narrow roped-off pathway along a center aisle with a dirt floor. He pointed. "There are doors at either end of the hoophouse, as you can see. Doc came in this way, the same way we entered. Both doors were opened when we arrived. The body's over here."

Candy had been in hoophouses before, and this one was no different than others she'd seen — just a wide aisle down the middle with raised beds on either side and a simple gravity-fed tube irrigation system. In the right-side bed was lettuce in two stages — a young crop and one in midcycle. On the left were rows of cherry tomatoes of various varieties, as well as Asian greens, purple mustard, cilantro, and what looked like endive — probably being grown for local restaurants and hotels, like the Lightkeeper's Inn, Candy surmised.

The center aisle was a little muddy down the middle, so they followed a narrow roped-off path that kept them close to the right-side bed and away from the wet earth, where footprints might have been left. The path skirted one area of the aisle completely, taking them up over the front edge of the bed itself.

From her raised position, Candy looked ahead. Two-thirds of the way along the aisle, on the left, stood a large metal rack with six or eight wide shelves, holding new plantings in small black plastic six-packs. Just past that, surrounded by two EMTs in dark blue uniforms and another officer from the Cape Willington Police Department, lay the body.

It was covered with a sheet. "The damage was too severe to be accidental," the chief said over his shoulder as he led her along the bed toward the actual scene of the crime. "It appears he was hit multiple times while standing and then again a few times while lying on the ground, with the flat side and edges of the blade."

"Blade?" Candy asked meekly.

"The blade of a shovel, Ms. Holliday," the chief clarified.

"A shovel?" Candy slowed. She wasn't sure she wanted to get any closer.

The chief stopped and waited for her to catch up, looking back at her now. "There don't appear to be any signs of a struggle," he continued in a soft tone, his head lowered toward her. "It looks like he was taken by surprise. Perhaps he knew the person who did it. Perhaps he was ambushed."

Candy shivered uncontrollably. "Someone hit him over the head with a shovel?"

The chief's mouth tightened. "It's over here. If you'll come with me."

He detoured around the body, following the path as it cut directly across the raised bed on the right. They walked on a plank that had been laid across neat rows of lettuce, so close to the sloping side of the hoophouse that the chief had to tilt his head away from the encroaching plastic wall.

After another half-dozen paces, he crossed back over on the other side of the bed, just past the body. At the edge he stopped and pointed down at the central aisle.

Candy followed him in silence. She stopped beside him and looked down.

An old farm shovel lay across the aisle, as if it had been dropped there by accident.

The wood handle was dark with age, the blade dull, marked by deep streaks and scratches from years of heavy use. Candy had seen dozens like it. They had several out at Blueberry Acres that could have matched this one exactly. It was a tool of the farmer's and gardener's trade.

"You'll notice," the chief said, still pointing, "that there's a marking on the handle."

"A marking?" Candy looked.

Indeed, there was.

It was faded but still legible. Just two thick letters, written in a steady hand with a black marker.

B.A.

"You have any idea what that refers to?" the chief asked, looking back at her with an odd expression on his face.

Candy felt a tightening in her stomach. Her mouth went suddenly dry. "I do," she said softly. "Doc marks a lot of his tools like that. They tend to get passed around sometimes, so he wanted to make sure they always found their way home."

She pulled her gaze from the alleged murder weapon and looked up at the chief, the shock evident in her voice as she spoke. "That shovel is from Blueberry Acres."

Six

Chief Durr grunted in acknowledgement. "Doc said the same thing. We just wanted to get your corroboration. That's why we had him call you, and asked him not to say anything to you about that shovel. So, Ms. Holliday." The chief's eyes bored into her. "I'm wondering how a shovel with the initials *B.A.* written on the handle made it from your farm all the way out here to Crawford's Berry Farm. And I'm wondering how it wound up at a crime scene as the possible murder weapon. You got any ideas about how that might have happened?"

There was nothing accusatory in his tone, but plenty of curiosity.

Candy gave him the most honest answer she could. "No, Chief, I don't. I'm as baffled as you are."

"Does the shovel look familiar to you?"

"Yes, of course."

"Do you remember seeing it out at Blueberry Acres?"

"Yes."

"So you can confirm it belongs to you and Doc?"

Candy hesitated, and blinked a couple of times. "Yes."

"When's the last time you remember seeing it?"

Candy had to think about that one for a while. "I don't know, really. We're busy out there. We come and go. We're both out in the fields a lot. Things get carried around by both of us, as well as by our helpers when they come out. We have a bunch of shovels, of different types. They're kept in the barn."

"Do you remember seeing this particular shovel recently, say, within the past week? Or the past month?"

"No."

"Within the past two months?"

A pause. "No. Not within the past few months."

"When do you remember last seeing it?"

Again, Candy had to take a few moments to think. "It was around the farm in the fall, I'm fairly sure of that," she said finally. "I remember getting it out to clean the chicken coop before winter. It went back in the barn then, into a back corner with the other gardening tools at the end of fall, when the snow shovels and rock salt came out. After that, I don't know."

"So it disappeared from the farm sometime within the past nine months?"

Candy carefully went back over everything in her mind before she answered. "Yes, I think that's correct, to the best of my recollection."

"Okay." The chief appeared to make a mental note. "That gives us a starting timeline, at least. Now we just have to pinpoint exactly when it disappeared and who was around the farm during that time period."

"You're surmising someone took it from Blueberry Acres?"

"It's one possible scenario," the chief said.

"Yes, I suppose it is," Candy admitted, scrunching up her mouth. It made her think. Could someone who had been out at Blueberry Acres recently taken the shovel from their barn, brought it out here to Crawford's Berry Farm, and used it to beat Miles Crawford over the head — more than one time, according to the chief?

Candy just couldn't conceive of it. No one who had visited Blueberry Acres seemed capable of such an act.

The chief was still giving her a hard look. "We'll need a list of everyone who's been out at Blueberry Acres over that period of time."

Candy nodded absently, her mind starting to assemble faces, dates, and names. "I'll put one together for you. But it could be a pretty long list."

"Would Miles Crawford be on it?" the chief asked matter-of-factly. "Could he have taken that shovel from Blueberry Acres himself?"

Candy shook her head. "Not as far as I know. I never saw him out there, though it's possible he stopped by sometime while I was away, and I just never heard about it, or something like that."

"Doc said the same thing," Chief Durr confirmed. "So it appears we have agreement on that point, at least. For now, we can rule out the possibility that Miles himself picked up that shovel at your farm and brought it here."

"And what are the other possibilities?" Candy asked.

The chief lifted his cap and scratched his head at the hairline. "Well, there are several, as I see it. One, I have to consider the fact that Doc was the first person on the scene, and the probable murder weapon belongs to him."

Candy felt a chill. "You don't think my

dad had anything to do with this, do you? I mean, with the murder?"

Chief Durr shrugged. "We have to consider all the possibilities."

"Is Dad a suspect?"

The chief didn't answer her question directly. "We just have to figure out what happened here, Ms. Holliday. Obviously you're both involved at this point."

"Obviously," Candy said, and she felt another chill as the reality set in.

They'd both been drawn into another murder in town.

Candy looked back down at the shovel. "My fingerprints are probably on that," she said after a few moments. "And Dad's."

"Probably," the chief agreed, his face tightening in thought. "We'll check that out, of course. I believe we have your prints on file from a previous case, but we'll ask Doc to stop by the station this afternoon."

"Of course," Candy said. She looked down at the sneakers on her feet. "Footprints?"

The chief tilted his head toward a number of small yellow flags, inserted at various spots in the wet dirt along the central aisle. "We found Doc's, of course. They're still fresh and well defined, so they're easy to spot. We've got them marked off. We're still examining the others we've found. We'll let you know if we need an accounting of your footwear."

He turned back toward her. "It's the shovel I'm most focused on at the moment, Ms. Holliday. Do you think it's possible Doc might have brought it out here at some point over the past few months, left it here by mistake, and then just forgotten about it? Maybe he doesn't remember leaving it out here."

Candy crossed her arms and took a deep breath. "Well, it's possible, I suppose. Doc *has* been a little forgetful lately. Senior moments, I think they call them. But I'm sure he'd remember if he left a shovel out here, especially given what's happened to Miles. Maybe he left it somewhere else, and it eventually found its way out here."

"Hmm, well, yes, maybe. But maybe it's something else." The chief's gaze turned steely. "I assume you can account for your whereabouts this morning?"

Caught off guard by the question, Candy took a moment to answer. "Yes, of course. I was at the office."

"What time did you arrive there this morning?"

"A little before nine."

"And before that?"

"I stopped in at the diner with Dad."

"I suppose I can find witnesses to corroborate your information?"

"Of course." Candy shivered. "What's this all about, Chief?"

He studied her for a moment before responding. "Here's the thing, Ms. Holliday. I've got a dead body here, who used to be a fine upstanding citizen of this community. I have an alleged murder weapon lying right next to the body — a shovel you just admitted is from your farm. And it was your father who discovered the body, with no apparent witnesses around to verify his testimony. I'm going to be frank — this is looking pretty serious for you and Doc right now. So if I were you, I'd put your two heads together and try to figure out how that shovel wound up out here at the berry farm. Make that list of everyone who's been out to Blueberry Acres since the beginning of the year — friends, neighbors, handymen, delivery trucks, whatever else you can think of. I've asked Officer Prospect to help you and Doc with that. I need you to get it to me as soon as you can."

He settled the cap back on his heat, turned abruptly, and started back the way they'd come, along the raised bed between the rows of lettuce. He spoke back over his

79

shoulder as he walked briskly along the cordoned-off path. "You can e-mail me whatever you put together. And call me if you think of anything else. You have my card?"

Candy nodded as she followed the chief along the narrow pathway. "In a pocket in the bag. I have several of them. I carry them with me at all times."

"Smart thinking, considering all that's happened in the community over the past few years." He stopped and turned back to her. "And there's one more thing I have to ask of you, Ms. Holliday. And your father as well."

"What's that, Chief?"

He gave her an enigmatic smile. "Don't leave town."

SEVEN

By the time she made it back down to the police cruiser, Officer Prospect had finished interviewing Doc, and they were in the process of putting together a list of recent visitors to Blueberry Acres.

Candy felt a little guilty as she checked the names on the list, realizing that every one on it was a good friend or longtime acquaintance of hers. There was Ray Hutchins, the local handyman, right at the top. Herr Georg and Maggie, both of whom had visited numerous times individually. And Maggie's daughter, Amanda, and her fiancé, Cameron Zimmerman, college students who had stopped by during spring break. All three of the boys in Doc's posse were represented — Finn Woodbury, Artie Groves, and Bumpy Brigham. Tristan Pruitt, an acquaintance of Candy's, had stopped by over Memorial Day weekend while in town to visit his aunt, Helen Ross Pruitt.

Marjorie Coffin, who supplied bees for the blueberry fields every spring, was on the list as well, along with several members of her growing brood.

Candy had almost forgotten that Colin Trevor Jones, the executive chef at the Lightkeeper's Inn, had stopped by around Eastertime for dinner and an informal interview conducted by Candy for the paper. Jesse Kidder, who worked at the *Crier* as a photographer and graphic designer, had driven her home a few times when she needed a lift. So had Judy Crockett, the paper's sales rep. The Reverend James P. Daisy had made an impromptu visit one warm spring afternoon, bringing along his statuesque wife, Gabriella. Even Wanda Boyle had stopped by a few times. The list went on and on, a literal who's who of Cape Willington, Maine.

Could they all possibly be suspects? It seemed insane. It *was* insane. Candy couldn't imagine any of them taking a shovel from the barn without permission, let alone sneaking up behind Miles Crawford and banging him over the head with it.

So if not any of them, then who?

Had the shovel actually been stolen from Blueberry Acres? Or had it found its way out to Crawford's Berry Farm by another route? Through someone else's hands?

That got her thinking in a different direction.

Who had a motive to kill Miles Crawford?

Candy mulled over the question, and briefly considered a number of possibilities. But one name stuck out above the others, for obvious reasons: Lydia St. Graves.

Lydia, rumored to have been involved in secret real estate negotiations with Miles for the sale of the berry farm. Lydia, who just a short while ago had almost run Candy off the road in her haste to get away from . . . what? A crime scene? A dead body? Incriminating evidence?

Had Lydia taken the shovel out to the berry farm? And if so, had she used it on Miles?

But why leave it there for the police to find? Why not take it with her after she had used it to do the dirty deed?

Candy waited until there was a break in the conversation between Officer Prospect and her father. "Dad," she interjected, "can I ask you a question?"

He turned toward her curiously. "Sure, pumpkin, what is it?"

"I was just talking to Chief Durr. He said there were no witnesses when you discovered the body."

Doc nodded. "That's right."

"So no one else was around?"

Doc squinted at her and answered without hesitation. "No one. The place was deserted, which I thought was a little strange, especially since it's berry-picking season."

"You didn't see any other cars?"

"Other cars? Where?"

"Here in the parking lot?"

"Nope, the lot was empty. No cars. Just my old truck — and Miles's vehicles, which were around. His truck and station wagon."

"No convertible?"

"Convertible? No, 'course not. Why?"

Candy shifted her gaze toward the house and the outbuildings. "Could there have been another car parked around here somewhere? On the other side of the house perhaps, or behind the barn?"

Doc looked out at the surrounding buildings as he considered the question. After a few moments he shrugged. "It's possible, I suppose. But if there *was* someone else out here, I didn't see 'em. I've already told that to the chief. Why?"

Molly Prospect leaned forward in the driver's seat and looked across at Candy, her thin black brows knitted together. "What's this all about, Ms. Holliday?"

"Honestly, I'm not sure."

"If you have any information that might help with the investigation, I'd sure like to hear it."

"Well . . ."

Candy hesitated. There were already plenty of rumors swirling around town. She didn't want to add to them without any real evidence of wrongdoing. Lydia could simply have been coming from some property she managed. Maybe she'd been showing a house to a potential buyer, and had been simply speeding back to town for another meeting. Any suspicions Candy had about her were purely circumstantial.

Still . . .

"Look, I'm not trying to get anyone in trouble, but I might have witnessed some suspicious activity on my way out here this morning."

The policewoman's dark eyes narrowed. "Might have? What type of suspicious activity are we talking about?"

"Well, I think I possibly saw someone fleeing the premises."

"The premises? You mean you saw someone leaving this farm? Who exactly are we talking about?"

Again, a hesitation, but Candy took a deep breath and pressed on. "Lydia St. Graves."

Doc looked surprised. "You saw Lydia out here?"

"Well, no, not out here at the farm. But I think I saw her driving away from it." And Candy explained how Lydia, in her silver BMW convertible, had come blazing out of nowhere and run her right off the road.

"And when did this happen? How long ago?"

Candy told her.

The policewoman checked her watch. "So about half an hour ago or so?"

Candy nodded. "That sounds right."

"I'd better let the chief know." Officer Prospect picked up a walkie-talkie sitting on the top of the dashboard, clicked a side button, and exchanged a few quick words with Chief Durr up at the hoophouse.

"We'll send a car over to her office to check it out," the policewoman told Candy after she'd finished talking to the chief, "and I'll need to fill out an incident report."

"Of course," Candy said, and ten minutes later, with that complete, they turned back to the list of visitors to Blueberry Acres. "The chief wants us to remain focused on the shovel," Officer Prospect informed Doc and Candy as she tapped the list, which was attached to a clipboard.

They wound up with twenty-seven names,

including Doc's and Candy's. That worried her, knowing they were suspects themselves. And even though she knew she could prove neither of them had anything to do with Miles's murder, their shovel had been found at the crime scene, and as the chief had said, that meant they were involved. At the very least they were responsible for letting the shovel slip through their hands, whenever and however that had happened.

As they reviewed the list again, Officer Prospect prodded Doc and Candy for additional information. "Can you think of anyone else who might have taken the shovel?" she asked in a coaxing tone. "Anyone out at the farm who might have looked suspicious? Anyone borrowing tools or asking odd questions? Or were there any strange incidents you can think of? Has something special or out of the ordinary happened over the past few months?"

Doc considered the questions, rubbing his chin. "Well, there were a few milestones, of course. I turned seventy a few months ago, in April."

The policewoman brightened. "Oh, I didn't know that! Happy birthday, Doc!"

He grinned. "Why, thank you, Molly."

"Sure thing." The policewoman's expression turned serious again. "So did you have a party? Was it out at the farm?"

"Yes, there was a party, but no, not at the farm."

"We held it at the Lightkeeper's Inn," Candy explained. "Maggie and I arranged it."

"How many people were there?"

Candy shrugged. "Forty or fifty."

"Any of them out at Blueberry Acres?"

"Other than the names on the list, no."

"Hmm." The officer thought a moment, but sensing a dead end, she moved on. "So was there anything else? Any other unique or out-of-the-ordinary events? Some time when you might have used the shovel — when you might have done some digging or something like that?"

Candy and Doc considered the question, and Doc looked like he was about to speak up, but before he could say anything, the walkie-talkie squawked to life. It was Chief Durr. "Molly, are you just about finished down there? I need you up here right away," he said amid a crackle of static.

Officer Prospect picked up the walkie-talkie again and clicked the side button. "We're just wrapping up here," she told him. "I'm on my way."

As she set the device back down, she turned to Doc and Candy. "We have enough here to get us started," she said, indicating the list, "but I really need the two of you to see what else you can come up with. We're looking for something solid. That shovel didn't walk out of your barn on its own. Someone took it. And if you didn't bring it out here, as you've said, then someone else did. We need to find out who."

As Doc climbed out of the cruiser's passenger seat, the policewoman handed him a card. She gave one to Candy as well. "You probably already have one of these, but take it anyway. Call me immediately if you think of anything else. And Doc," she added, leaning over and looking out at him, "we need you to stop by the police station so we can get you fingerprinted. As soon as you can."

After she was gone, headed up around the barn toward the hoophouse, Candy and Doc lingered in the parking lot. Doc gave his daughter a worried look as he ran a hand though his gray hair. "I don't have a good feeling about any of this," he said. "We'd better see if we can figure out what's going on, and fast, before they wind up arresting the both of us and charging us with murder, all because of that damned shovel."

Candy understood her father's concern, but she didn't want to overreact. "Well, I don't think it's going to get *that* bad," she said, trying to sound reassuring. More thoughtfully, she added, "At least, I hope not. But you're right about that shovel. One way or another, it links us to the murder scene, and it could spell trouble for the both of us." She said these last few words as lightly as possible, trying not to sound too ominous. But they both knew there was some weight behind them.

Her father sighed and shook his head. "I just can't figure out what's it's doing up in that hoophouse, lying next to the body of Miles Crawford. It just doesn't make any sense."

Candy hesitated, proceeding with a little caution as she asked the next question, since she didn't want to upset or accuse her father. "Dad, *you* didn't bring it out here, did you?"

Doc grunted as his eyes flashed with a moment of irritation. " 'Course not. But I know that's what the chief probably thinks, right? I had a senior moment? Becoming forgetful in my old age? Well, he's dead wrong. Despite what anyone else thinks, I didn't bring that shovel out here. I know that for a fact. And honestly, there's really no way Miles could have taken it from Blueberry Acres. He never came out to the place — and I can't imagine he sneaked into

90

our barn when we weren't around and stole it from us."

"I can't either," Candy admitted. "So how did it get here?"

"I don't have any idea. Do you?"

"Not yet," Candy said.

"What's that mean?"

"It means something doesn't fit right. In fact, it really doesn't make any sense at all."

"Which part?"

"All of it — or rather none of it," Candy said, trying to put her thoughts together. "Look, if we assume our shovel was actually used as the murder weapon, then what's it still doing here? Why did the murderer leave it behind? Why leave it at the scene of the crime, where it would be found?"

Doc mulled that over as he gazed up the slope toward the hoophouse. "I don't know," he said after a few moments. "What do you think?"

"I think whoever murdered Miles knew the shovel would be found and checked for evidence. They knew we'd all be trying to trace its whereabouts over the past few weeks and months. And they knew it would be used to incriminate either us or a second party. They were trying to divert attention, to pin the murder on another person — or persons."

Doc shielded his eyes against the sun as he looked inquisitively at his daughter. "So what are you saying?"

Candy took a breath before she continued. "I'm saying the shovel wasn't left there by accident, Dad. Whoever murdered Miles left it there on purpose."

EIGHT

Doc was silent for a long time. He stood almost stone-still, hands deep in his back pockets, face drawn. When he finally spoke, his voice was soft, edged with concern. "You're saying someone in this town left that shovel beside Mile's body to implicate *us* in this murder?"

Candy leaned in a little closer to her father and lowered her voice, just in case other ears were around. "When you put it that way, it sounds pretty dramatic. But yes, I think it's possible. At the same time, part of me says it's not very likely they were trying to implicate us specifically."

Doc was surprised by this comment. "How do you figure that?"

"Like I said, something about all this doesn't add up." Candy lowered her voice even more. "It just doesn't make sense — not when you think it through. Let's assume for a moment the shovel was left there on purpose to incriminate us. That means, one, the killer knew you were coming out here today, and two, the killer took the shovel from our barn months ago in anticipation of today's events. He or she held on to it all this time, until this morning, and then left it up there in the hoophouse for the police to find right after you stumbled across the body, all to incriminate you or me in Miles's murder. It's just too far-fetched. You made your appointment with Miles only a week ago. How would the murderer have known to steal the shovel from our barn last spring?"

"Hmm," Doc said, rubbing at his chin. "I suppose that makes sense."

"Then there's the question of motive," Candy continued. "What could the murderer have hoped to achieve by framing you or me for the murder? What's the point?"

Doc had a quick answer for that one, his eyes widening as he spoke. "Maybe the point was to get us both arrested and thrown into jail!"

"Yes, but again that's not realistic. Look at the facts," Candy pressed. "For one thing, we both have pretty solid alibis. We can both prove where we were today. I was at the office all morning before stopping at the bakery — that's where I got your phone call

— and you were at the diner with the boys all morning, right? That's where you were just before you came out here?"

Doc nodded. "I walked out of the diner at a quarter to ten," he confirmed.

"Right. And we're a few miles out of town here. By the time you walked out to your truck, started it up, sat in traffic at the light, and followed a long line of cars out of town like I did, it must have taken you, what, ten or fifteen minutes to drive out here? That means you arrived right around ten o'clock."

"A couple of minutes before ten," Doc confirmed.

"Okay, so you found the body right after that, just a few minutes later. What time did you call the police?"

"Ten-oh-seven," Doc said. "It's time-stamped on my phone. I checked it with Officer Prospect. She wrote it down in her report."

"Good, so we have a time frame. And overall it works in your favor."

"How do you mean?"

"Well, the window is too tight, isn't it? While it's certainly possible you could have driven out here in record time, tracked down Miles in the hoophouse, snuck up behind him, whacked him over the head, dropped the shovel on the dirt floor, and called the police, all in a space of about twenty minutes, the facts are your old truck just doesn't move that fast, and neither do you these days, with that limp of yours."

"I beg your pardon," Doc said with a hint of gruffness.

"Nothing personal, Dad. I'm just stating the facts. I'm pointing out that you didn't really have an opportunity to kill Miles, given the time constraints, and why it doesn't make sense for the killer to make it appear that way. Besides, we both know you're not a stupid person, right?"

"I certainly hope not!" Doc said, trying not to sound indignant.

"So if you *had* killed Miles, would you be dumb enough to call the police right away after the deed, without tidying up first, and then leave the murder weapon there at the scene of the crime for the police to find?"

"Of course not," Doc said, seeing her point. "At the very least I would have ditched that shovel in an out-of-the-way corner or tossed it outside the building — anywhere out of sight. But I think I have something even more concrete working in my favor."

"And what's that?" his daughter asked.

"The state of Miles's body."

It took Candy a moment to realize what he was saying. She crossed her arms and looked at him with renewed interest. "You have an idea about the time of death?"

"Not specifically," Doc admitted, "but I overheard one of the paramedics talking to Chief Durr. She said the body had already cooled a couple of degrees, and he was turning pale when I found him. According to some of those forensics shows we've been watching, that means he'd been dead for at least an hour, maybe two. At least, that's my guess."

"Right." Candy took a deep breath, nodded, and went on.

"So based on the state of the body, the fact that the killer couldn't have known you were going to show up when you did, and the unlikelihood of either of us actually committing the murder ourselves, we have to assume that we're not the targets here."

Doc looked impressed at his daughter's grasp of the situation. "Okay. So what's all that mean?"

"It means the shovel was left there on purpose, not to implicate us, but *someone else.*"

"Who?"

"That's what we've got to figure out."

"How are we going to do that?"

"I don't know yet."

"Well, we'd better come up with something fast," Doc said, "before the police actually *do* find a reason to throw us both into jail. It was *our* shovel, after all. Darnedest thing, isn't it?" He shook his head, and it was clear the events of the morning were puzzling him. "What about Lydia St. Graves? You think she might be involved in this?"

Candy was looking out at the sea again. A light breeze had picked up, and the treetops around them rustled. "Possibly. I have no way of knowing for certain, but her behavior was certainly suspicious."

"Well, given the rumors flying around town, I wouldn't be surprised if she's involved in this whole thing somehow. In fact, I'd almost bet money on it, if I were a betting man." He paused. "You think she could have . . . well, you know, killed Miles herself with that shovel? Is she capable of such a thing?"

Candy gave it some thought. "Again, I suppose it's possible. I just don't know her that well, but she's obviously a frail-looking woman. I'm not sure she'd have the strength to lift a shovel, let alone hit a man over the head hard enough to kill him. So for the moment I'm trying not to jump to conclusions. Besides, maybe we're both overthinking this. Maybe by leaving the shovel here, the killer meant simply to muddy the waters for a while — you know, confuse the police, send them off on a wild-goose chase."

"Like interviewing every person on that list we just compiled?" Doc let out a snort of air. "You and I both know none of those folks had anything to do with this."

"I hope you're right, Dad," Candy said softly.

"So what's our next move?"

"I think," Candy said, turning back to look at her father, "that you should head over to the police station and get yourself fingerprinted."

"I'd rather have my teeth pulled out," Doc said honestly. "Just the idea of it bothers me. To think I could ever do something like that to someone like Miles."

"I know, Dad, but it's just a formality. And it might help the police find the killer."

Doc seemed resigned to his fate. "Very well," he said, sounding a bit antagonistic, "guess I'll get it over with. What about you? Where're you headed?"

"Back to the office." Candy pointed at the Jeep with her thumb. "I have appointments this afternoon and I need to finish up some work. But on the way, I might stop at the house and check out our barn — see if I can remember the last time I saw that shovel. Maybe something will spark a memory. And I can check on the chickens."

With that, they parted. After a quick, reassuring hug, Doc climbed into the cab of his old pickup truck while Candy slid into the driver's seat of the Jeep. He waved half-heartedly as he drove off. She followed him out to the main road and trailed him for a few miles, until they reached the turnoff that led northward toward Blueberry Acres. She made a left, while Doc continued straight on toward town.

The blueberry fields behind the house and barn were at near peak. They'd start harvesting in another month or so, and they were beginning to put together their equipment and farm machinery. But in many ways this time period, from early to mid-spring, was the lull before the upcoming storm of activity. The blueberry season would last until mid-August, after which they'd turn their attention to the vegetable gardens, and later on into the fall they'd start mowing the blueberry fields. But for now all they needed was a little rain and plenty of sunshine to ripen the berries.

Candy pulled up in front of the house and climbed out of the Jeep. The place was amazingly peaceful, though she could hear the chickens cackling in their coop behind the barn. The wind was still blowing from the northwest, a light breeze running down toward the sea, bringing with it the smell of the woods and the ripening berries.

She checked her watch. It was nearly eleven thirty. She had to get moving.

She spread some feed on the floor of the coop, checked for eggs, which she collected in a wire basket, and headed into the barn. Near the workbench was a well-supplied tool rack. A quick glance at their collection of lawn and garden tools revealed the typical hoes and rakes, shears and pruners, scythes and axes, trowels and post hole diggers. They also had a number of spades and shovels, including several snow shovels, a wide wood scoop, a short-handled digging shovel, and a wood-handled, squared-off garden spade. Then there was the new long-handled digging shovel they'd bought earlier in the year. Its blade was still shiny.

Candy looked at the new shovel for several moments. When had they bought that? she wondered. Sometime in the early spring? Or was it during the winter?

As her mind worked back over the past few months, she was surprised to hear the sound of a vehicle coming up the dirt lane.

When she stepped out of the barn, she saw Doc's old pickup truck pulling to a stop in front of the house. She watched as he shut off the engine, climbed out of the cab, spotted her, and ambled in her direction.

"What are you doing back so soon?" Candy called to him across the driveway. "Did you get fingerprinted?"

Doc scowled and waved a hand. "It's a madhouse over there," he called back, and as he drew nearer, he continued, "Phones ringing off the hook. Everyone rushing back and forth. They told me to come back later today — or tomorrow. Too busy, short-staffed. I'll give them a call this afternoon and see when they want me to go in."

Candy nodded, and led the way back into the barn. "I was just looking over the tools," she told him. "You remember that new shovel we bought a few months back? When did we pick that up at Gumm's?"

Doc knew the answer right away. "March Madness sale. Got it for twenty-five percent off."

"But why buy a new shovel when we had one exactly like it in the barn?"

"You mean the one that's currently lying next to Miles's body?" Doc shrugged. "Because we needed it, I guess."

"But why? It's the same style as the old one."

"Well, you can never have too many shovels," Doc said, sounding a little defensive, "and like I said, it was on sale."

Still, Candy pressed him. "Yes, but *why*, Dad?"

It took Doc a moment but he finally realized what she was getting at. "Ahh," he said, throwing back his head, "I suppose I bought the new one because I couldn't find the old one when I needed it."

"Exactly," Candy said, holding a finger up in the air to make her point, "which means the old shovel disappeared sometime during or before March. Did we have anyone out to the farm at that time? Anything special going on that month that you remember?"

Doc scratched his head as he thought. "Well, just lots of snow. We had that string of snowstorms and roller-coaster weather. We wouldn't have used the digging shovel much during that time. We had the snow shovels out a lot, though." He paused, and his face clouded. "But there was that one time . . ."

He paused again, blinked several times, and snapped his fingers. "That's it!"

"That's what?" Candy asked.

"Those spring snowstorms we had. They

were pretty wet and heavy. The snow melted quickly during the day, then froze up at night."

"Icicles," Candy said. She felt a tinge of excitement as the realization dawned on her.

"That's right. I think I used that old shovel to knock some icicles off the house. They can get pretty long and scary-looking, you know. You don't want one dropping down on the top of your head as you're passing by. It could be mighty painful."

"So what happened to the shovel after you knocked down the icicles?"

"Well, after I finished here at our house, I ran into town to help some of the older folks knock down the longer icicles from under their eaves and make it a little safer to walk outside their houses."

"Do you remember where you went?"

"Sure do, now that I think of it." Doc nodded. "I made three stops that afternoon, first at Mrs. Fairweather's. Then I swung by Sally Ann Longfellow's place, and finally I ran out to see the Gumms, since Gus was out of action this spring due to that back surgery he had." Doc caught his daughter's eye. "I must have left the shovel at one of their places."

NINE

For a few moments both were silent, surprised by their discovery. "Wow, how about that?" Doc said finally, sounding a little pleased with himself. "We actually figured something out."

"We did," Candy said, "and it just might help us find out what really happened to Miles."

"It certainly might," Doc agreed. "I can't believe I didn't think of it earlier. I guess my brain isn't working right today."

"It's to be expected, after what you've been through," Candy said supportively. "At least you remembered."

"With your help. It's like you said — I bought that new shovel for a reason. I just didn't remember why."

"It'd be hard to prove in court, though," Candy said thoughtfully, "if it ever came to that, I mean — to prove it wasn't in your possession when Miles was killed. Are you

105

sure that's what happened to it? You left it at one of your stops that day?"

"I'm positive." Doc nodded a single time for emphasis. "I remember throwing it into the back of the truck and driving into town. It's clear as day in my mind right now."

"Then you know what this means?"

"What?"

"It means that one of those three or four people you just mentioned — Mrs. Fairweather, the Gumms, or Sally Ann — might be the person who killed Miles Crawford and left the shovel beside his body."

Doc snorted. "That's impossible. Those folks are all in their seventies or eighties. Some might be pushing ninety. I think Mrs. Fairweather is in line for the cane, isn't she?" It was a tradition in some New England villages to award an honorary cane to the oldest person in town. "I'm not sure she could even lift a shovel, let alone swing it that hard. Neither could any of the others."

"What about Sally Ann?" Candy asked thoughtfully.

"Well, she's a tough old bird, all right. She still wrangles those goats pretty well."

"And Mr. Gumm? He still gardens and he's active."

Doc eyed her skeptically. "You really think Gus could do something like that?"

"No," Candy admitted, and then she turned toward her father, eyeing him curiously. "Could *you*?"

"Could I what?"

"Could *you* lift and swing that shovel?"

Doc took a moment to answer. "I'm not sure why you're asking me that," he said finally, "but of course I could, if I had to. But why would I ever want to?"

Candy let his question pass. "My point," she said instead, "is that right now we shouldn't rule out anyone as a suspect — even if it's someone we know, even if it's someone who we think is incapable of committing such a deed. People do strange things, for strange reasons. If there's anything I've learned over the past few years, it's to assume nothing, and to consider everything, even if it's highly unlikely. So for the moment, we don't take anything — or anyone — off the table."

Doc shuffled his feet and frowned. He didn't seem happy with this latest development. "Then maybe I just shouldn't have said anything at all," he muttered, his voice sounding a bit strained. "The last thing I want to do is get any of those nice old folks into trouble with the police. I don't want to point the finger of blame at anyone — especially them."

"Neither do I," Candy said.

Doc was about to respond, further arguing the point, but he paused, and considered what his daughter had just said. "So what do *you* think we should do?"

Candy hesitated only a moment before responding. "I think we should call the police right now and tell them we just figured out what happened to that shovel."

"But that won't work," Doc said with a shake of his head. When this daughter said nothing in reply, he continued, "For two reasons, since you asked. First, they're so darn busy at the station that I'm not even sure I could get anyone on the phone if I called over there right now. They didn't have time to see me today. Who knows if they even want to talk to me?"

"They'll talk to us if we have information about the shovel," Candy said, playing devil's advocate.

"Yes, but that's just it. And brings me to my second point."

"Which is?"

"It would just traumatize those old folks if the police came calling on them."

Candy had to agree with him on that point.

"Which is why I think we should just go and find out what happened to that shovel ourselves," Doc concluded.

"Conduct our own investigation, you mean?"

"No. Go talk to our friends. See if we can figure out what happened. Once we know where I left that shovel, and figure out how it made its way to Crawford's Berry Farm, *then* we'll contact the police and tell them what we've learned."

Candy nodded. "Okay, agreed. But no matter what we find out, we call the police this afternoon and fill them in."

"Agreed." Doc seemed pleased with their compromise.

"So where do we start?"

Doc shrugged. "With Mrs. Fairweather, I guess. She was my first stop that day."

"I'm not sure that's necessary then," Candy said, "because if you *had* left the shovel at her house, you wouldn't have had it when you got to Sally Ann's place, or the Gumms'. You needed it to knock down the icicles at all three places."

"But that's just it," Doc said. "I remember taking the shovel with me that day, and I remember where I stopped. But I think I also used their shovels at some of the places. I just can't remember which is which."

"Okay, so we'll visit all three." Candy

turned on her heels and headed toward the house. "I'll get my keys. We'll take the Jeep."

TEN

On the way back to town, Doc fiddled relentlessly with the radio dial, searching for any news of the town's most recent incident. But he found nothing other than the usual classic rock, oldies, and talk radio stations, as well as a Spanish language channel and one devoted exclusively to polka tunes. Giving up, he shut off the radio, scratched at his leg, looked out the window, scratched his leg some more, and made a face. "I know what you're thinking," he said finally, in a tone that had a defensive edge to it.

Candy glanced over at him, a half smile on her face. She had grown used to her father's many moods. "And what am I thinking, Dad?"

"You're wondering if this is the right thing to do."

"Which part?"

Doc let out a sigh. "You know — talking to these people ourselves, rather than going right to the police."

"Ahh." Candy slowed the vehicle as they came to a line of traffic on the outskirts of town. "So you're having reservations?" She'd thought that might happen. "Should we head over to the police station instead?"

Doc waved a hand dismissively in the air, as if swatting away a fly. "No, no, that's just it. I've thought it through, and I'm convinced we're doing the right thing."

"Really?" Candy found herself somewhat amused. Usually she was the one who went off on her own investigations, while Doc took a more levelheaded approach, cautioning her to follow protocol and leave the detecting to the experts. "And why is that?"

"Because we're the ones with the best chance of finding out what happened here."

"How so?"

"Well, look. If we'd gone to the police first, they'd have rushed over to see these folks and started questioning them. Then it would have spread around town, and people would think those folks were mixed up in the murder somehow, and it would have turned into a huge mess."

"You're saying we should be more discreet?"

"Not even talk about the murder," Doc confirmed. "Just a few friendly little chats.

Besides, if we start talking about dead bodies and murder weapons, that would just get everyone worked up. It'd probably scare the bejesus out of Mrs. Fairweather to know she might be tied up in a murder case. She'd probably just clam right up — get so confused she wouldn't know what to say. And you know Sally Ann can be pretty cantankerous at times. She doesn't get along well with the police, mostly because of those goats of hers, which have caused some trouble around town. But she likes me, so I can talk to her. And, of course, we both know Gus pretty well."

That was true. They were frequent visitors to Gumm's Hardware Store, and Candy and Maggie had managed Mr. Gumm's pumpkin patch for him for the past two years, so she had a good relationship with him.

"So it's best to do this ourselves, and keep a low profile — for now," Doc concluded.

"Got it, Dad. Good thinking."

He pointed out the windshield, toward the upcoming intersection and traffic light. "Let's stop by the hardware store first and see if Gus is around. Then we'll head over and see the others."

They indeed found Augustus "Gus" Gumm behind the counter of his hardware store on Main Street. They entered as nonchalantly as possible, as if they'd stopped by to do a little browsing around the store. Doc started talking about the weather, and Candy mentioned something about the pumpkin patch, but Mr. Gumm saw through their charade right away. He eyed them both with a look of cold logic. "I don't suppose this little drop-in has anything to do with the events taking place this morning out at the Crawford farm."

Candy and Doc exchanged a glance, knowing they'd been found out. "Well now, Gus," Doc said, shuffling his feet a little, "you know if it did, we really couldn't say."

Mr. Gumm had a quick response. "So does that mean if you *aren't* saying, then it really *does* have something to do with that murder I just heard about?"

Doc cleared his throat and smiled obligingly, though Candy noticed his smile looked a little forced. But considering the circumstances, he made a pretty good actor. *He's getting the hang of this,* she thought as she stood off to one side and let her father do the talking.

"Actually we're here about a shovel," Doc said, making it sound as if he'd lost his favorite pair of socks.

"A shovel? Got plenty of those along the

back wall." He pointed toward the rear of the store.

"No, this is one of our old shovels we had out at Blueberry Acres. It's got the initials *B.A.* on the handle. I had it with me when I came out to your place last March, when we had those snowstorms, remember? I helped knock the icicles off your house? But I lost the darn thing somewhere along the way. Thought I might have left it at your place. You seen anything like that around?"

"Well, now, let me think." Mr. Gumm plopped himself on to an old varnished wooden stool behind the counter, rubbed the stubble on his chin, and rolled his gaze to the ceiling. But finally he shook his head. "Don't recall seeing a shovel around the house with any initials on the handle," he said after a few moments. "Of course, we got lots of tools out in the sheds. Got three toolsheds in all, you know. Dozens of shovels and rakes and what have you. Could be in there somewhere. But if it is, I don't recall."

"Do you remember seeing a strange shovel lying somewhere around the place, maybe on a walkway or leaning up against the building?" Doc pressed. "Somewhere I might have left it by mistake?"

"Sure don't, Doc."

"What about Mrs. Gumm?" Candy asked.

"Could she have picked it up?"

Mr. Gumm shrugged. "It's possible. Any tools she finds lying around, she leans them up against one of the sheds, so I can sort them out. You got to keep them in order — otherwise you'll never find what you want. So she leaves that up to me."

Sensing they were getting nowhere, they thanked Mr. Gumm and headed back out to the Jeep. The day had grown warmer, so Doc rolled up his sleeves as he climbed into the cabin, and opened the passenger side window. "No sense searching those sheds. Sounds like a dead end," he said as Candy started the engine. "Let's see what Sally Ann and Mrs. Fairweather have to say."

They made a quick jog back out to the Coastal Loop, headed north a block, and then made a right turn on River Road, which ran parallel to Main Street. Rachel Fairweather lived closest to them, near the corner of Pleasant Street and Shady Lane, just a block over from Gleason Street and two blocks from Rose Hip Lane, in the older, historic section of the village. Sally Ann Longfellow's place, an old Cape Cod-style house, was just a little farther out, where Gleason met Edgewood Road at the outskirts of town. So they'd decided to stop at Mrs. Fairweather's first.

Time was becoming an issue, since Candy had meetings in the afternoon, so they agreed to keep their conversations as brief as possible.

They parked in the gravel driveway in front of Mrs. Fairweather's house and hopped out of the Jeep. Her home was a modest chocolate brown bungalow with white trim, and she'd done her best to keep the place neat. The hip-high white picket fence around the property had been recently painted, and window boxes held colorful cascades of flowers in red, yellow, and violet, while well-tended gardens encircled the house, meandering artfully from dual walkways that ran to either side and met somewhere around the back.

Doc ambled right up the front walkway, climbed the steps to the porch, and knocked on the front door, while Candy wandered around to the left side of the building, admiring a wisteria-covered archway and a row of sunflowers hugging the building, almost shoulder high. She spotted a rose garden a little farther on, and could see part of a large vegetable patch out back with several bean teepees. She looked over when she heard the front door open, and noticed the surprised look on Doc's face.

"Oh, hello," he said hesitantly to the

person who opened the door. "I'm looking for Mrs. Fairweather. Rachel Fairweather? She's still around, isn't she?"

"Yes, hi." A slim, dark-haired woman pushed open the screen door and stepped out onto the porch. She looked to be around Candy's age, in her late thirties or early forties. She wore a knee-length flowery print dress, loosely belted at the waist. She was barefoot.

"I'm Morgan," the dark-haired woman told them. "Aunt Rachel's niece — or rather, her grand-niece, or something like that — I'm not really sure, to be honest. You'd have to ask her, I guess." She laughed pleasantly.

"Well, it's very nice to meet you, Morgan," Doc said with an affable grin. "I'm Henry Holliday. Doc, actually. Well, that's what everyone calls me around here."

"Nice to meet you, Doc." They shook hands, and Morgan turned to wave at Candy. "And you must be the famous local detective — Candy Holliday, right?"

"That's me," Candy said lightly, and when Morgan came over to the porch rail, leaning toward her and reaching over, Candy walked forward, and they shook hands also.

"It's so good to meet you both," Morgan said, looking back at Doc. "I've heard so much about you two."

"All good, I hope," Doc said with a grin.

"Oh yes. Aunt Rachel has told me quite a bit about your exploits. You're both fairly famous around here, you know. Almost like local celebrities."

"Well, I don't know if I'd go quite that far," Candy said. "We're just regular villagers, working out at the farm most of the time, and doing what we can to help out when needed."

Morgan's eyes widened. They were a rich, deep brown, framed by long dark eyelashes. "Don't underestimate yourselves! From what I've heard, you two have been involved in catching a few very bad criminals around here. I hope the townspeople realize what gems you both are. You should be congratulated."

"I can't take the credit for any of it." Doc motioned toward his daughter. "She's the one with all the talent. She seems to have an instinct for solving these local cases."

"More like an instinct for getting myself into trouble," Candy said with a wry smile, "something I've promised to stop doing."

"Well, I hope you don't mind if I disagree. You've been doing a great job, and I think you should continue doing it," Morgan said sincerely.

"Yes, well." Doc cleared his throat. "It's actually other business that's brought us out here today — farm business, you could say. We seem to have lost one of our garden tools — an old shovel — and we've been trying to track it down. It's possible I left it here when I visited your aunt a few months ago. The initials *B.A.* are marked on the handle. I wonder if you or your aunt might have seen it?"

"Well, I wish I could help you out, Doc, but I haven't seen it around anywhere," Morgan said. "But why don't we ask Aunt Rachel? She's moving a little slowly today — she's almost eighty-five, you know, but her mind is still sharp as a tack. If your shovel is around here, she'll remember. She's out back, relaxing in one of the gardens. Here, I'll walk with you."

Morgan took Doc's arm and guided him down the stairs, then came around the porch toward Candy. "I was in the area on business and I just stopped in for a brief visit today," she said as they headed along the side of the house toward the back, "but it's always wonderful to see Auntie, even if it's only for a couple of hours. I live down in the city and I don't get up here as much as I'd like to check on her, but I do my best. The whole family helps out whenever we can. And she seems to be doing well enough on her own, for the most part. She still cooks and bakes and takes care of herself. She has a strawberry pie baking in the oven at this very moment."

"Isn't that a wonder," Doc said, genuinely impressed.

"So you're from Boston?" Candy asked.

"Actually, I'm working in New York City right now," Morgan said. "I'm with a financial firm. We're in commercial real estate, property management, investments, that sort of thing. It's fairly dull work, so I like to get away and come up here whenever I can. Cape Willington is just so beautiful at this time of year, and of course Auntie always loves the company — as long as I don't interfere with her gardening."

It was clear Mrs. Fairweather spent a considerable amount of time in her gardens, for they were quite verdant, and smartly laid out, making them easy to tend, with pathways, stepping-stones, and numerous places to sit, relax, and enjoy the flowers. Candy paused frequently to admire a small lush strawberry patch, an herb garden thick with lavender and chives, the neat rows of black-eyed Susans, lupines, phlox, and asters.

They found Mrs. Fairweather in a small alcove near the back of the yard, seated in a bright yellow Adirondack chair, wearing a wide-brimmed hat, with a basket of fresh cuttings beside her. As Morgan had said, she was resting in the sun with her eyes closed. She appeared to be taking a nap.

"Oh, here you are, Auntie," Morgan said as they approached. "Are you awake? I've brought some visitors. Candy and Doc Holliday have stopped by to see you."

"Who?" Mrs. Fairweather's eyes eased open and focused on her guests. A faint smile came to her face. "Oh, hello you two. What an unexpected surprise. Tell me what you've been up to."

That got the conversation started, and soon enough Doc was able to angle it around to the shovel, but again, they came up empty-handed.

"I remember that day when you came out," Mrs. Fairweather told him. "And I vaguely remember the shovel. But I don't remember seeing it anywhere around the house after you left. And I tend to pick up all my tools every afternoon — I don't leave anything lying around these days. I keep everything locked up in the garage. You're welcome to take a look if you'd like." She pointed to a narrow, low-roofed building nearby.

"I don't think that's necessary," Doc said.

"Got so full I have to keep the car in the driveway," Mrs. Fairweather went one. "Can't fit it in the garage anymore. But I'm going to clean it all out one of these days and have a yard sale. Maybe this summer yet, if I get around to it."

"Well, if you need help doing that, just let me know. I'd be glad to lend a hand," Doc said. They talked for a little while longer but had a schedule to keep. So after saying their good-byes — and declining an invitation to stay and have a slice of warm strawberry pie — they were off again, to see Sally Ann Longfellow.

ELEVEN

They drove over to Gleason Street and
turned left, which took them past Sapphire
Vine's old house halfway up the block.
Sapphire had been a local Blueberry Queen
and community columnist for the newspaper, as well as a gossip and a blackmailer,
before her untimely death in that house a
few years ago. More recently, some spooky
happenings had taken place there — Candy
remembered them well, for she'd been a
central part of them. But the house had
finally given up all its secrets and let go of
its ghosts, and like the rest of them, with
the passage of time, it had moved on.

As they approached the house, Candy
slowed the Jeep a little, so she could get a
good look at the place. A young family had
bought it and moved in last fall, and they
were in the process of fixing it up. Bright
curtains decorated the windows, well-used
rockers swayed on the porch, the cocoa-

colored trim around the outside had been recently painted, and a new swing set was set up in back. The yard was neatly trimmed, and the flower beds were in bloom. The house looked lived in again. Candy couldn't help but feel a surge of happiness as they passed by.

Sally Ann Longfellow lived a little farther out, at the end of Gleason Street. She was a longtime resident of the town and something of a local legend. She claimed to have familial ties to the famous poet, and she apparently had a few dusty old volumes inscribed by the author as proof. In her rebellious youth she'd eloped and married a farrier from Dover-Foxcroft, who died suddenly right before his twenty-seventh birthday, kicked in the head by a horse he was shoeing. Sally never remarried and in time took back her maiden name, choosing to live by herself for the better part of half a century — until one day, on a lark, she purchased two female goats, whom she named Cleopatra and Guinevere. Sally Ann developed a great affection for the goats, and took them with her to events and parades around town. They were popular with children and families, but the neighbors weren't quite as enamored with the animals, especially when they broke loose of their tethers or wheedled their way out of their pen, on a quest for greener pastures.

Those goat adventures had caused quite a bit of friction in the small, close-knit community, especially in the early years. In time, though, the villagers became accustomed to the animals — or at least learned to tolerate them — and accepted them as part of the landscape, despite their sometimes cantankerous nature, which could mirror their owner's at times.

Sally Ann was not known for her social graces. She could be civil when she wanted to be, but that wasn't very often. She lived on a tight budget and rarely updated her wardrobe, so she could appear a bit raggedy at times, much to the consternation of out-of-towners, who sometimes mistook her for a bag lady and offered her a meal or a place to stay. Needless to say, Sally Ann did not take to such insults kindly, however well intentioned they might be.

Whatever her eccentricities, she was also solid New England stock. She was tall and strongly built, with a mane of long gray hair that fell halfway down her back. She combed it out every day and sometimes put it in a braid, or wore a headband or straw hat. Her hands were big, those of a laborer. Her word was her bond. She spent a lot of time by herself, respected other people's privacy, and expected the same. But should anyone be in need, she was always among the first to offer help.

Her house was nothing fancy on the outside — just white clapboard and black shutters, with a low side profile, high end gables, a steeply pitched roof, and a small red-brick chimney protruding from the top. Behind the house was a small animal shed with a sloped tin roof and an attached pen, but there were no other outbuildings. A long dirt driveway, fringed with leftover gravel, led to a parking area beside the house. A pile of recently delivered firewood stood to one side, ready for stacking. Shade trees — maples and oaks and chestnuts, dressed in the fresh green of spring — populated the front and side yards, but the back was given over to extensive gardens. Along one side, a line of lilac bushes insulated the house from the road. And the two goats were tethered in the front yard, morosely cropping at the thick grass while intently looking around for something better.

As Candy and Doc pulled into the driveway, the goats bleated belligerently and the kitchen curtains fluttered. A few moments later the side door opened and Sally Ann emerged from the house. She was dressed in her work clothes — baggy khaki pants, a red flannel shirt, a dark green down vest, and brown clogs. She stood with one hand shading her eyes, the other on her hip, as she watched her visitors emerge from the Jeep. "I was just having lunch," she said when they were within hearing distance, "but you might as well come on in."

Doc slowed. "Oh, now, Sally Ann, we didn't mean to interrupt your meal," he said apologetically. "We can come back another time."

Sally Ann waved a hand, more annoyed that he was thinking of leaving rather than staying. "Heck no, it don't matter. I can always reheat it anyway. Nothing too fancy, just chicken noodle soup and crackers. So what brings you two out today?" Sally Ann gave them a firm look that was not un-friendly, but not necessarily friendly either.

"Well, we've come on farm business," Doc said. "We're looking for a shovel that I might have left out here a few months back, when I dropped by to knock the icicles off your house. I brought it along with me from Blueberry Acres. It had the initials *B.A.* on the handle. Does that ring a bell?"

Sally Ann nodded and answered right away, without having to give it any thought. "Yup, I remember that," she said. "Have you lost it again?"

"Again?" Doc echoed, surprised.

"Yeah, the shovel with the initials on the handle, right?"

"That's the one, but . . . you've seen it *again*?" Doc didn't quite understand what she meant.

"No, just the one time, when you left it here a few months ago."

"Oh, well, that's what we're inquiring about," Doc said, brightening, and he looked over at Candy and winked. "So do you know what happened to it?"

"I sent it back to your place — months ago."

Doc's brow furrowed. "But we never got it. Did you give it to one of us personally?"

"Well, no," Sally Ann said. "I gave it to Ray Hutchins." She was referring to a local handyman, who often did small jobs for Candy and Doc out at the farm. "He stopped by in April to help me take down the pen in the kitchen. He helps me with that pen every year. I keep the girls inside during the winter, you know," she said, pointing with her chin toward the goats. "Just in the kitchen — they're not allowed in the rest of the house. Me and Ray block off a little area for them." She squinted. " 'Course, they don't make great house guests, and they practically eat me out of the place, and they're noisier than a bar full of drunks, but the shed gets too cold for them in the dead of winter, and I can't let them freeze, can I?"

"Well, no," Candy agreed. "It makes perfect sense. We talked about your goats a year or two ago, if you recall. I wrote a story about them for the paper's community column. We had great response to it." Candy paused. "So you gave the shovel to Ray?" she prompted.

"That's right. He spotted it leaning up against the house. I didn't even notice it — I just get so busy around here. He said he was headed out to your place and he'd make sure it got back to you." She eyed the both of them. "And since you're here looking for it, I guess I can assume that didn't happen."

"Unfortunately, no, it didn't," Doc said. "I wish it had, though."

"Then Ray's still got it," Sally Ann assured him. "He must have just forgotten he had it — though that's not like him. He's usually pretty careful about things like that. He's as honest as the day is long, you know. That's why I like him. It's just a mix-up. Give him a call, and you'll get to the bottom of this in a jiffy."

TWELVE

"So," Candy said when they were back out in the Jeep, "the plot thickens." She turned toward her father, a contemplative look on her face. "What's the likelihood Ray killed Miles Crawford with that shovel?"

"Zero. Zilch," Doc said, scoffing at the very idea of it. "You know as well as I do that's just not possible. We went through this once before with him. He's just not capable of such a thing. Ray's a gentle sort."

Candy nodded and reached for the phone in her back pocket. "I agree completely," she said as she swiped the screen and poked at it, looking for Ray's number. "But Sally Ann's right about one thing — Ray's usually a pretty conscientious person. He wouldn't just forget to return the shovel to us. Something must have happened to it between Sally Ann's place and Blueberry Acres. And whatever it was, Ray's the only one who knows."

It took three rings but Ray Hutchins finally answered. He was out on a job, he told her, down at the docks along the English River, working on a motor for a boat crane. It took Candy several attempts to try to explain why she was calling, since he was distracted by his present job and anxious to get back to it. But he finally focused in on what she was saying and recalled the incident. "Oh, that's right, the shovel. I remember it now. I found it out at Sally Ann's house. I offered to return it to you."

"We never got it back, Ray," Candy said in a nonaccusatory tone. "We're just trying to figure out what happened to it. We thought you could help us out."

Ray sounded surprised by this revelation, and the story quickly came out. He'd been planning to head out to Blueberry Acres with the shovel, he told her, but before he could swing by, he got a call from Judicious F. P. Bosworth, another villager who was a bit of a recluse. Judicious lived in an isolated log cabin on the outskirts of town, on family-owned property along the river. The place had once belonged to his father, and his father before him, both judges, so it had a fairly extensive library, with a heavy focus on law and politics. But Judicious had avoided the family profession, choosing instead to travel to Europe and Asia, where he sought enlightenment. Decades later he returned to Cape Willington as a quiet man in his forties, with the fervent belief that he could turn himself invisible. It was an outlandish claim, and no one really believed he had such a skill, but over the past few years he had convinced at least a few people around town that he could, indeed, disappear at will.

Despite his unique ability, however, Judicious still apparently faced real-world problems around the house. One day while walking home, so the story went, Judicious flagged down Ray and asked for his help getting an old tree stump out of the ground at his place by the river. With Ray on a long-handled pickax and Judicious on a shovel, they'd managed to get the stump out of the ground, but the effort had cost Judicious his tool. The handle of the shovel cracked down near the blade. As Judicious had more work he needed to finish up, Ray loaned him the shovel from Blueberry Acres, with the promise that Judicious would return it to Doc and Candy when he'd finished with it. And that's what Ray assumed had happened.

Like Sally Ann, he was apologetic for not

following up. But they all trusted one another, as those in a close-knit community do, and assumed their neighbors could be counted on to follow through on a promise.

It all made sense, in a Cape Willington sort of way, Candy thought as she keyed off the phone — and even thought it a little amusing that their shovel had turned into a hot potato, making its way from hand to hand. Good thing Doc marked their tools.

Her father caught the gist of the conversation with Ray and furrowed his brow. "So Judicious had it next, right?"

"Sounds like it got passed around quite a bit." Candy slipped the phone back into her pocket and snapped on her seat belt. "Up for one more stop?"

She had no phone number for Judicious, and honestly didn't know if he even owned a phone. Neither did she know his address, since he rarely shared personal information. Like others in town, he kept to himself, but he could be social when he wanted to. It just didn't happen very often.

Candy knew where he lived, though, so they drove out Edgewood Road to the Coastal Loop and turned left, heading northward.

A five-minute drive brought them to a single-lane dirt turnoff on the right, which led down toward the river. The lane was tight, with low trees and shrubbery pressing in on either side, and at times thin limbs and branches reached out to rake the sides of the vehicle. The lane twisted first one direction, then the other, and passed under a thick canopy before emerging into a clearing. A small log cabin, half-hidden by foliage, was nestled back among the trees. The lane continued on a little farther to the river.

No car was parked in front of the cabin — Judicious didn't own one, as far as Candy knew. On nice days he sometimes rode a bike, but mostly he walked, following a trail that wound along the river, past other small cabins and fish camps. It eventually ended near the River Road bridge and boat docks, where Ray Hutchins was currently working.

Judicious came into town once or twice a week, when he needed something from the general store or wanted to attend an event. He was always at the Town Hall meetings every March, and usually made appearances at the community's frequent festivals, cook-offs, bashes, and fairs — though most times he hovered around the edges of the activities, preferring to keep a low profile and rarely taking a central part in them.

Candy parked in front of the cabin and they both got out. This time Candy walked up on the porch and knocked, while Doc surveyed the territory. It was mostly natural landscape. No flower or vegetable gardens that Doc could see. Just trees and shrubbery, mostly pines and undergrowth. The cabin sat on a slight rise, putting it above the river's floodplain. A screen of trees on the north side probably did a good job sheltering it from the fiercest winds in the winter, while a cleared area to the south and west allowed some sunlight through the canopy. Several paths led off into the woods in various directions, many in the general direction of the river. Doc noticed a couple of fishing rods leaned up against one side of the cabin. And he spotted an area of disturbed earth nearby, where it looked as if a few tree stumps had been removed.

A few minutes later Candy was back down beside her father. "No answer," she said.

Doc glanced around, narrowing his gaze. "Maybe he's gone into town." He pointed toward the river. "Let's check over that way."

They walked rather than drove, since it was just a short distance to the riverbank. After little more than two dozen paces, the woods fell behind them and the landscape

136

opened to give them good views both upstream and down. The English River flowed
from left to right, zigzagging between rocky
banks and a grassy, wildflower-strewn
stretch before curving around a dogleg
farther along and disappearing from view as
it made its way toward the village and the
sea beyond. To their left, they could see a
fairly long distance upstream, until the river
curved farther up as well. Silently they
studied both directions for several moments, turning one way, then the other, then
back, scanning the banks and the surrounding woods and fields. But they saw no one.

Doc let out a sigh and slid his hands into
his back pockets. "Well, I suppose we could
search the woods," he said, "though I'd hate
to get lost, and I have no idea which direction he might have —"

"Hullo!" a voice called suddenly from
behind them.

They both turned.

A figure was walking along the dirt lane
toward them, waving a hand in the air. He
was tall and lanky, with long dark hair, wearing a wide-brimmed straw hat that shadowed his face, a loose-fitting shirt, dark
pants, and black rubber boots. In one hand
he carried a thick walking stick made from
a tree branch. Across his chest was a tan

canvas strap attached to a bag that hung at his hip.

Candy waved back. "Hi, Judicious."

"Afternoon," Doc called.

"This is a surprise," Judicious said with an easy smile as he approached them. He stopped close by and planted the bottom of the walking stick on the rock-strewn riverbank, clasping it near the top with both hands. "It's good to see the both of you. You're looking well," he said.

"It's good to see you also, Judicious," Candy said. "It's been a while."

"It has. I've been around," he said, "but with the arrival of spring there's just so much to do in the woods." He patted the bag at his hip, which looked full. "Today I've been out mushroom hunting. The woods are full of them this time of year, especially after a good rain."

"What do you use them for?" Candy asked curiously.

"Soups. Stews. And some I dry for use later."

"You'll have to show me how to do that sometime."

"I'd be glad to," he said.

Doc cleared his throat, anxious to get on with the matter at hand. "Hope we're not disturbing you by showing up unannounced like this, Judicious," Doc said. "It's an impromptu visit."

"Actually, Doc, I've been expecting you."

"You have?" Candy said, a little surprised, though a moment later she realized that nothing about Judicious should surprise her.

"I don't suppose your visit has anything to do with that murder this morning out at Crawford's Berry Farm?" he asked.

"Gosh dang it!" Doc said. "Does everybody in town know about that already?"

"Word gets around fast," Judicious said. "What can I help you with?"

"Well, we're looking for a shovel," Doc said, and he explained about the icicles, and how he'd left a shovel with the initials *B.A.* on the handle at Sally Ann Longfellow's house, and how she'd given it to Ray Hutchins to return to Blueberry Acres, but he had supposedly lent it to Judicious.

"I do remember that," Judicious said when Doc had finished his explanation. "I don't have a car or a phone, as you know, so I wasn't sure how I was going to get it back to you. But fortunately someone stopped by, and she promised she'd return it to you. I put it in her car myself."

Candy and Doc exchanged glances. "And who might that be?" Candy asked.

"She came out one day, a couple of

months ago, to talk to me about some real estate my family owns up north," Judicious said. "I invited her in for tea. We talked for a while. I asked if she'd return the shovel to you, and she agreed." He paused, and looked from Candy to Doc and back again. "I gave it to Lydia St. Graves."

THIRTEEN

"Well, I guess that's it, then," Doc said once they were back in the Jeep and headed toward town. "Sounds like your instincts were right again. Lydia must have been fleeing the scene of the crime when she ran you off the road this morning — just like you thought."

"Yup, sounds like it," Candy agreed, thinking through all they'd just discovered. "Judicious gave her the shovel, so she could return it to us, but for whatever reason she never made it out to our place. She must have still had the shovel in her car when she went out to the berry farm this morning. Maybe she had an argument with Miles about the sale of his property, or something like that, and at some point she just snapped, so she took the shovel from her car and hit him over the head with it." She shrugged, an indication that she was not totally convinced. "Pretty simple, I guess."

"An open-and-shut case," Doc agreed, missing his daughter's subtle gesture. "We need to let the police know what's going on, so they can take it from here." He flicked a finger out the windshield, in the general direction of the Cape Willington Police Station, which was located a mile or so ahead of them around a few curves. "No need for both of us to go in. You can just drop me off. I'll bring them up to speed."

Candy was a little surprised by his suggestion. "You don't want me to go in with you?"

Doc waved a hand. "Not necessary. I'll make a statement for the both of us and you can fill in any details I missed later on. Besides, I still need to have my fingerprints taken, so I might as well kill two birds with one stone. I'll probably be there for a while. No point you sitting around waiting on me."

"But we're in this together," Candy protested.

"True, but I've got absolutely nothing else on my schedule today, and you have a busy afternoon planned. Several meetings, if I recall. And you still have a paper to get out, right?"

Candy nodded. "Yes, that's true."

Doc reached over and patted his daughter on her knee. "Look, your life is stressful enough right now, what with the paper and the farm and now this. So why don't you let me take care of the police? I'll be fine. And you can make your meetings and catch up on your work."

"How will you get back to town?"

Now it was Doc's turn to shrug, as if that were the least of his concerns. "I'll hitch a ride with one of the police officers. They seem to enjoy ride-alongs. Or maybe I'll just walk. It's a nice afternoon for a stroll. Meet you at the diner at five to catch up?"

Despite her misgivings, Candy let her father out at the police station, waited until he disappeared inside the building with a wave, and drove back to town.

She felt a little guilty leaving him there to face the police alone. A part of her argued that she was skipping out on her civic duty, especially given her involvement in the morning's events.

But another part of her appreciated her father's gesture. Once the police heard what he had to tell them, they'd most likely put out word to locate and detain Lydia St. Graves. But they'd also have a lot of questions for Doc. It could turn into a long session — an hour or two at least, maybe more. She honestly didn't know if she could afford the time for that. Doc was right. She *was* late for meetings, and she *did* have a lot of work to catch up on. Besides, she'd already told Officer Molly Prospect everything she knew about her encounter with Lydia that morning. There wasn't much else to add. Doc knew the rest. The police didn't really need to talk to both of them right now. She could drop by later and give her perspective. In the meantime, she had a busy afternoon ahead — and she wasn't necessarily looking forward to it, given the events on her schedule and the folks she was meeting.

Maybe it'd actually be easier to go back to the station and hang out with the police, she thought idly as she pulled into a parking spot along Ocean Avenue. *At least they'd probably be civil.*

She climbed out of the Jeep, pulling her tote bag from the backseat, and pushed through the door at 22B. She was halfway up the staircase before she heard the chatter from above.

The door to the *Cape Crier*'s office on the second floor of the building stood halfway open, and she could hear the voices of several females.

They're here, Candy thought, checking her watch. And she was late. *Oh boy.*

She listened for a few moments, took a

deep breath, and plunged ahead.

Out of the frying pan and into the fire.

There were five of them in all, standing on either side of the office suite's central hallway. They were conversing back and forth, clucking like hens, making their opinions and annoyances known to one another. Most wore scowls on their faces or had their arms crossed, a clear indication they didn't appreciate being kept waiting.

They were the ladies of the Cape Willington Heritage Protection League.

"She's nearly twenty minutes late," a dark-haired woman was saying. Her name, Candy recalled, was Cotton Colby. She was one of the group's founders. Candy had met her a number of times before around town and they'd exchanged a few words, but never took the time to talk at length.

"We had an appointment at one o'clock," Cotton continued in a high-pitched, quick-paced tone, while the other ladies paused to listen. "We can't afford to be kept waiting. We're busy people, you know. We have a lot to do, with the Strawberry Fair coming up on Saturday."

As Candy came through the door at the far end of the hall, she saw that Cotton was addressing Betty Lynn Sparr, the *Cape Crier*'s part-time receptionist and office manager. As the great-granddaughter of a sea captain, Betty Lynn liked to joke that she had salt water in her veins, which in turn (she claimed) enabled her to ably handle the most stressful and chaotic of situations with a reasonable amount of grace and aplomb. It made her an anchor around the office, her coworkers often told her, especially on the days they uploaded digital files to the printer, when dozens of things were happening at once. So finding herself in her current situation, as the primary focus of a group of moderately perturbed women, was generally a piece of cake for Betty Lynn.

"Oh, that should be a wonderful event," Betty Lynn said to Cotton, her eyes brightening. "Whoever came up with that idea is a genius. I don't use that word lightly. And yes, you're exactly right about the meeting, Mrs. Colby. I wrote it down on the office schedule. I can show you if you'd like. One o'clock, it says. Sharp as the nose on my face. She's well aware of it, I promise you that. I'm sure she'll be here as soon as she can."

"But she's supposed to be here *now,*" Cotton intoned, her voice expressing her impatience. "Where *is* she, if I may ask?"

Candy took a few steps into the hallway and cleared her throat. She stood behind the ladies, who were all facing away from her, toward Betty Lynn. "Here I am," she said as breezily as she could manage. "Good afternoon, ladies. Sorry I'm late. I was unavoidably delayed."

As she spoke, six pairs of eyes shifted around to look at her. At least one pair was friendly and looked relieved to see her. The others were scrutinizing at best, and bordering on unfriendly at worst.

Good thing they're not daggers, Candy thought.

With a fervent hope she hadn't ruffled too many feathers, she forced a smile and closed the door behind her. "If you'll just give me a few moments to put down my things, we can get started. Betty Lynn, I think we can fit everyone in my office. Would you bring in some extra chairs?"

As Betty Lynn dashed off to help get the ladies seated, Candy nodded appreciatively and started forward, winding her way past the ladies of the Heritage Protection League. They watched her pass in silence, though she could feel the power of their stares. Once past them and a little farther along the hall, she turned into her new office.

Or rather, Ben Clayton's old office. He had taken a few of his books and personal items with him when he suddenly relocated to San Francisco more than a year and a half ago, but he'd also left a lot behind. Candy could still see reminders of him everywhere she turned, in every drawer she opened. His chewed pencils were still in the top middle drawer, files with labels written in his hand were still in the cabinet. He'd even left one of his old Red Sox ball caps behind. Perhaps for that reason, she had avoided moving over here from her old office, which was located farther back in the rabbit warren of hallways, doorways, and offices that meandered through the building. But she'd found herself increasingly going into his then-vacant office to retrieve a file or look for an e-mail address on his computer, or to check one of his reference books, so she'd finally decided it was more efficient to just move in.

A couple of months ago she'd brought over some of her own things, including photos, books, files, and office equipment. She'd been moving over more items ever since, a few at a time, and the place was finally starting to look like her own. She didn't know how long she'd be here in this office, but at least she'd be comfortable until she decided on her next move.

Betty Lynn burst in with an armload of

metal folding chairs, and behind her came the ladies of the Heritage Protection League. Candy set down her tote bag on a corner of the desk and turned to help. "Please, have a seat," she said as she took a couple of chairs from Betty Lynn and started setting them up. They arranged the chairs in a semicircle around Candy's desk, with everyone equal distance away. It wasn't a large office, but it had a good-sized open space in the middle, since the modular L-shaped desk was pushed into one corner, and a long credenza that doubled as a filing cabinet was tucked back against the outside wall, under the tall window that looked out over Ocean Avenue.

Candy greeted the ladies in turn as they entered.

Cotton Colby was the first one through the door, walking with quick, precise steps. She was the youngest and the most vocal of the group — and also the most ambitious, Candy thought. One of the group's two founders, Cotton had thick, shoulder-length dark brown hair, parted on one side and neatly brushed to the other, with a carefully positioned swirl across her forehead. She was dressed to impress, in a gray narrow-cut jacket, cream-colored blouse, and black formfitting skirt, with contrasting jewelry and mirrorlike black pumps.

Alice Rainesford came in right behind her. She was older than Cotton, perhaps in her mid-to late-forties, and less flashy in appearance. She had a studious look, owing in part to her thick horn-rimmed glasses, which she wore on a thin silver chain draped around her neck. She was dressed more casually than Cotton, in beige slacks that showed wrinkles in places, a light-colored blouse buttoned up to the neck, and a pale pink sweater. Straight light brown hair, interspersed with a few streaks of gray, framed a narrow, reddish face with prominent cheekbones and a sharp chin.

Candy shook hands with both women, escorting each to a chair, and then turned to face the next three ladies, who entered more or less in a group, clutching their purses in their hands as they stepped into the room with some uncertainty. They were older than the other two, all in their fifties and about the same height. They all wore print dresses in various shades of green, blue, and purple, and had on their best shoes. They looked like they might just have come from church. They surveyed Candy's office with great interest, as if they were entering a secret inner sanctum where amazing wonders took place.

"You're Brenda Jenkins, right?" Candy said to the first of the three, shaking her hand. "We've met once or twice around town, I think. Won't you please have a seat?"

Brenda nodded, eyeing the place with interest as she moved toward a vacant chair. "I've never been in a newspaper office before," she said. "Where are the printing presses?" She glanced under the desk, as if they might be hidden there, and then looked back out into the hall.

"The newspaper is printed at another location," Candy said. "We only do editorial and production work out of this office, as well as sales and accounting."

"Oooh," Brenda said, absorbing this intriguing bit of information.

The next woman in line, wearing a blue print-patterned dress, reached out a tentative hand toward Candy. "I'm Della Swain," she announced in a firm tone. "I don't think we've met before. I'm new in town."

"Oh, well, it's nice to meet you," Candy said pleasantly, "and welcome to Cape Willington. How long have you lived here?"

"Seven years," said Della without batting an eye. "I'm still finding my way around and getting to know everyone in town. It's such a wonderful community, isn't it?"

"Yes, it is."

"Is Ben still working for the newspaper?" Della asked. "I enjoy reading his articles but I haven't seen them in a while. Is he sick?"

"I'm afraid Ben Clayton's left the paper," Candy said. "Some time ago."

"Oh my." Della looked crestfallen. "I'm afraid I didn't realize that. He seemed like such a nice man. Who's writing for the newspaper now?"

"There are a number of us who are trying to fill his shoes," Candy said evenly. "And we've brought in some new writers lately."

This seemed to appease Della for the moment. As she sat, Candy turned toward the last woman, who still stood in the doorway.

She was the group's other founder, and unlike Della, she had been in town for as long as anyone could remember. And she had an unmistakable air about her that made sure everyone knew it. Elvira Tremble had family roots in Cape Willington that went back generations, to around the time of the Civil War. Like Betty Lynn, she claimed a maritime-affiliated ancestor, a Captain Ezekiel Tremble, who had piloted steamboats along Maine's nineteenth-century coastline. From what Candy had read, Captain Tremble made quite a bit of money as the part owner of a regional transportation company that still maintained a small percentage of some of the ferry lines around the state. Her purple ensemble was complemented by expensive jewelry and a designer purse. She held her head aloof as she entered the office, studying it with a discerning eye. She managed to look down her nose as she turned to Candy and spoke.

"So is this *her* office?" Elvira asked, without any sort of introduction or pleasantries.

Uncertain what she was asking, Candy shook her head and said, "This is Ben Clayton's old office. I recently moved in, until they hire a new full-time editor."

"So is *she* here?" Elvira pressed, her dark eyes narrowing in like a vulture's.

Candy blinked several times and looked around the circle, from one woman to another. "Is who here?"

"The editor," Della Swain said.

"I'm the editor," Candy answered as she plopped down into her padded office chair. "At least, temporarily. I'm filling in — for now."

"There's been some mistake, then," Cotton said from the end of the row. "We were supposed to meet with the *other* editor."

"The other editor?" Candy shook her

head, confused. "Who's that?"

Elvira Tremble made a sound in the back of her throat, as if this was something she'd expected from such a shoddily run operation. "The woman we wanted to meet with is the same person who writes the community column. You know who she is."

Candy nodded as the realization stuck her. "Ahh, yes. Our community columnist. You're talking about Wanda Boyle."

FOURTEEN

It had been, Candy thought, an act of total desperation. And it had worked out better than she could have ever expected.

Her decision — an over-the-top gamble, really — had grown out of the events of a cold uncertain winter, when the newspaper's fate had hung in the balance, and rumors of financial troubles and even the paper's closing had been rampant around town. Candy hadn't known where the stories were coming from, but they hadn't been far off base, she eventually came to discover. As it turned out, the unexpected resignation of Ben Clayton and the rapid departure of two subsequent editors had caused instability at the newspaper, which was compounded by a lack of direction, support, and communication from the paper's then-owner, who was based out of Rhode Island.

At the same time, the increased popularity of a local community blog called the *Cape Crusader,* owned and written by a local woman named Wanda Boyle, challenged the newspaper's status around town and drained off some of its readers, which in turn caused ad sales to drop. Budgets were tightened and hours reduced. The paper's volunteer staff grew fretful and undependable, despite Betty Lynn's best attempts to keep up morale around the office by putting a positive spin on the latest news, whatever that might be.

The situation worsened right before Thanksgiving, when the then-owner announced that the paper was indeed up for sale. Shocked villagers sent the rumor mill spinning into high gear. Because of uncertainty about the paper's future, ad sales faltered even more. Financially the *Cape Crier* teetered on the brink. For a few desperate weeks at the end of the previous year, everyone associated with the paper, including Candy, prepared for the worst while hoping for something — anything — even remotely positive to happen.

As all this was going on, Candy had expected Wanda Boyle, through her *Cape Crusader* blog, to rejoice in the paper's problems. Wanda's primary competitor in town appeared to be on its last legs. Certainly this was what she had wanted all along, Candy remembered thinking.

Their relationship had been a rocky one over the past few years. Wanda remained upset that Candy had been hired by Ben as the paper's community columnist, and as a result they'd butted heads a number of times since. It was the primary reason Wanda had started her own community blog — as a way to rattle the town's established newspaper, which had, in her opinion, rejected her.

However, Wanda surprised everyone by coming out strongly in support of the *Cape Crier*. Decrying the possibility of its demise, she called the paper "a local treasure" that was "essential to the village's lifeblood," and considered it "a vital source of news and information for the people and businesses of our community." Over a series of blog posts, Wanda had whipped up local support for the paper, and even started an online petition to protest the paper's possible closing. Within a week she had several hundred signatures, and to date more than a thousand people had put their names to the document.

Once the paper's new owners had taken over after the beginning of the year, things had quieted down a bit. Still, the paper struggled financially. After all the negative publicity through the fall and into the winter, they'd lost quite a bit of readership and advertising, and didn't expect to get it back until the tourist season started up in late May. Candy wasn't sure the paper would last that long. The end seemed imminent. To prevent that from happening, she knew she needed to come up with a way to boost readership and ad sales as quickly as possible.

With Ben gone, no new editor in sight, and only a handful of part-time and volunteer workers left in the office, Candy took it upon herself to try to find a solution. So one cold February morning, she sat down at her office computer and drafted an e-mail to the new owners, who were located on Commercial Street in Portland, outlining several options.

Some of her ideas, such as reducing the number of issues they published each month or completely closing down the office for a day or two each week to save on utilities and other overhead costs, were practical but painful to envision. So she added a more creative solution, one that had actually been suggested by Betty Lynn on a dismal winter morning, when they were in Candy's office reading one of Wanda Boyle's blog posts describing the proper way to plow a drive-way after a heavy snowstorm. The four-paragraph piece included interviews with local snowplow drivers and a handy bulleted list of do's and don'ts.

"She's turning into a pretty good reporter," Betty Lynn had observed at the time. "Too bad she's not working for us."

It was true. Wanda had a prickly personality that made her hard to get along with. She could be snobbish when she wanted to be, and she sometimes resorted to mockery and sarcasm to make her points. Her fashion tastes were distinctive, to say the least. But she was good at what she did. She was a clever entrepreneur who worked hard and made smart decisions. She demonstrated tenaciousness and creativity. She knew just about everyone in Cape Willington, and she'd developed a strong following on her social media accounts, thanks to her on-the-spot reporting of the community's many events and activities.

And she'd always wanted to work for the paper.

Candy thought: *Why not?*

Maybe it was just what the paper needed — something fresh, something different, something to shake up the status quo.

Candy's outside-the-box proposal

prompted a flurry of e-mails with the paper's new owners, and after receiving approval, she approached Wanda with a novel concept.

By the end of the April, Wanda Boyle's first column had appeared in the *Cape Crier.*

The idea had been a simple one — offer Wanda what she'd always wanted by naming her the paper's new community correspondent, and launch a new print version of her blog, which would be prominently featured on page three of every issue of the paper. Wanda would also continue to write for her online blog on a regular basis, but now it would reside on the newspaper's website.

There were obvious benefits both for the paper and for Wanda. By joining forces, the paper could draw in all Wanda's followers. Maybe that would be enough to give them the boost in readers and sales they needed. And Wanda gained the prestige of working for an established print publication. She was thrilled with the idea, because she finally got what she'd always wanted — the title of community correspondent.

They decided to call Wanda's new column the *Cape Crusader,* just like her blog, and it replaced the paper's existing community column, which had been titled *Blueberry*

Bits. Candy herself had written the column for the past several years, ever since she'd been hired by Ben for the position.

During the exchange of e-mails with the owners as the details of the new arrangement were being worked out, Candy had agreed to relinquish the title of community correspondent, which she'd had for four years, and temporarily step into the position of managing editor. She had plenty of experience for the job, having worked closely with Ben all those years. And although it meant more work for her, it also meant more money, since her hours at the paper would increase. In the end, despite her reservations, she had agreed to give it a try.

It many ways it was a bittersweet transition for her. She'd had fun writing the *Blueberry Bits* column over the past few years, and had learned a lot from the process. But now she would turn her attention more toward editing, assigning, and managing, and less to writing.

Just as they'd all hoped, Wanda's column took off, creating a buzz around town. Issues of the paper started selling out again. They increased their press run. More copies started popping up around town, and advertisers were suddenly intrigued by the paper's resurgence. In the end, financial disaster was averted, and the paper moved onto stabler financial ground, especially with the tourist season now in full swing.

Of course, the new arrangement meant Candy and Wanda had to learn to work together — which hadn't been easy for either of them at first. But they both knew they needed each other, and so they'd developed a relatively civil working relationship — which mostly consisted of Candy biting her tongue a lot. For her part, Wanda had developed a more professional demeanor, and tried her best to keep her outsized personality in check. And as expected, she took her work very seriously. Her social media accounts thrived, and she quickly established herself as a recognized voice for the paper.

As Wanda's fame had grown, Candy had taken a few steps back out of the spotlight, concentrating her attention on the activities in the office.

So it wasn't surprising to hear that Cotton Colby, Elvira Tremble, and the other ladies of the Cape Willington Historical Protection League thought that Wanda Boyle — and not Candy — was the editor of the newspaper.

FIFTEEN

"She's such a wonderful writer," Della Swain said, trying very hard to keep the swoon out of her voice. "I've learned so much about the village while reading her articles over the years. And now to see her with her own column in the newspaper!" She puckered her face in excitement. "What an honor it must be for you to work with her!"

"Um, yes, it's . . . quite an honor," Candy said hesitantly. "Wanda's a great asset to the *Crier,* of course. I don't know what we'd do without her. Excuse me for a minute."

She slipped out of her chair and went to find Betty Lynn, who was in a conversation with Jesse Kidder, the paper's photographer and graphic designer. Candy broke in to ask if Betty Lynn knew the whereabouts of Wanda. "These ladies want her to sit in on the meeting," she explained.

Betty Lynn leaped right into action. "Let

me see if I can get hold of her," she said, dashing off to her desk.

Jesse grinned at Candy's evident discomfort. "Tough crowd?" he asked, raising an eyebrow.

Candy blew out a breath. "You have no idea," she said, and returned to her own office.

"We're trying to track Wanda down right now," Candy explained to the ladies once she was seated again. "Just so I can understand what went wrong, did you talk to Wanda personally when you set up the appointment with me, um, with *us*?"

"I believe she was CC'd on our e-mails with Betty Lynn," Cotton informed her primly.

"That's right," Della confirmed. "I made sure Wanda was included."

"Della is our e-mail expert," Brenda Jenkins explained helpfully, "so if she says Wanda was notified, then she's telling the truth!"

"But I don't want to get Wanda into trouble," Della responded, sounding horrified.

"Wanda's not in trouble," Candy assured her. "It's just a little mix-up."

"We *asked* for a meeting with the *editor*," Elvira clarified, bunching together her dark

164

eyebrows. She had finally seated herself, though she perched on the edge of her chair with her tightly folded hands resting uneasily in her lap, as if she wanted to be ready in case she needed to spring to her feet and make a hasty exit.

Candy was tempted to say, *Well, you* are *meeting with the editor* — she was certain that was what the ladies had requested in those e-mails, and Betty Lynn had complied with their wishes — but she held herself back. She also wanted to ask them why *she* hadn't been included in this apparent exchange of e-mails, but let that go as well. Today was not a good day to upset the ladies of the Heritage Protection League and stir up even more problems for herself.

So instead, as pleasantly as she could, she said, "Well, then, I'm sure Wanda will be here shortly to meet with you. In the meantime, if there's any way I can help, I'd be glad to do what I can."

The ladies were silent for a few moments. They exchanged furtive glances, as if silently coaxing one another to say something. Finally they all looked at Della, who cleared her throat, straightened her shoulders, and asked, "What is it you do again?"

As she spoke, studious Alice Rainesford leaned forward and pulled out a notebook from her tote bag. She flipped it open and took up a pen, apparently prepared to make notes of the meeting.

Candy eyed all five of them. "Hmm," she said.

How to answer?

She finally reached around, took a pile of business cards from her desktop, and passed out a card to each lady. "I'm a writer and a reporter for the newspaper," she told them in a clear tone, as if talking to first graders. "I was the community correspondent before Wanda. For most of my time here I wrote a column called *Blueberry Bits.* I also covered a number of news stories about events in town. Now I'm the interim managing editor."

"I thought Wanda wrote *Blueberry Bits,*" Della said, tapping a finger to her chin.

"No, Wanda writes a new column called the *Cape Crusader.* It's based on her blog. It replaced my column a few months ago."

"You have a blog?"

"No, Wanda has a blog."

"Then who have I been reading all these years?" Della asked, sounding confused.

"You've probably been reading all of us," Candy said. "My column, Wanda's blog, Ben's editorials —"

"I really did enjoy reading Ben's articles,"

Della said wistfully. "Are you sure he's not still around?"

Elvira Tremble waved her hand, interrupting them. "I have a question," she said in a somewhat haughty tone.

Candy looked at her expectantly. "Yes?"

"What is an *interim managing editor*?" She made the last three words sound like something she'd expect to find at the bottom of a drain pipe.

Candy gave her a polite answer. "It means I've temporarily taken over the editor's duties here at the newspaper until they can find the right full-time person. Currently, I'm responsible for assigning, writing, editing, and proofing all the content in the paper. I work with Jesse and the production department on layout. I write headlines and photo captions. I meet with people and take phone calls. That sort of thing."

"Oh, I see." Elvira considered this. "So you say you're a writer?"

"Yes, well, I try to be."

"Will you be covering the Strawberry Fair this weekend then?"

"Of course," Candy said. "Both Wanda and I will be there, along with our photographer."

"And what exactly will you be writing about?"

167

Candy tilted her head slightly. "What do you mean?"

Cotton Colby spoke up in response. "You realize how important this event is to our organization?"

Candy was silent for a moment as she thought about that. "I'm not sure. In what way?"

Cotton straightened herself in her chair and launched into what sounded like a carefully rehearsed spiel. "We need to preserve our way of life — our heritage — here in the village," she said with great seriousness. "Our group is not antigrowth or antibusiness. In fact, it's just the opposite. We believe the village needs to maintain its small-town atmosphere in order to survive and thrive. That's what brings all the summer visitors here and helps keep the village humming along. So we, as civic-minded citizens, believe we must guard against anything that might threaten Cape Willington's small-town charm."

"Of course," Candy said. "Anything in particular you're referring to?"

"Well, since you asked," Elvira said, "we're opposed to the unfettered building of large commercial establishments on historic farmland that contributes to the health and vitality of this community, especially without the voice of the people being heard on the subject."

"Ah. You're talking about the alleged real estate deal out at Crawford's Berry Farm?" For the moment, Candy avoided any mention of her own involvement in the events of the past few hours. Instead, she said, "Yes, Wanda's been writing quite a bit about that over the past few weeks, hasn't she?"

"Her articles have been very informative," Della agreed with a nod of her head.

"Is that why you wanted to talk to Wanda?" Candy asked. "To find out information about the berry farm? About this supposed sale?"

"We want to make sure our voices are heard," Cotton said. "We want to make sure our event gets the coverage it deserves. And yes, we were hoping Wanda could tell us the latest about the situation at the berry farm and this new resort we've heard about. We want to keep our berry farm intact. We don't want some big conglomerate moving in. So we're very concerned with what's going on out there."

"Especially after what happened *this morning,*" Elvira said in a tone so low it sounded like a growl.

Again, they were all silent for a moment, until Candy finally said, "Yes, yes, from

169

what I've heard, it's very . . . unfortunate."

Elvira leaned forward from her perch on the chair. "As the interim managing editor, as you call it, have *you* heard any behind-the-scenes information you could share with us?" she asked craftily. "Do they have any idea who did it?"

"Any clues you could share with us?" Della added breathlessly.

"Just so we know how to proceed in order to better protect our village from further harm, of course," Cotton clarified.

Candy had known the question might come up, and she'd already formulated her response. "I only know what the police have officially released."

"I see," Cotton said with a stern look. "It's been a shock for all of us, of course. We held an emergency meeting of our executive committee this morning to discuss whether we should proceed with the Strawberry Fair or cancel it."

"I was late for the meeting!" Della cut in. "I was out running errands. I didn't even know we were having one!"

"A few people were late," Cotton confirmed, and her voice rose just a bit in pitch. "As I said, it was an emergency meeting to make a decision about the Fair. We had a quorum. Of course, the decision was easy.

Too much time and money has already been spent to turn back now. We agreed unanimously to proceed as planned. Besides," she added, "we all think the Fair might just be what the community needs to get us through this difficult time."

"We're having pony rides!" Della said excitedly.

"And we'll have speeches and performances as well," Brenda added, "with food booths and several contests. I'm helping out at the strawberry shortcake tent," she said proudly.

"The Pruitt Foundation has helped us fund the event," Elvira noted. "Of course, we're grateful to them for their support."

"Really? The Pruitt Foundation?" Candy had not heard that. Established by one of the town's wealthiest families, the foundation supported a number of local civic and charitable events. "That's not the type of thing they usually do, is it?" Candy asked. She was a little surprised.

"They respect the town's heritage as much as anyone," Cotton said. "They're helping us preserve our way of life here."

So does that mean the Pruitts oppose the rumored sale of the berry farm? Candy wondered.

It was food for thought.

171

She was about to say something else when they all heard heavy footsteps on the wooden staircase leading up to the second floor. The main office door creaked open and then slammed shut. A tornado swept down the hallway toward them.

Wanda Boyle had arrived.

Sixteen

She rushed into Candy's office, a whirlwind of red hair and energy. "My, what a day it's been!" she exclaimed in a measured tone, as if she'd chosen her words carefully before she'd arrived. Wanda could be a formidable woman when she wanted to, given her large frame, wide shoulders, and big hands. In the past she'd been known to haul around lumber and pound a few nails with her husband, Brad, who owned a remodeling and construction business. But she'd smoothed off some of her rougher edges over the past few years, and slimmed down as well. She'd toned down her wardrobe too. These days, she opted for a business-casual, small-town newswoman look that fit well in a low-key Maine coastal village. She favored khaki pants, flowing pale blue blouses, and penny loafers, like she wore today, sometimes accented by a scarf, a tasteful necklace, or a vest. It was a carefully honed image, Candy knew, but it worked, since it made everyone around her more at ease — which enabled her to manipulate the situation to her advantage, something she was very good at doing.

Wanda surveyed the room in a single glance, then went straight to Cotton Colby at the far end of the semicircle. She leaned over gracefully and gave the dark-haired woman a quick, warm embrace before anyone knew what was happening.

"There you are. And you're looking just wonderful today, as usual. I'm so sorry I'm late, but you will *not* believe who I just talked to," Wanda told Cotton in a casual tone, as if she were sharing a secret with a close friend. "He's the older brother of a prominent senator's hairdresser. This was quite a coup for me, I don't mind telling you. I've been after this person for weeks!" As she spoke, she moved on down the line, greeting each lady in turn, pecking a cheek here, shaking a hand there, dolling out hugs everywhere. "But hard work pays off, I always say. I finally tracked him down. He gave me some wonderful anecdotes about growing up with such a talented sister — as well as some inside news about the latest happenings with the senator! I can tell you, it's going to make a great story. I'm going to write it up for the next issue of the paper."

The ladies all looked a little bewildered as Wanda spoke. No one seemed to know what to say to her, or even what Wanda was talking about. But no one seemed to care. Her casual, talkative attitude had completely disarmed them — even Elvira. All the fire had gone out of her eyes. Wanda had won them over before they'd had a chance to say a word to her.

"Now, I understand you ladies are here for a very important reason," Wanda continued, her tone lowering and becoming more serious as she stepped back and dramatically put her hands together. "We have a Strawberry Fair coming up, right? So we're going to put our resources together and see if we can build some positive energy around here, right!"

"Yes, you're absolutely right," Cotton said with a surprised smile. "That's exactly what we're hoping to do."

"And we're not going to let the events of this morning" — here Wanda wheeled around briefly, speaking in a low tone so only Candy could hear — "which you and I need to talk about, by the way" — before flipping back around and continuing — "stop us from helping out our community any way we can. After all, we need to protect our village's heritage, right?"

"We couldn't agree more," Elvira said, nodding approvingly, and the other ladies gave their consent as well.

"You know what?" Wanda said, and she clapped her hands together. "I have a wonderful idea. Why don't we get out of this stuffy old office and reconvene someplace that's a little cozier, where we can have a nice cup of tea and chat about the Fair and this wonderful new group you've founded."

The ladies perked right up at that idea. Knowing she had them in the palm of her hand, Wanda continued, "On my way up here, I stopped by that new tea shop downstairs and reserved us a table. Why don't we let Candy get back to her work, and we can reconvene downstairs in" — she dramatically checked her watch — "shall we say ten minutes? How does that sound?"

The ladies all agreed it sounded like a splendid idea, and started chatting excitedly among themselves. They rose as a flock, and within a few minutes, after some brief final words, they were gone.

Wanda lingered, though. She leaned out the doorway of Candy's office and waved to the departing ladies. "I'll catch right up with you," she called as they headed down the hallway and out the door. "Be sure to save me a seat!"

When they were out of earshot, Candy said, "Well, I have to admit, Wanda, you handled that brilliantly."

The red-haired woman waved the comment away with a mild look of annoyance, as if she were batting away a fly. "Piece of cake," she said as she fished her phone out of a pocket. "I got their lingo down to a science. You just have to know how to charm them. It's not that hard."

Candy knew there was a dig intended for her somewhere in there, but she let it go — again. Instead, as Wanda scrolled rapidly through the contact list on her phone, Candy said, "Apparently there was a mix-up. They thought they were meeting with you."

"And I thought they were meeting with *you,*" Wanda said flatly, her eyes still focused on her phone. She touched the screen and held the device to her ear. "They said 'the editor' in their e-mails. They must have thought I was the editor. I've had that happen a lot around town lately. Common mistake, really, don't you think?"

"I suppose so."

"Good thing Betty Lynn texted me," Wanda continued. "I was right around the corner, just about to get my nails done, and rushed straight over."

"So when did you have time to reserve a table at the tea shop?"

Wanda held up a finger and said into the phone, "Yes, hello, this is Wanda Boyle. I'm with the *Cape Crier* newspaper upstairs?" She listened a minute. "Well, thank you!" she said, her face brightening. "It's so nice to talk to you again too. Listen, would you be able to do me a huge favor and set up a table for a group of six? Yes, right away, if you could. They should be walking in your door right about now. And would you be able to bring us a nice green tea, maybe something with mint or jasmine? And could we also get a fruit infusion — maybe a Turkish apple or a ginger peach, something like that? What's that?" She listened again for a few moments. "That sounds perfect! I'm on my way down. I'll see you in a few."

She lowered the phone and poked at the screen. "I have to run, but a couple of quick things before I go. First, we have to figure out what to do about the berry farm."

"In what way?" Candy asked guardedly.

"I need to know who's covering what, so we don't duplicate our efforts."

"Oh, right! Like figuring out the angles,

divvying up the assignments, that sort of thing."

Wanda nodded. "I have Jill the intern working on a few sidebar items about the Crawford property, and a volunteer who knew Miles is writing a tribute. If it's okay with you, I'm going to focus on the investigation. This could be big, you know."

"I know," Candy said, again holding back details of her own involvement with the murder — at least for the time being.

"This is the stuff they give out Pulitzers for."

"Let's not get ahead of ourselves," Candy cautioned. "Let's just try to get the next issue out on time."

"Right. So I'm heading over to the police station as soon as I'm done with the league ladies, and I'll put together some ideas and e-mail them to you a little later on."

Candy nodded. "Sounds good. Anything else we need to talk about?"

The red-haired woman glanced at her watch and edged toward the door. "Just the office situation — I'm going to move all my things into your old office this evening."

"My old office?" Candy was caught off guard by this pronouncement.

"Sure, that's where the community correspondent has always worked, right? Out

179

of that musty office back in that dark corner of the building?"

"Yes, but . . . why would you want that office? You already have a desk," Candy said.

Wanda waved a dismissive hand. "I'm tired of working in that little cubbyhole up front with the interns and the volunteers. When people walk in, they always ask me for directions to the bathroom or want me to help them unclog the printer. I need a place where I can close the door, so I can think, write, and do some interviews. Besides" — she twirled a finger in the air, motioning around the room — "you've moved in here. You don't need your other office anymore."

"Yes, but I still have stuff in there," Candy said.

Wanda shook her head, her red hair flying. "Not much, really. I checked. Just scarves and mittens and such, and some dusty old files in that beat-up filing cabinet pushed back into the corner. I glanced at them but they look worthless. I'll throw them out if you want me to."

Candy tried to make her reaction as casual as possible. "No, I'll take care of them. Those are . . . some personal files of mine. I'll box them up and take them home. In fact, you're right. I'll finish cleaning out that office this afternoon and you can have it. It'll be ready for you to move in by tonight."

Wanda was gone a few moments later, satisfied she'd gotten what she wanted once again. But Candy knew she'd just escaped a rather delicate situation.

I should have taken care of those files years ago, she thought, angry at herself for her letting them linger there as long as they had. *They should have been destroyed right away.*

Betty Lynn scrounged up a few empty boxes for her and offered to help her do whatever she was doing, but Candy declined, saying she just needed to clean out a few papers and files. She carried the boxes to her old, dark office and tossed them into the middle of the floor. They landed with dull thuds, which echoed dimly in the hollow room.

Over the weekend, Candy had taken down the last of the posters she'd hung up on the walls to brighten the place. She'd also removed the old calendars and production schedules, the handwritten Post-It Notes, and Betty Lynn's HR memos, which had dotted the walls. She'd relocated a large cork board to Ben's old office — *I guess it's officially my office now,* she told herself — a few days ago. She'd already cleaned her stuff out of the drawers but had left behind some general items — boxes of paper clips and rubber bands, rulers and pens that barely worked. There wasn't much left, as Wanda had pointed out — just a few old scarves and a battered folded umbrella hanging from a wall peg, and some mittens and gloves on a lower shelf.

She wasn't sad to leave this office. The memories were too mixed, too scattered. But she'd spent a lot of time in here, tapping out stories on her computer. That, at least, was something to dwell on, at least for a few moments.

She had moved most of her files over to her new office as well. But she'd left one drawer in the filing cabinet untouched.

It was the drawer at the bottom, the one labeled *S.V.*

SEVENTEEN

The files in the bottom drawer had once belonged to Sapphire Vine, the paper's community columnist before Candy took over the job. Sapphire had been struck down in the living room of her home on Gleason Street several years ago, and upon her unfortunate passing, her work files had found their way into Candy's hands. She'd also inherited lesser-known personal files Sapphire kept squirreled away in a secret attic hideaway.

In the files, Candy had found evidence that Sapphire was spying on some of the local villagers, and using the information she'd learned to blackmail certain people. Candy had resolved most of those issues years ago, but felt there still might be a few bombshells hidden deep within those files, though she'd resisted looking for them herself, wary of what she might find.

She still wasn't completely sure why she'd

kept the files this long. Her brain had told her, many times, that it would be best simply to destroy them — shred them, burn them, bury them, whatever, and get rid of all the uncomfortable secrets they held — but her instincts made her hold off on doing that, for she suspected the information they contained might prove useful someday. So she'd dumped them into the bottom drawer of the filing cabinet in the corner and left them there to gather dust, until she decided what to do with them.

As it turned out, her instincts had been right. Two or three times over the past several years, she'd dipped into the files, searching for information she hoped would help her solve a mystery or two. At those times she'd gone through only specific files, such as the ones devoted to Wanda Boyle and the wealthy Pruitt family, so she knew those at least contained nothing particularly damaging. That was how most of the ones she'd seen had been — filled with random clippings and aging photos of townspeople going about their everyday lives. Sapphire had assembled the files more for informational purposes than anything else, but a number of them held secrets and revelations that could ruin reputations if the information leaked out, and a few were meticulous

in detail about their subjects' lives —
evidence of Sapphire Vine's snooping and
far-reaching schemes. For that reason,
Candy had kept the files to herself, not hiding them but not putting them on full public
view, hesitant to let anyone else — especially
someone like Wanda — get a good look at
them.

Still, Candy knew someone might someday stumble over them, as Wanda had. For
whatever reason, Wanda hadn't yet made
the connection between *S.V.* and *Sapphire
Vine.* Maybe the events of those days had
simply, finally, faded from memory.

But Wanda was right about one thing —
the files were now too old, and the information they contained too outdated, to be of
any use anymore. It was time to destroy
them — and the secrets they contained —
once and for all.

Candy pulled a box over toward the filing
cabinet, sat cross-legged on the floor in
front of the bottom drawer, and slid it open.
In quick order she started lifting files out of
the drawer and loading them into the box.
She'd been back through the files before —
she knew what the labels read. No need to
dwell on them, she thought. The quicker
they were gone, the better. She'd made up
her mind. She filled up one box and reached

185

for another.

Some of the files were thicker than others. All had labels and descriptions written in various colors by Sapphire's own hand, often embellished with curlicues and whimsical designs. Candy tried hard not to let them distract her as she pulled them out of the drawer and stacked them into the box, but she couldn't help glancing at some of them. Eventually curiosity got the better of her, and in the end she allowed herself to take a quick peek inside two files — one devoted to Miles Crawford, and the other to Lydia St. Graves.

Since the files hadn't been updated in years, they wouldn't contain any recent information, she knew, but they might provide a tidbit of information or some unknown background detail to help her better understand what had happened between those two.

The Crawford file contained only a handful of clippings from the *Cape Crier,* including a couple of community news briefs written by Sapphire herself. Most of the articles were about the strawberry fields, written for issues published in late May or early June to coincide with the start of the picking season. There were a few old recipes as well, and a few photos of a younger Miles, including one with his family, Candy guessed — a wife and two teenaged sons, both with long, reddish-brown hair. It looked like the photo had been taken sometime in the nineties, long before Candy had arrived in town. There was also a faded clipping about some legend connected to the farm, but a major part of the article was missing. Candy could make neither heads nor tails out of it. None of it, she decided quickly, was of any value.

She tossed the file into the last box and picked up Lydia's folder, but it, too, contained only a few random clips — Lydia as Realtor of the year, Lydia giving a talk at a business luncheon, Lydia closing a deal on a well-known property. The clips were at least four or five years old, and many of them were older than that. Again, nothing that Candy could use.

It only confirmed her decision to destroy the files once and for all, she thought as she tossed Lydia's file on top of the others. So she sealed up the boxes and started carrying them down to the Jeep, one or two at a time.

Betty Lynn had gone out. Jesse had disappeared. The front office where the volunteers and interns worked was empty. The place was deserted, so Candy was left to load the boxes in the Jeep herself.

She pounded up and down the staircase a couple of times, and on the final trip down she almost ran into Rachel Fairweather, who was coming up the stairs. Candy barely avoided knocking the elderly woman backward, sending her all the way to the bottom.

"Oh my!" Mrs. Fairweather exclaimed as Candy halted herself and backpedaled up a step or two. She teetered a little before catching her balance. When she had her footing again, she held the boxes over to one side so she could see around them. "Is that . . . Mrs. Fairweather? Are you all right? I almost ran over you."

The elderly woman held tightly to the side rail with one hand, and clutched a serving dish in the other. "Yes, yes, dear, I'm fine. Thank you. Just a little surprised."

Candy took another step back, and up. "What are you doing here?"

"Oh, I hope I'm in the right place," Mrs. Fairweather said. "I'm looking for the newspaper office."

"Well, yes, this is the right place, but —"

"I have an appointment. For a meeting. At two o'clock," Mrs. Fairweather said. "I'm supposed to meet with Wanda Boyle, the editor. You see, I'm the secretary for the

Cape Willington Heritage Protection League. I'm not late, am I?"

EIGHTEEN

"No, you're not late," Candy told the elderly woman a few minutes later, when they were back upstairs in her office. She set the boxes down on top of the desk and motioned Mrs. Fairweather to a chair. "At least, not for a two o'clock meeting." Candy checked her watch. "In fact, you'd be about ten minutes early. The only problem is, the meeting was scheduled for one o'clock. I'm afraid the other ladies have been here and gone."

Mrs. Fairweather looked deflated. "Does that mean I've missed it again?"

Candy nodded. "I'm afraid so."

"Oh dear. I seem to keep missing these meetings. What will the other ladies think of me?"

"Actually," Candy said, "you're in luck. They relocated with Wanda Boyle to the tea shop downstairs, and might still be there. Why don't I walk down with you and we'll see if we can find your friends?"

Mrs. Fairweather's face lit up. "Oh, that would be wonderful!" She looked down at the plate, which she'd set down on her lap. "Oh yes, I almost forgot this. It's the most important part." She handed the plate over to Candy. It held something under a covering of tinfoil.

Candy lifted an edge and peeked inside, but the aroma gave it away almost at once. "Strawberry pie?" she asked.

"Fresh out of the oven," Mrs. Fairweather confirmed. "I brought two big slices for you. I made it myself this morning. The crust comes from an old family recipe. I've heard you worked at the bakery for a while. Let me know what you think of it."

"I will," Candy said, "and it certainly smells wonderful." She set the plate down on her desktop, saving it for later.

"I'm quite a cook, you know," Mrs. Fairweather said as she rose. "I'm making bean soup this afternoon. You really should stop by and try some later today or tomorrow. It's from an old family recipe."

Her expression grew serious as she looked at Candy with melancholy gray eyes. "This morning, when you visited me at the house, I hadn't yet heard about what happened out at the berry farm," she said softly. "But after

191

you left, I got a call from a friend of mine, who told me what happened to Mr. Crawford. I've been on the phone ever since. Everyone's talking about it."

"I imagine they are," Candy said. "Word gets around town pretty fast these days."

Mrs. Fairweather took a few steps toward the door. "I suppose that's why I mixed up the time about the meeting this afternoon. It has me in a bit of a tizzy, I'm afraid. I didn't know him very well, but everyone agrees his death is a great loss for this town."

"I couldn't agree more," Candy said, rising as well.

"You know," Mrs. Fairweather continued, "that property has been a berry farm for as long as I can remember. It was a dairy farm before that, and a homestead before that. My mother used to go out there when she was a little girl for eggs and milk, fresh from the farm. I've taken my own children and grandchildren there for berry picking since before they could walk." She sighed and shook her head. "I've heard the rumors around town just like everyone else — that Mr. Crawford was going to sell the place, and somehow that horrid real estate woman was involved in the whole thing. I heard they were going to tear up the strawberry fields and turn it into a big resort. Can you imagine that? We can't allow things like that to happen around here, can we? We can't lose our special places. We must protect them." She said these last words quite emphatically for an eighty-five-year-old woman. "So that's why I joined the Heritage Protection League. I'd hoped we might convince Mr. Crawford to change his mind. We had a meeting scheduled with him for next week, you know, just to tell him how we all felt about his place. But now he's gone and, well, that changes everything, doesn't it?"

"I suppose it does," Candy acknowledged.

"But what will happen to his place now?" Mrs. Fairweather asked worriedly. "Will it stay a berry farm — or will they change it into something else?"

Candy shook her head. "I don't know. We'll just have to wait and see, I guess. Come on, I'll walk you to the tea shop."

Halfway down the stairs, Mrs. Fairweather paused, looked back up at Candy, and said, "I don't suppose your visit this morning had anything to do with that terrible business out at the berry farm?"

Candy sidestepped the question, as she had before. "We were just trying to find out what happened to that old shovel of ours."

"And did you?"

"Yes, I believe so."

"Good! I'm glad you found it. Your father is a very nice man, by the way. How's everything going out at the blueberry farm?"

They chatted pleasantly as they walked the rest of the way down the stairs, out the door, and up the street to the tea shop.

They found the reserved table easily enough. Some of the league ladies, as well as Wanda, had already departed, but a few remained. Candy stopped in only briefly to reunite Mrs. Fairweather with her friends, and then she was out the door and headed across the street to the Pruitt Opera House for her two o'clock meeting with the town council chairman, Mason Flint.

Located halfway down Ocean Avenue, the opera house not only served as the town's most prestigious and historic entertainment venue, but it also housed the town offices in the basement. Named for its principal benefactor, Horace Roberts Pruitt, it dated back to 1881 and featured a controversial but picturesque widow's walk at its peak.

Candy hurried up the granite steps and in through the large, heavy front doors into the building's atrium. She was a frequent visitor to the opera house, so she knew her way around. Once inside the front doors she turned right, heading past the closed ticket window and information desk, toward a staircase at one end of the room, which led down to the basement. But before could start down the stairs, she came face-to-face with Mason Flint, who was headed up.

A lean, elderly gentleman with a full head of white hair, the town council chairman was accompanied by a small entourage, and looked like he was on his way somewhere in a hurry. But he spotted Candy as he reached the top of the stairs and beckoned her over with a crook of his finger.

"I had someone call your office but you must have been out," he told her without preamble, giving her a grim look. "I'm afraid I have to postpone our meeting this afternoon. I suppose you've heard what's happened out at the Crawford place."

"I've heard."

"I'm headed out there right now." He looked over his shoulder at his companions, who had bunched up on the stairs behind him. "I'll be right with you," he told them, and motioned Candy aside. "Can we have a few words in private?"

Candy reacted with mild surprise. "Of course."

Mason led her to an alcove, where they were more or less out of earshot of the others. He lowered his voice as he spoke, just to make sure. "What's this I've heard from the chief about a shovel?" Mason asked. "From Blueberry Acres? What's that all about?"

Briefly, Candy explained how a shovel with the initials *B.A.* on the handle, found in the hoophouse near Miles Crawford's body, had made its way from Blueberry Acres to Sally Ann Longfellow's place, and eventually into the hands of Lydia St. Graves. "Doc's over at the police station right now, explaining it all," Candy finished. "It seems to confirm our suspicions that Lydia was involved in some way with the murder. I suppose they'll bring her in for questioning and go from there."

"So all those rumors about her and the Crawford place are true?" Mason asked, his brow furrowing.

Candy agreed there appeared to be some truth to them.

"Well, that just takes the cake," Mason said, not trying to hide his irritation. He gave Candy a hard look. "Do you think she did it?"

Candy shrugged. "That's for the police to decide."

Mason nodded and glanced at the members of his entourage, who were cooling their heels near the large front doors, checking their phones and shuffling around impatiently as they waited. "I've got my folks looking into it right now," he told her. "We've got to get to the bottom of this thing as quickly as possible. I want to find out what's going on with this real estate deal, and I want to know who's behind it, if it exists at all. Those league ladies have been pestering me about it, you know."

"They have?"

"Met with them earlier in the week," Mason said with a nod. "They're all worked up about that berry farm. They're trying to get me to intervene and stop the deal — but I haven't been able to confirm any sort of deal exists. There's nothing on paper, as far as I can tell. It's just smoke and mirrors at this point. That's why I want you to help me out."

"Me? How?"

Mason's gaze narrowed on her. "By doing what you do." He made a downward twirling motion with his finger, as if he were stirring a pot. "You have some experience with these sorts of things, right? Ask a few questions. Check in with your sources. Do a little research. Stir things up a little — and find out who or what's behind all these rumors. I want to know if they're true or not. If Lydia and Miles really were involved in some sort of secret deal, I want to know what it was. Then let's end this thing once and for all. Tourist season's upon us, and I don't want to ruin it with any more problems. So what do you say — can you do me this favor?"

Candy nodded quickly. "Of course. I'll check around and see what I can find out."

"Good!" Mason seemed pleased by her response. "I made a promise to bring stability to this town, and that's what I intend to do. We haven't let any of these murders stop us so far — and we're not going to let them now."

He nodded sharply. "You have my number. Call me if you find out anything. If not, I'll see you Saturday at the Fair." He gave her a toothy grin. "I'm really looking forward to having some strawberry shortcake, aren't you?"

Then he spun on his heels and was off.

NINETEEN

Candy moved the last couple of boxes down to the Jeep and spent the rest of the afternoon working in her office. People drifted in and out. Betty Lynn came and went several times. A volunteer or two stopped by, said hello, worked for a while, and left. Candy had missed lunch, so she ate a slice of the strawberry pie Mrs. Fairweather had dropped off as she proofed some of the pages Jesse had laid out. Then she wrote several photo captions, did quick edits on a couple of articles, checked the calendar items for the next issue of the paper, and assembled a short news brief section to fill an open quarter-page.

With those tasks complete and everything else out of the way for a few minutes, she opened a new file on her desktop and starting keying in some notes about the morning's events, while they were still fresh in her mind. She'd have to put together an article for the front page, but she hadn't decided yet what she'd include in the next issue, and what she'd leave out. It all depended on what happened over the next day or two. But at least she'd start a record of the sequence of events so far, and some descriptions of what she'd seen and heard. She'd update and add to it as the story unfolded. And maybe the process would give her some insight into the murder of Miles Crawford.

As she wrote, she began to realize there were big gaps in the story. When she visualized the events, questions began popping into her mind. Not just about the shovel, but about bigger issues, such as motivation and timing.

Why would someone want to kill Miles Crawford? she wondered. He'd been a berry farmer for thirty years, a hard worker, and a bit of a loner. So why would someone hit him over the head with a shovel?

As she considered the possibilities, the words of Mason Flint echoed in her mind: *If Lydia and Miles really were involved in some sort of secret deal, I want to know what it is.*

A secret deal. That was what the rumors said. But was it a reality — or a fantasy?

So far she'd mostly discounted the rumors surrounding the berry farm as typical small-town chatter. *Somebody* was *always* upset about *something* around town, she'd learned after working at the paper for a few years. Gossip and rumors circulated all the time. It was just the way people were. In fact, Candy thought, that was why local newspapers existed in the first place — to sort the truth from the fiction and tell people what was happening with their neighbors.

So she always discounted rumors until they were backed up by facts. But what if the stories about the Crawford place were true?

In fact, now that she thought about it, the rumors probably *were* true. Candy had seen Lydia coming from the direction of the farm. She must have been out there this morning. That seemed to confirm she'd been talking to Miles, and leant credence to everything Candy had heard over the past month or two about a deal between the two.

But if all that was true, why would Lydia kill Miles? What could she hope to gain? Certainly the berry farm was a coveted property. Any deal for its sale would involve a lot of money — money that could become a motivation for murder. Had something gone wrong with their arrangement? Did they have a falling out? Had Miles tried to back out of the deal?

Or had it been something else?

And if Lydia *did* kill Miles, why would she leave the murder weapon at the scene of the crime — a shovel she must have known could be traced back to her?

That was the point that nagged at Candy the most.

She heard Mason Flint's voice again in her head: *We have to get to the bottom of this thing as quickly as possible. Ask a few questions. Check your sources. Do a little research. . . .*

Maybe he was right.

Since she'd left Judicious's place and parted ways with her father earlier in the day, she hadn't had much time to consider what all their earlier discoveries might mean. Obviously Lydia was the likeliest suspect in Miles's death, based on her appearance on the road this morning. Once they'd found out how the shovel got into her hands, Candy had left it at that, deciding it was an issue for the police to handle.

But maybe she'd been too hasty.

Maybe, she thought, she was seeing what someone *wanted* her to see, rather than what was really there.

So what was real, and what wasn't?

Ask a few questions. Check your sources. Do a little research. . . .

If she wanted the latest inside information on all the rumors floating around town, the best place to start, she knew, was with Wanda Boyle. Wanda always had her ears to the ground, and had been following the story about the secret real estate deal for several weeks. If anyone knew the real scoop, it would be her.

But Candy wasn't ready to drag the red-haired community columnist into her confidence right now. Wanda would ask too many questions, and demand to know answers. She could make things uncomfortable for everyone. In a delicate investigation like this, she'd be more of a hindrance than a help.

So instead, Candy turned to her computer screen, called up archived files of the past several issues, and dropped her chin into an upturned palm as she started reading through Wanda's old columns.

Ten minutes later she closed the last of the files. They weren't as informative as she'd hoped. Facts were nonexistent, and details were sketchy at best. Wanda had started a few weeks earlier with several teasers about the rumors, but she'd never progressed much beyond that. There just wasn't much to go on.

Still, maybe Wanda knew more than she

was telling. Or maybe she'd uncovered something more recent that hadn't yet made it into a column.

A quick call could resolve the issue, Candy knew. But again she hesitated.

Maybe there was another way. Maybe Wanda kept something at her desk — a notepad or file that might contain some helpful information. Candy could easily slip down the hall and take a quick peek.

But she nixed the idea almost immediately. She wasn't about to start snooping around like Sapphire Vine — at least not yet.

Besides, how could she look for answers when she didn't really know what all the questions were?

So instead she pulled a legal pad from a nearby shelf, took up a pen, and started making a list of key questions to help her direct her thoughts. As she did so, the whole situation became clearer:

- *At what time did Miles Crawford die?* This could help establish exactly who had the ability and capability to kill him. Alibis could become important. As a side note, she wrote, "Establish a timeline."

- *Where was Lydia St. Graves going when*

she ran Candy off the road out by the berry farm? Had she been fleeing the scene of a crime?

- *Did the alleged secret real estate deal have anything to do with Miles's murder?* Why? Who was behind the deal? Who was Lydia working for? Surely she must have been representing a client of some sort.

- *Most importantly, if Lydia killed Miles, why leave the shovel — the alleged murder weapon — right there beside the body?* Why not just take it with her and dispose of it someplace where it wouldn't be found? For that matter, why use the shovel from Blueberry Acres? Why not just use a shovel or another farm implement lying around the berry farm? Surely Miles had sledgehammers and axes in the barn. Why a shovel at all?

Candy paused a moment and read back through her list. It seemed like a good start — but she still felt she was making an unproven assumption about Lydia's guilt. So she added a few more questions at the bottom:

- *Did Lydia St. Graves* really *kill Miles Crawford?* Or had she been set up in some way? If so, by whom?

- *If Lydia hadn't killed him, then who?* And why?

By the time she'd finished and looked up at the clock, it was nearly quarter to five. Almost time to meet her father at the diner.

Before she left, she read back through the list one more time, and frowned. There were more unanswered questions than she'd realized. Mason had told her to talk to her sources, to do some research. But the realities were harder than the expectations. She wasn't sure where to start.

At the beginning, she thought.

She dug through a pile of business cards she kept on her desk, found the main office phone number for Lydia's real estate business, and called the number. She strongly doubted she'd get Lydia herself on the phone — though you never knew. More likely, she thought, she could talk to a secretary or an assistant who could help her piece together Lydia's schedule that day, so she could begin to work out a timeline.

But no one answered the phone. After three rings voice mail picked up. Candy ended the call without leaving a message.

She sat back in her chair and thought a few moments. "Okay," she said to herself. "What's next?"

She checked her watch again. It was time to go, but if she hurried, she could make a quick stop on the way.

She put her computer to sleep (a habit she'd picked up from Ben), grabbed her tote bag, shut off all the lights in the office, set the alarm, locked the door, and headed down the stairs to the street.

The village was busy for a Thursday afternoon in late June. She started up Ocean Avenue against a fairly strong headwind that had kicked up, and through an oncoming wave of strolling pedestrians. The crowds lightened as she reached the top of the avenue, where it intersected with Main Street. She continued northward across the street and then jogged left, heading for the Black Forest Bakery. Herr Georg usually closed up the shop in late afternoon, but there was a chance they'd still be open, and she could catch Maggie if she was still around.

The door was indeed still unlocked, and the OPEN sign still hung in the window, so Candy pushed her way inside.

But the place was empty. No customers.

No Maggie. No Herr Georg.

"Hello," she called out, "anyone here?"

There was a burst of muffled voices from the back kitchen area. She heard what sounded like a quick whispered conversation. Then Maggie called out, "Be right there!"

A few moments later she burst through the doorway, tucking in a loose shirttail and sweeping up her hair as she went. "Oh, it's you! I thought I had a customer."

Candy gave Maggie a quick look up and down, then gazed through the doorway. "So what's going on back there?"

"Nothing!" Maggie said quickly. "Nothing at all. Herr Georg was just . . . um, just showing me how to knead the dough."

"Ahh," Candy said with a sly smile, "and has he been kneading anything else?"

Maggie mustered up her best indignant look. "I'm sure I haven't the slightest idea what you're talking about."

"I'm sure you don't. So are you two . . . you know . . . getting chummy?"

"Well" — and Maggie paused to clear her throat — "Herr Georg has been very instructive. He's taken a special interest in my skills."

"Hmm, I'm sure he has — and your other assets as well," Candy said. "Anyway, I'm really happy for you two, but I have another issue to discuss with you right now."

"Something to do with the berry farm?"

"How'd you guess?"

"Whenever there's a mystery around town, you're usually at the center of it. What can I help you with?"

Candy got right to the point. "This morning, when I stopped by for tea, you said Miles Crawford personally dropped off some fresh berries earlier in the day. Do you remember what time he was here?"

Maggie thought about it a moment. "It would have been early. Herr Georg usually gets here around six or six thirty. But let me find out."

She disappeared in an instant, popping back through the doorway. Candy could hear the low murmur of voices again, and a muffled squeak, before Maggie reappeared, a carefully composed look on her face. "He says it was around seven thirty or eight. And he says to say hello."

"Tell him I said hello as well. Listen, I'm headed over to the diner to get something to eat with Doc and the boys. Want to join us?"

"You know, normally I would," Maggie said, "but Herr Georg has offered to take me out tonight. He says he knows of a quiet

Italian place with soft lights and candles on the table."

"Hmm, I think I know exactly the place you're talking about," Candy said, "so have fun, you two. And *guten appetit!*"

TWENTY

Five minutes later she slipped into the corner booth at Duffy's Main Street Diner, taking a seat next to her father. He was with his three best friends, whom Candy sometimes referred to as the "posse." To Doc's right, in the center of the booth, sat Artie Groves, while Finn Woodbury and William "Bumpy" Brigham were across the table. They were fishing and golfing buddies who played poker religiously every Friday night and camped out here in the corner booth for an hour or two every weekday morning, and whenever else they had a chance during the day. It was, in a sense, their collective office, where they hashed over the latest news while enjoying their favorite comfort food.

Juanita the waitress swung by the booth to take Candy's order and then dashed away again. The place was buzzing as usual today, given the after-work and early dinnertime crowd, but the atmosphere around the table in the horseshoe-shaped booth, which overlooked the northern end of Main Street, was uncharacteristically subdued. As Candy settled herself and tuned in to what her father was saying, she quickly understood why.

Doc was providing an account of his trip to the police station that afternoon.

"Took me forty-five minutes to get finger-printed," he said, holding up his splayed fingers and turning his hand one way and then the other so everyone could see the ink marks. "After that I talked to a couple of officers and a detective over from Augusta. I think I had to explain my story something like fifteen times. Maybe twenty. I thought we'd never finish. Anyway, they made some notes and that was about it. But while I was there, I heard they're on the lookout for Lydia. They're saying she's a 'person of interest.' "

"I called her office a little while ago, just to see if she was around, or if anyone had heard from her," Candy told them, "but there was no answer."

"She's probably on the run," Bumpy surmised, wrinkling his forehead. He was a barrel-chested man in his late sixties who, like Wanda, had lost a little of his winter weight, especially around his waist. To celebrate, he'd bought a few new spring shirts to spiff up his image. He wore a bright green one today. "Though if she was wise, she'd turn herself in."

"That's exactly what she should do," Finn agreed.

"It's the automatic fight-or-flight response," Artie said knowingly, pushing his wire-rimmed glasses up on his thin nose. "She must've got into an argument with Miles and things got out of hand, so she snapped and hit him over the head with a shovel. And then she panicked. When she realized what she'd done, she left him there and ran. Classic story. She's probably long gone by now."

"Could be," Doc said, gazing reflectively out the window. "If she's smart, she'll head north, where she'll be harder to find. There's a lot of empty land up there toward the border. Lots of places to hide out."

"She's a real estate agent," Candy said. "She could have property anywhere. Maybe she's got a rental place that's currently vacant where she can lie low for a while, or a camp or something like that. She could be anywhere."

"If they're looking for her, they'll find her," said Finn, who was an ex-cop. "It's

213

only a matter of time."

"What will happen when they do?" Candy asked.

Finn let out a sigh. "It all depends on the evidence — what they found in that hoophouse. They'll question her, of course, just like they did Doc. And they can hold her for a few days until they decide whether or not to file charges."

"I hope for her sake it's all some big mistake," Doc said.

"We all do," Finn agreed, "but whatever happened, Miles Crawford is gone. That's going to shake up this town. He'd been out at that berry farm forever, and that strawberry patch of his is as much a part of the community as anything else. Think of the traffic he brought through here. Heck, they're starting a whole new event that's essentially a tribute to his product. But what happens now? This town has been buzzing about that berry farm for months, and this will only stir things up even more. Folks are going to want to know what's happening out there, especially if they sell it and turn it into something else — something we don't necessarily want."

"What about the next of kin?" Candy asked.

Finn nodded with his whole head and

214

shoulders. "They're trying to locate them now."

"I've heard the same thing," Doc said. "They were talking about it at the station."

"Two boys," Candy said, remembering the contents of Sapphire Vine's file on Miles Crawford. When she saw everyone looking at her with eyebrows raised, she explained, "I saw a photo of him today, with two teenagers and a woman I assume was his wife — or ex-wife, I guess."

"Must have been a really old photo," Finn said. "He was alone out at the place for years. Now that you mention it, though, I think I do remember seeing him with his boys around here. But that was a while ago."

"If they do find the boys," Artie put in, "the place belongs to them. And then the question becomes, what will they do with it? Will they keep it or sell it?"

"Which brings us back to the shady real estate deal," Bumpy said.

Candy looked over at Finn. "What have you heard about it?"

Finn had a secret source inside the Cape Willington Police Department, and sometimes found out information before it was made public. But he shook his head. "Can't say I've heard much of anything. This real estate thing hasn't been on their radar down at the station — so far it's just local gossip. But now with Miles gone, they might start looking into it."

"Well," Artie said, "whoever winds up with that place will be getting a valuable property. With its location and acreage, it's got to be worth a pretty penny."

That piqued Candy's interest. "How much, do you think?"

Bumpy, who was a retired attorney and still followed local business news, shrugged. "We could be talking half a million. Could be talking a million."

"I heard of a place up the coast — it went for a little over four million," Finn said.

"Another place on the water over in Rockport went for eight," Artie said.

Candy whistled. "That's a lot of cash."

"Good motivation for murder," Finn said, which silenced them all for a few moments.

"It's all about the view," Bumpy informed them. "They're raising the property values of houses with scenic ocean views. It's what everyone's paying for these days."

"And the Crawford place certainly has those in spades," Candy observed.

Doc let out a deep sigh and shook his head. "Yeah, it's such a darn shame, though. Miles worked really hard on that place, view or not. He had it looking good."

"Too bad there's not a way we can all pitch in and keep the picking operation going through the season," Bumpy said. "Sure hate to see all those strawberries go to waste in the fields."

"You hate to see any food go to waste," Artie pointed out in a moment of levity, and Bumpy nodded in agreement.

"I hate to see it happen too," Doc said. "So we'll have to see if we can do something about it. Fortunately, the fields are fine for now. The berries need another day or two to ripen anyway, so we have a little time, maybe a week, before we start losing them — as long as it doesn't get hotter or dry out. But more berries are going to ripen for sure, and pretty fast. If we don't catch them in time, they'll start to rot."

"The fields were well picked earlier because of the Strawberry Fair," Candy said, and thought that whatever the Fair contributed to the town, there was at least that. "They're going to need more on the day of the Fair, but Miles made some deliveries this morning, so right now everyone seems to have enough berries."

"Except us," Doc said, and his shoulders slumped forward. "I'd hoped to get a few quarts when I was out there this morning."

Candy patted him on the arm sympathetically. "I'm too busy to make anything with them right now anyway," she said. "Besides, we'll all have our fill of strawberries on Saturday."

"Hey look, here come the appetizers!" Artie said.

"Just in time," added Bumpy. "With all this talk about strawberries, I'm starving."

They'd ordered fried mozzarella sticks with marinara sauce, stuffed mushroom caps, and loaded potato skins, and after they'd dug in and wiped out the appetizers, their entrées arrived. Candy had opted for Maine crab cakes with coleslaw and a freshly baked corn muffin, a specialty of the diner, while Doc indulged in homemade chicken pot pie.

Candy was almost finished with her crab cakes, and was discussing with her father whether they should share a piece of strawberry swirl cream cheese cake, when she caught Finn giving her a strange look. At second glance, she thought he was making goo-goo eyes at her. And then she thought it might have been a series of winks.

She almost said something out loud to him, asking what he was up to, but he shook his head so subtly it was almost unnoticeable, the slightest gesture.

She hesitated, and watched as he flicked

his eyes to the right, toward the far side of the diner, and then looked back at Candy.

He did it again.

She finally realized what he wanted. "I'll be right back," she told Doc, and slipped out of the booth, headed to the restrooms at the back of the diner.

As she expected, Finn was waiting for her when she came out. "What's the heck's going on?" she asked in a low tone. "Why all the strange eye signals?"

"I needed to talk to you alone," he said.

Candy turned suddenly serious. "Why, what's up?"

Finn lowered his voice to a bare whisper. "I heard something this afternoon that's somewhat sensitive. I didn't want to tell the other guys because, well, I didn't want it to get around town — at least not yet. I'm not even sure I should be telling you, but, well, you're pretty good at solving these mysteries, so I thought it might help you."

"What have you heard, Finn?"

He paused for only a moment before he continued. "Well, you were out there today, right? At the berry farm? In the hoophouse?"

Candy nodded but said nothing.

Finn continued, "Then you know there

were all sorts of footprints around the body, right?"

"Right," Candy said, recalling the scene. "Some of the footprints had little flags beside them."

"Well, the forensics team spent several hours sorting through them all. They've identified some of them — most were made by Miles himself, of course. But they've identified one set of footprints that they're particularly interested in. The prints were made with some type of rubber boot. Everyone around here's got a pair — well, at least, anyone with a garden does. But these particular boots had a unique pattern on the bottom — made to stand out from the others."

That got Candy's attention. "What kind of pattern?"

Finn leaned in closer. "It's a star pattern, on the heel," he said. "Apparently it's quite distinctive. They're trying to track down the manufacturer right now. Then they can figure out where the boots might have been sold and go from there." He paused. "They're also starting to wonder what types of boots people around here might be wearing — people like you and Doc."

He let that hang in the air for a moment. "So a word to the wise: When you get home tonight, you might want to check the pattern on the bottom of your boots. And don't be surprised if the police come snooping around Blueberry Acres tomorrow, asking a few questions. Just thought you should know."

He gave her a firm nod, and headed back to the table.

TWENTY-ONE

Forty-five minutes later Candy walked into the kitchen of their old farmhouse out at Blueberry Acres and turned to her right, focusing in on a line of shoes beside the door, arranged neatly along the outside wall beneath a peg rack for hats and coats and, farther along, a window that looked out over the porch. They didn't have a mudroom like many New England homes, so they made do with a series of floor mats and rugs, placed side by side along the kitchen floor. Here they kept sneakers and casual shoes, plus boots in the spring, fall, and winter, and flip-flops and boat shoes in the summer. Though Candy tried to keep control of the footwear, and shift out-of-season shoes to the back of a closet somewhere to get them out of the way, there often could be ten or twelve pairs of shoes lined up along the wall.

Near the end of the row were a couple of

pairs of black rubber boots. Even though mud season was long gone, Candy had left them out because they were still needed on rainy or mucky days, though she'd shifted to her low-cut spring boots for most of her yard and garden work.

She glanced around. Doc was still outside, walking the property, as was his custom in the early evenings. Sometimes he walked back through the blueberry fields, toward the far ridge, and sometimes he just made a quick tour of the lower gardens. He could walk into the house at any time, especially if the bugs were biting, so she made quick work of it.

But she needn't have worried. Both pairs of rubber boots had patterns on the bottom, yes — pronounced rubber nubbies of a geometric design arranged for maximum grip, especially on the heels and toes. But nothing that resembled a star pattern. Not even close.

She set the boots back down and, just to be safe, checked a few other older pairs stashed in the back of a downstairs closet. Same thing, though the boots were more beat up and the nubbies were worn down. But nothing resembling a star pattern.

There might be a few older pairs of boots around the house somewhere, she knew, but they weren't in regular use. So . . . at least she could prove those star-patterned footprints hadn't been made by either her or Doc — if it came to that.

As she pondered what it all might mean, she headed back outside, glancing at the clock as she went. It was almost seven. Still enough daylight left for a bonfire.

She checked the chickens, scattered some feed on the ground of their coop, carried a few eggs inside, and then returned to her Jeep, where she started unloading the boxes containing Sapphire Vine's old files.

Years ago, they'd made a shallow fire pit behind the barn and chicken coop, at the edge of the fields. They'd stacked a few rocks around the circular pit to keep the fires contained, and had even pulled over a few logs, in case they wanted to sit nearby while a fire blazed.

Candy had hauled most of the boxes over to the fire pit when Doc appeared. He came out of the gathering shadows along the northern ridge, dropping down through the thick blueberry bushes, stopping to check them periodically. He finally saw her, waved, and walked over to join her.

In the light of the lowering sun they talked for a few minutes, before Doc looked down, appearing to notice the boxes at her feet for the first time. "What are those?"

Candy explained where they'd come from and what she planned to do with them.

Doc had seen the files a few years earlier, sitting inside the house on their kitchen table; Candy had brought them home to examine them after Sapphire Vine's death, before eventually taking them back to the office. "I didn't even know they were still around," Doc said, his eyebrows contracting.

"I've kept them in a filing cabinet at the office."

"They've been there all this time?"

Candy nodded.

"Have you looked through them?"

"Only a few. Now and then. Whenever I needed help with a case."

"So why burn them now?" Doc asked.

"Because it's time," Candy said. "They've outlived their usefulness — and I don't want them to fall into the wrong hands. They might still contain a few secrets that could cause trouble around town. I probably should have burned them years ago."

That seemed to make sense to Doc. He'd learned to trust his daughter's instincts. "Need help?"

Candy considered his offer, but finally said, "I only have a couple more boxes to

225

carry over. I think I'm okay."

Doc caught the meaning between the words, and sensing she preferred to perform the fiery deed on her own, he left her to it with a warm pat on the shoulder. He also fetched matches for her from the junk drawer in the kitchen. "I'll be inside. Call me if you need anything," he said. "Maybe I'll bring out some marshmallows when you get the fire going."

Once alone, she combed the yard for twigs and branches, then settled onto an old log just outside the ring of stones. Pulling over a box, she lifted the lid and began to empty it, stacking the files at her feet. In the fire pit she laid down a bed of larger branches first in a lattice-work design and covered it with a layer of pages from the files. Over that she made a teepee-shaped arrangement of longer twigs and branches to keep the pages from flying away.

Striking a match, she lit the edges of the papers all around and leaned back as the fire sprang to life. The flames rose quickly.

She let the fire burn for a while to establish itself, and when it was going well, she started feeding in more pages, a handful at a time, letting the flames lick at them and take them away. Sparks and charred bits of paper rose into the air, dancing on the slight breeze. She went through the first box and started in on the second.

As the sun sank behind the tops of the trees to the west, the fields fell into shadow, and the chirping of the crickets intensified. But the smoke from the fire kept the bugs away, for the most part. She started in on the third box, watching as handful after handful of papers were consumed by the flames.

Doc kept to his promise, and after a while brought out a few marshmallows, which they attached to the ends of long sticks and roasted. They chatted for a while, and as she started on the last few boxes, he went back inside.

Night was close when she finally placed the final few pages on the fire and watched them erupt into flame. The longest days of the year were upon them, and the sun didn't set until around eight thirty at this time of year. But a few clouds had bubbled up on the horizon, blocking out the sun's fading light, and the twilight deepened.

By the time the fire started burning low, darkness had settled around her. The crickets mellowed out as well, and the bugs dispersed. The wind calmed. She watched the glow of the fire die, until finally she rose and kicked a little dirt over it. Then she carried the empty boxes into the barn. After a last check of the chickens, she went inside.

Doc was asleep in his chair with the TV on, set to some historical program with the volume low. She let him sleep, and cleaned up a little in the kitchen. When she took the trash out to the bins in the barn, she made a last pass by the pit, to make sure the fire had gone out.

As she crossed back toward the house, she saw a flash of light to her left, out along the dirt lane that led to the main road. She stopped in her tracks, surprised, and watched, not sure if she'd really seen something or just imagined it.

But there it was again, a quick flash of light that cut through the darkness.

Two lights.

Headlights.

In the miasma of shadows and grayscapes beyond the well of faint illumination cast by lights on the porch and barn, she could barely make out the black outline of what looked like a vehicle — a low-slung car, parked at one side of the lane, half-hidden behind a fan of dark bushes.

A few moments later she heard a low, raspy voice, calling her name.

"*Candy.*" A pause. And again, "*Candy, it's me.*"

"Who's there?" Candy called hesitantly into the darkness. She looked back at the house. They kept a shotgun in the broom closet in the kitchen. She toyed with the idea of going to get it but she remained rooted to the spot upon which she stood.

Someone called her name again — a woman's voice, she could tell this time, though still low and harsh.

"Who are you?" she called back.

In response, the headlights flashed again, on and off, so quick and unexpected they made her eyes burn. But this time she was able to better identify what she was seeing.

It looked like a sports car.

She hesitated a few more moments, wondering what to do. Finally she made a quick detour into the barn, where she picked up a hoe, so she'd have something to protect herself with if it came to that. Back outside, she took a deep breath and started walking away from the farmhouse and out toward the dirt lane and the darker shape of the car against the shadowy landscape. She heard and could vaguely see the driver's side door swing open. A dark figure stepped out, holding a flashlight aimed down at the ground. In the pool of light, Candy caught a glimpse of very expensive-looking shoes.

She glanced behind her. The house — and

the security it offered — was receding from view. But she tightened her grip on the hoe's handle and kept going forward, toward the car and the black-draped figure that now stood beside it, half-hidden behind the opened door. In the reflecting light from the downward-cast flashlight, Candy could make out a thin frame, bony shoulders, pale hair, and even the frames of silver-rimmed glasses and a glint of jewelry.

"It's you, isn't it?" Candy said, stopping a few feet away. "What are you doing here?"

"I have to talk to you," the figure said. "It's urgent." And she turned the flashlight upward, so Candy could see her thin face.

It was Lydia St. Graves.

Twenty-Two

Lydia lowered the flashlight, but rather than pointing it at the ground, she aimed it toward the car, moving it with a quick jerk of her hand. "Get in," she said. "We have to talk."

"About what?"

"You know what. Something very, very wrong is going on around here, and I need you to help me figure out what it is."

Candy held the hoe across her body and stayed right where she was at. "Lydia, what's this all about? The police are looking for you. You need to go to the station right now and turn yourself in."

"I can't," Lydia said.

"Why not?"

Again, Lydia flicked the flashlight toward the car. "I won't take much of your time, but you need to hear my side of the story. That's all I ask. Then I'll be on my way."

Still, Candy hesitated. She wasn't quite

ready to get into a car with a possible murderer. "Did you kill Miles?" she asked pointedly.

Lydia's reaction was quick and sharp. "Of course not. It's a ridiculous question. That's why we need to talk." After a few moments, she added, "I had no reason to kill him. I'm being set up. Why, or by whom, I don't know. But I need your help figuring it out, so I can clear my name."

"The best way to do that is to go to the police right now," Candy said again, "and let them help you."

But Lydia would not be swayed. For a third time, she swung the flashlight toward the sports car. Candy could see its black leather seats and dark walnut interior trim.

She also spotted the tip of a black rubber boot lying on the floor behind the driver's seat.

Her gaze shifted back to Lydia. "Where are we going?"

"Nowhere. I just don't want to talk out here in the open. I'm being a little cautious right now — and maybe a little paranoid, as you can probably imagine. I'll feel safer if we talk in the car."

Candy still hesitated, but when she caught a glimpse of the ragged look on Lydia's thin face, and noticed the woman's tense stance, she finally complied. "Doc's right up at the house," she said. "All I have to do is yell and he'll come running with the shotgun." She refrained from telling Lydia that nothing short of an earthquake could wake Doc when he fell asleep in front of the TV set — and she wasn't sure even that would work.

She walked around the front of the car, leaned the hoe up against the side of the vehicle, opened the door on the passenger side, and climbed inside.

Lydia followed on the driver's side. They both pulled their doors closed.

The convertible top was up and the windows were closed. The plush cabin enclosed them. The car smelled of leather and wood and expensive perfume, though now that they were inside with the doors closed, Candy couldn't see much more, since the dome lights had gone out. Again, they were left only with the muted light from the house and barn.

Lydia sat stiffly for a few moments, eyes straight ahead, hands absently gripping the steering wheel, as if she wasn't quite sure where to begin. But finally she said in a voice so soft Candy could barely hear, "I didn't kill him."

The words hung in the air between them for a few moments. Finally Candy said,

"You were there, though, weren't you? I saw you leaving the farm. You almost ran me off the road."

Lydia's head swiveled toward her, though her face was lost in shadows. Only her eyes were visible, reflecting pinpricks of light. "I didn't know it was you at first. I only realized it later, when I regained my senses and thought about what had happened. I had to hide out for a while on one of the back lanes at the farm until the coast was clear. I sat there for nearly half an hour, waiting for the right time. I thought I could make a clean escape, until I ran into you."

"Did you see the body?"

Lydia was about to respond but then clamped shut her mouth and shook her head. It appeared she wasn't ready to answer that question, at least not yet, so Candy asked another. "Where have you been all day? I called your office."

When Lydia spoke again, she sounded dazed. "I don't know, really. Driving around. Hiding out on back roads and a few spots I know out in the woods. Trying to figure out who's attempting to frame me, and why." She let out a warbling breath, as if she was working very hard to control her emotions. "I can't tell you what an awful day it's been. If I had known what was going to happen

234

out at that berry farm this morning, I would've stayed home. Better yet, I would've stayed in bed and shut off the phone."

"What *did* happen this morning?" Candy prompted. She kept her voice low and non-accusatory. She wasn't interested in laying blame just yet. She only wanted to learn the facts.

"*Not* what you think," Lydia said defensively. "I was lured out there."

"*Lured?* To the berry farm?" Candy couldn't keep the disbelief out of her voice.

"I was framed," Lydia clarified. "Set up."

"How? By who?"

"I don't know. That's what I want you to find out for me."

Candy had to think this over. After a few moments she said, "Why don't you tell me what you *do* know, and we'll go from there."

"Okay." Lydia nodded and let out a few deep breaths, gathering her thoughts. "It all started this morning around eight, when I received an e-mail from Miles Crawford. He asked me to come out to his place. He said he wanted me to meet him in the hoophouse out at the berry farm at ten. He said it was urgent business. And he told me not to respond to the e-mail message he'd sent, after I'd read it, but to delete it instead, which I thought was very strange. But I

235

complied with his requests. I deleted it and then drove out to the farm a little early. I got there about nine forty-five."

"Did he say why he wanted to meet with you?" Candy asked. "Do you have any idea what he wanted?"

"Not specifically, but I figured it was because" — here Lydia hesitated a few moments before continuing — "because Miles and I had been working on a business deal together. We'd already met a few times — though never in a hoophouse, which I also thought was a little strange. But Miles could be eccentric. I thought he wanted to talk business."

"Ahh," Candy said, "so all those rumors flying around town about a secret real estate deal really *were* true."

Lydia noticeably grimaced. "Yes, but not in the way you think. I've heard what people are saying, and most of them are wrong."

"Okay . . . so what's the truth?"

"Well, for one thing, no one wants to buy that old berry farm and turn it into some fancy resort — at least, not that I'm aware of. I have no idea how that story got started. And for the record, I wasn't twisting Miles's arm, trying to get him to sell the place, as some of the rumors claimed. From what I've heard, they're portraying me as some sort of interloper who puts money over people, which just isn't true. I've been a stalwart citizen of this community for more than twenty-five years. And just to be clear, I'm not working for some rich mysterious out-of-town client who wants to come in here and destroy the village's atmosphere, like all these ladies are saying. That's just ridiculous. I would never do something like that."

"Then who *are* you working for?" Candy asked.

"Well, that's what is so ironic," Lydia said, "and the most frustrating part of this whole thing. Because I wasn't working for some-one else, trying to get Miles to sell his place. It was the other way around. *I* was working for *him.*"

"Working for who?" Candy asked.

"Miles," Lydia said, and she looked over at Candy, the pinpricks of light in her eyes turning hard-edged. "*Miles Crawford* was my client," she said. "*He* hired *me.*"

TWENTY-THREE

"Hired you?" Candy tilted her head, surprised by this revelation. "To do what?"

"To help him sell his place," Lydia said.

"So he really *was* selling the berry farm?"

"Yes, but — well, I don't know the whole
story. Only bits and pieces of it."

"Then tell me what you know."

"All right," Lydia said, glancing nervously
down at her watch, which was faintly lumi-
nescent in the dark, before looking up and
out the vehicle, turning her head in both
directions. "I can't stay much longer," she
added, "so I'll be quick." She returned her
attention to Candy. "A few weeks ago, out
of the clear blue sky, Miles calls me and
asks me to come out to his place 'after
hours,' was how he put it. Naturally, I was
suspicious about that request, not knowing
his intent. But I needn't have worried. He
said he simply wanted to meet when no one
else was around, since he didn't want

rumors to get started around town. Of course, the rumors got started anyway, but that's a different part of the story. That first night we met, Miles was all business, right from the start. He told me he wanted to hire me, as I've said. And I can tell you, no one was more shocked than I. He's been out at that farm for as long as I've been a real estate agent. You don't think I haven't tried to get him to sell it a few times over the years? You don't think I made a trek out there every time a viable client — one with a hefty bank account, that is — sought an incredibly desirable rural property with some of the most stunning ocean views in the world? Of *course* I approached him with the idea of selling, numerous times," Lydia said, the exasperation she felt, even at the mere memories, coming through in her voice. "I told him he was sitting on a gold mine. I told him he could retire for the rest of his life. But he adamantly refused to consider the idea. He told me he wasn't ready to sell, no matter the money — which struck me as odd, because we'd never discussed a price. And he said a few other things that made me suspicious."

"About what?"

"I began to suspect that I wasn't the only one inquiring about the place. To be honest, I got the feeling he was getting other offers. I discreetly asked around, to find out if any other agents from around here were talking to him, but I came up empty. However, *something* else was going on in the background, I'm sure of it," Lydia said. "I just never found out what it was."

"So," Candy said, as she tried to make sense out of what Lydia was telling her, "if Miles was so adamant against selling the farm, why all of a sudden would he hire you to help him sell it?"

"That," Lydia said, "is the million-dollar question, isn't it? I've been trying to figure that one out for weeks, ever since this whole thing started. That first time we met out at the farm, he told me he'd changed his mind. He wanted me to help him find a buyer for the place — but the *right* buyer, he said. Someone who would respect the property, keep it as it was, as a berry farm. He wasn't interested in selling to a speculator or developer, no matter how much money they offered. He told me he wanted to find a nice family who would take over the farm and continue what he'd been doing for thirty years. But," Lydia added, holding up a thin finger, "he wanted me to do all this off the record. No advertising, no MLS listings, no public release of information or acknowledgement whatsoever about the sale. He told me he wanted to keep it private, a secret — just between him and me for now."

"But why?" Candy asked.

Lydia shrugged her bony shoulders. "He had his reasons — though he never shared them with me."

"So you were looking around for a buyer?"

"I was," Lydia said. "Miles was my client, so I did as he asked. I did some searching and was in the process of identifying a few prospects. As I've said, whoever I found had to meet certain criteria. I sent him a report every week or two, bringing him up to date. But I didn't hear back from him until this morning. I thought that's why he wanted to meet — to talk about my progress, to see where we were at. Of course, all the secrecy — the e-mail message, the request to delete it — struck me as odd, as I've said. But I thought Miles was just being cautious, given all the rumors that have sprung up."

"Which brings us back to the hoophouse," Candy said.

"Yes, the hoophouse." Lydia swallowed and rubbed at her forehead. "I can't believe what happened," she said after a few moments. "I can't believe he's gone. I can still see him there, lying facedown on the ground, his body all twisted around and crumbled randomly, with his limbs at odd angles, as if he'd just dropped where he'd stood. For a split second, when I first spotted him, I thought he might be looking for something or trying to make some sort of repair or something like that. But when I got closer, I knew right away he was dead. At first I thought he might have had a heart attack. But then, well, I saw his head."

Her voice dropped off, and her hands fell into her lap. A silence built inside the car. Hesitant to interrupt, Candy waited until the other woman started again. "I never touched him," Lydia said softly. "I just backed away as soon as I realized what had happened. I left him right where he was."

"So you didn't approach the body?" Candy asked. "Check for a pulse or —"

Lydia shook her head quickly. "No, no, I . . . I couldn't go near him. I couldn't even move. If there was any way to help him, I would have. But I knew he was dead right away. That was plain to see from . . . the body."

Candy nodded. She'd been inside that hoophouse too.

"It all happened in a flash," Lydia said, her voice starting to sound tired. "At a moment like that, when you realize what you're looking at, your heart tells you it can't be true but your mind tells you it is."

"Why didn't you call the police?" Candy asked. "If what you're saying is true, and you found him already dead, then you're innocent. You haven't done anything wrong."

"But that's just it," Lydia said. "I can't *prove* I did — or didn't do — anything. And I knew right away, as soon as I walked into that hoophouse and saw that dead body, that I was being framed somehow. I didn't know how or why at first. It took me a little while to figure it out. But eventually it hit me."

"The shovel," Candy said softly.

Lydia nodded. "When I saw it lying there next to the body, I knew something about it was familiar, but I couldn't figure out what it was. Only later, when I was driving around, running through everything in my head, did I remember where I'd seen it before."

"Judicious gave it to you," Candy said.

Even in the shadows, the shock on Lydia's face was evident. "How could you possibly know that?"

"Because Doc and I tracked down its whereabouts today," Candy said, and she explained how she and her father had traced the shovel from Sally Ann to Ray Hutchins

243

to Judicious F. P. Bosworth, "who says he gave it to you," Candy finished.

"That's right, he did." Lydia's head nodded absently as her memories took her back to previous events. "This was . . . well, I guess maybe six or seven weeks ago, maybe two months, something like that. Since Judicious doesn't have a car and has to walk everywhere he goes, I told him I'd return the shovel to Blueberry Acres for him. And that's exactly what I planned to do. But I had to make a stop first, at the beauty shop in town. It was one of the first warm days of the year, and I remember I had the top down on the car, so I just tossed the shovel on the floor behind the front seats. I didn't bother putting the top up because I wasn't inside the hairdresser's that long. And I parked right out in front of the shop, where I could look out and see the car whenever I wanted to. It wasn't as if I'd parked in some dark alley or in downtown Boston. Besides, there wasn't anything valuable inside to steal. I keep all my important stuff, like boxes of brochures and signs, locked up in the trunk. Who's going to steal a worthless old shovel, right? But when I came out, it was gone."

"You're saying someone took the shovel out of your car while you were inside the hairdresser's?"

Lydia made a sound of frustration in the back of her throat. "I know how it sounds — like I made all this up. But it's true. That's the only place someone could have taken it out of the car. Why, I don't know. I didn't think about it much, really. I thought someone had just borrowed it again, or maybe you or Doc had seen it and took it, since you work right around the corner, and the bakery shop is just a few doors down. I meant to call you and tell you about it, but to be honest, I got busy with other things and it slipped my mind. Only today did I realize that someone stole that shovel right out from underneath my nose, used it to kill Miles Crawford, and then *left* the shovel there on purpose, knowing it would probably lead back to me — which is exactly what happened, of course."

She paused a moment as she looked down at her hands in the darkness, before she continued. "With all those rumors swirling round town, saying I was trying to get Miles to sell his farm — well, that just provides motivation, doesn't it? It makes me the perfect villain. I heard the police stopped by my office this afternoon, and at my home. Of course, I wasn't at either place. But it just proved that I was being set up to take the fall for Miles's murder. And that's why I'm here. I need you to figure out who stole that shovel from my car. Help me find the person behind this, so I can clear my name. I'll pay you — I'll do whatever it takes. But as I've said, I can't go to the police, because I have no proof and they won't understand. They'll just throw me in jail. I need someone on my side. So will you do it? Will you help me?"

Candy thought about Lydia's request for several long moments, then held out her left hand. "Can I borrow your flashlight?"

It took Lydia a few moments to react, but finally she nodded and relinquished the flashlight.

Candy opened the passenger side door, climbed out, reached around the seat, and found the latch that flipped it forward. She shined the light behind the seats. "Have you cleaned the car since you had the shovel back here?" she asked.

Lydia craned her thin neck around so she could look at the floor. "I don't know. I don't think so."

Candy reached down, running her hand over the thick carpeting, her fingers searching.

"What are you looking for?" Lydia asked curiously.

"Something like this." Candy held up a small clump of dried dirt, about half the size of her little fingernail. "It could be dirt from the shovel. It could be something else. Mind if I look at your boots?"

"My boots?" Lydia echoed, shifting around even more.

"It'll just take a second." Candy lifted one of the black rubber boots she'd seen on the floor behind the driver's seat and shined the light at the heel. "Did you wear these boots this morning out at the berry farm?"

"Well, I, ah . . ."

Candy checked the bottoms of both, just to be sure. "It doesn't matter," she said. "It's not the pattern I'm looking for."

"What do you mean?"

"It's nothing." Her search complete, Candy returned the seat back to its regular position. Then she climbed back inside, closing the door. She turned back to Lydia and handed over the flashlight. "The truth is, I'm not sure how much I can help you. But I'll do what I can. However, I highly suggest you go see the police first thing in the morning."

"I'm afraid I won't be doing that," Lydia said. "I'm headed out of town tonight. I'm going to make one more stop and then lay low until this whole thing blows over."

"Where are you going?" Candy asked.

But Lydia shook her head. "I won't say, but it's a safe place. I have just one more stop to make tonight before I'm gone."

"How will I contact you if I find out anything?"

"You won't. I'll contact you. I'll give you a call tomorrow evening, and we'll go from there. It won't be from my regular number, so be sure to answer your phone if you see an unfamiliar number."

She reached over and placed a bony hand on Candy's forearm. "I can't tell you how much this means to me. You're the only friend I have at the moment. I want you to know I appreciate your help."

A few minutes later, she was gone.

The next morning, she was dead.

TWENTY-FOUR

Candy's phone rang first thing. It was Finn. "You'd better get over here."

"Why, what's happening?" Candy was still upstairs, dressing. Her father was already outside on the porch with his first cup of coffee and the morning paper.

"There's a lot of chatter going on over at the station this morning. The police have found something."

"What?"

"I'll tell you when you get here."

"Where are you?"

"The usual place. We're keeping a couple of spots reserved for you and Doc."

She finished combing out her hair and dressing and hurried downstairs. For a few moments she lingered in the kitchen. She disliked rushing out like this, first thing in the morning, without a few minutes to get herself organized and take care of a few chores. But there was one chore she couldn't ignore. She grabbed her tote bag, did a quick sweep of the kitchen to see if she'd forgotten anything, and headed outside.

Doc had his phone out and was looking down at it. "I just got a text," he said.

"From Finn, I'll bet." And she told her father what she'd just heard.

Doc folded up the paper as he listened, and swallowed the rest of his coffee, then rose. "I'll lock up the house and meet you over there," he said as he started toward the door. But he stopped after a couple of steps and looked back at her. "Hey, did someone stop by the house last night?"

Candy gave him a brief wave of acknowledgement as she headed down the steps and around the porch toward the chicken coop. "I'll tell you about it at the diner."

The chickens were clucking and pecking at the ground, content as usual. She went about her daily routine, collected the eggs, and ten minutes later she was in the Jeep, headed toward town.

She was the last one to arrive in the corner booth. Doc and the boys were working on a plate of doughnuts and fruit-filled croissants. As she slid into the booth, this time next to Artie, a cup of coffee instantly appeared in front of her, delivered by Juanita.

A warm blueberry muffin and a small

chilled bowl with freshly made honey butter arrived a short time later. Despite Candy's protests, Juanita continued to provide her with free food, because of an earlier episode between the two. For a long time Candy had protested the special treatment, but after a while, rather than fight it, she'd learned to accept it. Instead, she'd simply started leaving larger tips, which worked out to be a comfortable compromise.

Finn waited until they'd all settled, with their food served and coffee cups filled, then leaned forward toward the center of the table, resting his elbows lightly on the edge. "The news is about to break," he said in a low voice, "so I'm not telling you anything you wouldn't know in a few minutes anyway. But they've found Lydia St. Graves."

Candy didn't say anything but Doc sounded surprised. "They have? Where?"

"Up on Route 1. She was in an accident overnight. Her car ran off the road and hit a tree sometime around midnight. Apparently no one saw her, since she wound up pretty far off the road, so she wasn't spotted until daybreak. They got her to a hospital but she didn't make it."

Candy was about to take a bite out of her muffin, but it dropped to the plate as a shocked expression came to her face.

"Lydia's dead?"

Finn nodded grimly. "That's what they're saying."

"How is that possible?"

Finn shrugged. "These things happen."

"What about the airbags?" Doc asked. "Didn't they go off, especially in that fancy car of hers? That thing must have six or eight of them at least. And doesn't that model have some sort of automatic alert system, which sends out a signal in the event of an accident?"

"Good points," Finn said, "and yes, her BMW had accident assist and GPS, but both had been disabled. She'd also apparently discarded her phone. She must have known she could be traced that way. As for the airbags, her vehicle had four, since it's a convertible. Front and side airbags. They deployed exactly as they were supposed to, which is what makes the death so mysterious."

"Mysterious?" Candy echoed. She didn't like the sound of that. "In what way?"

"Well, she was out there all night in her car," Finn said, "but her injuries weren't necessarily that severe, from what I've heard. As Doc said, the airbags went off, so she was fairly well cushioned. She might've had a few bruised ribs, maybe even a broken bone or two. She would have been dehydrated when they found her, of course, but she didn't appear to be fatally wounded."

"But you said she died," Candy pointed out.

"That's just it. She *did* die. But she *shouldn't* have."

Candy scrunched up her face. "So what are you saying?"

"I'm just reporting what I've heard. No one knows what happened yet. They're still trying to figure it out. But there are a few theories floating around."

"Such as?"

"Well, as I said, when they found her, she wasn't in bad shape physically. They got her into an ambulance and checked her out on the way to the hospital. At first they thought she might have had a heart attack, though they were able to rule that out. And they also thought she might have overdosed on her medication. Now, however, they have a new theory. They think she might have been poisoned."

TWENTY-FIVE

After she left the diner, Candy swung by the Black Forest Bakery briefly to say hello to Maggie and Herr Georg, but stopped in the doorway when she saw the crowd in front of the counter. Maggie waved to her but was obviously too busy to talk. "I'll come back a little later," Candy mouthed to her friend.

Back outside, she headed down the street and up the stairs to her office, where she pulled her phone out of her tote bag, tossed the bag onto a side chair, and closed the door behind her. She could hear a few voices around the office, and she preferred to make her next phone call in private.

She scrolled down through the contacts until she found the number she wanted. But when she made the call, she was sent straight to voice mail. She left a quick message — "It's Candy Holliday. We need to talk. Call me as soon as you can" — and ended the call.

She dug back through her contacts and found another number that might work. This time someone answered. "Cape Willington Police Department. How may I direct your call?"

"Chief Durr, please."

"The chief is unavailable at the moment. Is this a personal matter, or can I direct your call to someone else who might be able to help?"

"It's a personal matter," Candy said, and left her name and number, along with a request for the chief to call her back as quickly as possible.

"I'll make sure he gets the message," Candy was informed, and she ended the call.

That was all she could accomplish on the phone at the moment, she decided. Now she'd just have to wait for the chief to call her back. So she set the phone aside and reached across her desk for the list of questions she'd made the previous afternoon. She had a number of new questions to add. She found a clean page and wrote down her thoughts quickly, while they were still fresh in her mind:

- *Why would someone poison Lydia? What was the motive?*

- *Why did the alleged murderer set up Lydia by leaving the shovel from Blueberry Acres next to the body in the hoophouse?* The motive appeared to be an effort to frame Lydia for Miles's murder, Candy thought, which was exactly what the real estate agent had claimed last night. But was that what really happened?

- *Is there a connection with the beauty shop?* Lydia said she'd parked right in front of the shop when she went inside. Could someone already inside have spotted the unattended car with the convertible top down and waited until an opportune time to steal the shovel? It was certainly a possibility, Candy thought. But why would someone steal the shovel from Lydia's car and then hold on to it for a couple of months before taking it out to the berry farm? That would indicate a long-term intention — premeditated murder.

- *Did the same person kill both Miles and Lydia?* Candy suspected the answer was yes. The berry farmer and the real estate agent were certainly connected, and she now knew the rumors about a secret deal were true, though not in the way everyone suspected. Had someone else been involved — a third party perhaps? But if so, why murder both Miles and Lydia? And why poison? Which brought up another question:

- *How was Lydia poisoned?*

According to Finn, Lydia had been out there along that road all night. She'd only died in the morning, while either on the way to or upon arrival at the hospital. Finn hadn't been specific about the time of death. But if Lydia came into contact with the poison sometime between nine and midnight — either by drinking it, eating it, inhaling it, or being injected with it — then it was reasonable to assume the poison had started taking effect within an hour or two, but had taken six to eight hours to end Lydia's life.

From nine to midnight. A three-hour window.

Candy wrote again:

- *Where was Lydia between nine P.M. and midnight?*

She straightened. Now that she thought about it, she recalled Lydia saying something about making one more stop before she left town. She planned on visiting someone, she'd said. But Lydia had never mentioned a name.

What had she said exactly? It came back to Candy after a few moments:

I'm headed out of town tonight. . . . I'm going to make one more stop and then lay low until this whole thing blows over.

One more stop. . . .

She must have met with someone after she left Blueberry Acres, eaten or drunk the poison, and then driven up to Route 1. But she hadn't made it much farther than that.

Poisoned, Finn had said.

Why?

One possible answer came to Candy almost immediately. *To prevent her from talking,* Candy thought. *That means she must have found out something about Miles's murder.*

And before she could talk, she'd been murdered herself.

Candy knew what that meant: Lydia had been telling the truth. It meant she hadn't killed Miles. Instead, it sounded like someone else had killed Miles, and used the shovel to incriminate Lydia — just as she'd said.

The shovel, Candy thought. *It's at the center of this whole thing. I thought we were done with it, but it's back in play.*

Candy put it all together in her mind with the information she now had. The shovel had gone from Doc to Sally Ann Longfellow to Ray Hutchins to Judicious F. P. Bosworth. Judicious had given it to Lydia, who promised to return it to Blueberry Acres. She had thrown it into the backseat of her BMW convertible. But first she'd stopped at the beauty salon, and when she'd come out, the shovel was gone.

If that was all true, then it meant many of Candy's theories were right. Someone had taken the shovel from the back of Lydia's car, held on to it for a couple of months, used it to kill Miles, and then . . . what? Lydia said she'd been lured to the berry farm. She'd mentioned an e-mail Miles had sent to her, instructing her to meet him at the hoophouse around ten A.M. And he'd asked her to delete the e-mail after she'd read it. Lydia had thought that was strange — and it *was* strange.

Why delete an e-mail message?

To cover up a paper trail, Candy thought.

But why would Miles want to cover up his own paper trail? It was a question she didn't have an answer for at the moment.

But something else stuck in the back of her mind — something Lydia had said last night.

She said she'd received the e-mail message from Miles at around eight in the morning. But if Candy recalled correctly, Maggie had told her that Miles had dropped off some fresh strawberries at the bakery sometime around seven thirty or eight — the same time he'd allegedly sent an e-mail to Lydia.

How had he e-mailed her? It's possible he had contacted her on the run using a smart phone. But Candy had never pegged Miles as the smart phone type. He seemed more low-tech, like Doc. So how had he e-mailed Lydia when he was out making strawberry deliveries?

She made a note to check on it.

And then there was the final question, perhaps the most important one: If Lydia hadn't killed Miles, then who had? Candy wrote down on the sheet of paper:

- *Suspects?*

She thought about that for a few minutes.

Why would someone want to kill Miles? she wondered. *Who had the motivation?*

Again, a possible answer came to her: *To prevent Miles from selling the farm.*

That led her inevitably to think of a very vocal group that had recently started a high-profile campaign with just that purpose. The ladies of the Cape Willington Heritage Protection League were vehement in their opposition to the sale of the berry farm. Could their passions have progressed to something deadlier?

Before she had a chance to ponder that harrowing line of thought, her phone rang. It was Chief Durr. She answered it and told him she had some important news concerning Lydia.

"Where are you?" he asked when she'd finished.

"In my office."

"Stay right where you are. I'm coming over. I'll be there in ten minutes."

TWENTY-SIX

True to his word, the chief arrived in nine and a half minutes. "I hope you don't mind the impromptu stop-in," he said after a brief greeting. "I thought it might be easier to meet over here. It's quieter. Lots of phones ringing and people talking over there." He waved a hand in the general direction of the police station.

"How's the investigation coming?" Candy asked.

Chief Durr removed his hat and ran a hand back across his steel-colored hair. "Well, we're making progress. I suppose you've heard the latest about Lydia St. Graves. I'm unable to say much about the accident at this point — and everything we talk about here today is off the record, of course — but we're following up on a number of leads, including that shovel of yours. I appreciate the effort you and Doc made in tracking that down." He slid into a chair and looked over at her expectantly. "So you said you had a 'personal' matter you wanted to discuss. Anything to do with the shovel?"

Candy cleared her throat. "Yes, well, that's part of it." Before she proceeded, she motioned toward the door and waggled her fingers.

The chief looked over, rose from his seat, gently slapped it closed, and resettled himself. "So what have you learned, Ms. Holliday?" he asked, his brow furrowing.

As she often did, Candy hesitated a few moments, giving herself a little extra time to collect her thoughts before she plunged on. She told the chief about her unexpected meeting with Lydia the previous evening, touching on the details of their conversation. She mentioned the e-mail Lydia allegedly received from Miles yesterday morning, requesting a meeting at the hoophouse, along with instructions to delete the message after reading it. She gave Lydia's side of the story, explaining that Miles had been dead when Lydia arrived at the hoophouse. "Lydia claimed she was innocent," Candy added. "She said she was framed."

"But if that's true, why not just contact us right away and let us sort it out?"

"Because she was scared," Candy said,

"and she felt trapped. So after she found the body, she fled."

"And that's when you saw her, right?" the chief asked. "When she ran you off the road? I read Molly's report."

"That's right. She said she hid out at the farm until the coast was clear and then headed back toward town, which is when I saw her."

"Sounds like she was running from the scene of a crime."

"It does, I admit, but I'm just telling you what I've heard."

The chief nodded, accepting that explanation for the moment. "What about the shovel, then?"

"Lydia says it was stolen out of her car while she was parked on the street outside the beauty shop on Main Street," Candy explained. "Whoever stole it must have held on to it for several weeks before leaving it next to Miles's body in an attempt to incriminate Lydia. Oh, and there's one other thing — Lydia said she intended to make one final stop last night before heading out of town."

The chief frowned at this bit of information. "She say where she was going?"

"Someplace 'safe.' "

"Too bad she didn't make it. Anything else?"

"That's about it — for now. Mostly I wanted to let you know that Lydia stopped by the farm last night."

The chief nodded and was silent for a long while, staring down at the floor, as if processing all that she'd told him. Finally he looked up. "Well, I wish you'd mentioned some of this earlier — last night, for instance, right after you talked to Lydia. But I appreciate the fact you're telling me now. And — again off the record — it matches up pretty well with our assumptions. There was quite a bit of evidence at the scene. Someone, for instance, tried very hard to cover up his or her tracks, using an old broom. From what you've just told me, it's possible that person was Lydia. But there were other prints out there that are more interesting to us right now. Those are the ones we're currently tracking down. But there's something else — something you might be able to help with."

"Oh?" Candy's voice rose in surprise.

The chief nodded and leaned forward, resting his elbows on his knees, holding his hat between his hands. "You know a lot of folks around town, right?"

Candy nodded.

"Do you know of anyone with the initials *M.R.S.?*"

"*M.R.S.?*" Candy repeated. *"As in Mrs.?"*

"That's just it. Could be either one," the chief explained. "Could be Mrs. Somebody or Something-or-other. Or it could be someone with those initials. We're not sure which. Here's the thing — we found a few, well, *baskets* out there, near the body."

"Baskets?"

"Yeah, you know. Like someone was going strawberry picking and brought along a few baskets from home — those wicker or straw ones with the handles on the ends." He made a general shape with his hands. "Frankly, they looked out of place, not like something Miles would have owned — and, of course, the initials don't match his. We swept his house and the rest of the buildings out there. He had stacks of commercial strawberry baskets in the barn — those little green plastic ones, as well as more industrial-sized containers. But he wasn't a basket collector — not in the traditional sense."

The chief paused, looking Candy in the eye. "These particular baskets had the initials *M.R.S.* woven into them, like they'd been made personally for someone. Maybe as a family heirloom or a Mother's Day gift?

Something like that. Since you get around town quite a bit and know a lot of the people, and you have connections in the farm community, I thought you might've seen something like that, or might know someone with those initials. So . . . does any of this ring any bells? Anyone jump to mind?"

He stopped and waited, giving her time to think. But Candy was still too astonished he was actually asking for her help. Usually, in the past, he'd warned her vehemently to stay out of local murder cases, giving her stern looks and speaking in gruff tones. But here he was, sharing an actual clue with her, bringing her into his confidence and giving up a valuable piece of information about the investigation. Why the change of heart?

In the end, it made no difference, because she couldn't think of anyone who fit the bill. She ran over a list of possible names in her head and scrolled through the list of contacts on her phone, but no one jumped out.

"I'll give it more thought, though," she told the chief with a shake of her head. "I'll let you know if I come up with anything."

Chief Durr accepted her answer in stride. "I knew it was a long shot anyway," he said with a forced grin. He rose and replaced his hat atop his head. "You did the right thing calling me. I need both you and Doc to stay in touch. I expect to hear from you again if you think of anything else that might help us out. And like I said, this is all off the record. Please keep anything we just talked about to yourself. I don't want to see it on the front page of the paper."

With that, he swung open the door, touched the tip of his hat, and headed back down the hall.

Candy let out a long breath as his footsteps receded toward the front door.

The meeting had actually gone better than she'd hoped. She'd envisioned another lecture, cautioning her about her involvement in a local murder case, warning her to stay out of police business. Instead, she found herself strangely gratified that he'd asked for her help.

The moment burst quickly, though, as Wanda Boyle poked her head in through the doorway. "Hey, was that Chief Durr? What was *he* doing here? What's the scoop?"

"There's no scoop. It's just personal business," Candy said vaguely, turning back to her computer and clicking open some work files. She wasn't trying to be rude to Wanda, but she also didn't want to encourage the woman. Wanda could be tenacious when it came to ferreting out information, and Candy has just been told to keep certain aspects of the current case to herself.

But Wanda wasn't so easily deterred. "Personal business? What's that mean? And since when does the chief of police visit the local newspaper editor? What's that all about?"

"It was just a routine visit."

"Routine? Hmm." Wanda drummed her long, freshly painted fingernails on the wooden doorjamb. "If I didn't know better, I'd say it had something to do with the Crawford murder."

"I really can't say anything about it."

"No, I suppose not," Wanda said with a touch of sarcasm. "Fine thing, too, when a newspaper editor sits on information that could help find a criminal."

Candy had to admit she had a point.

"Okay, you're right, I *am* sitting on information. And *no,* I'm not going to tell you what it is — at least not yet. That's just the way it is, so there's no point in pursuing this conversation any longer. Besides, more than likely you'll hear about it soon enough."

Despite the stern words, Wanda grinned. She slipped inside the office and perched on the edge of one of the chairs. "Did he say anything about the ladies of the Heritage Protection League?"

Candy looked over at Wanda again, holding the other woman's gaze this time. "What makes you ask that?"

"Well, it makes sense, doesn't it? I've heard the latest scuttlebutt at the police station. Things are buzzing over there since Lydia's death. They're calling it 'suspicious.' Poison, they're saying. If that's true, then it could mean that Lydia didn't kill Miles. Maybe someone else killed them both."

"And you think the ladies of the league might have had something to do with it?"

"Don't you?" Wanda threw her hands up into the air. "It doesn't take a genius to figure this out! I could certainly see one or two of them taking a swing at Miles's head with a shovel. Cotton Colby seems like a woman who always gets her way, and Elvira Tremble has the demeanor for such a thing. And think about it: Who has the most to gain from Miles's death? Who's been bugging everyone around town about the rumored sale of that berry farm? Who's launched a secret campaign against Lydia?"

"You mean they're the ones behind these rumors of a secret deal between Lydia and Miles?"

"It's coming from somewhere," Wanda

said, "and it just makes sense. They always seem to have the best information, don't they? Maybe they have another agenda. Maybe they're starting these rumors because there's something else they're after."

"Like what?"

"I don't know." Wanda shrugged her big shoulders innocently as the corners of her mouth turned up. "I'm just speculating."

"But I don't understand. I thought they were your friends."

Wanda made a face. "What, you're talking about yesterday? I know how to schmooze them, yes, but I don't sit around and drink tea with them all day and chat about the weather and who wore white after Labor Day, if that's what you mean. I treat them the same way I treat everyone else in town. You get more bees with honey. It pays to be friendly and chatty. That's how to get people to tell you their stories. It's something you learn when you write a community column — but I don't have to tell you that, do I? I learned it from you."

This surprised Candy. "You did?"

"Of course. Everything I know about this business I learned by watching you. Of course, I put my own spin on it. Improved on it."

Candy couldn't help but smile faintly. "It

271

almost sounded like there was a compliment in there somewhere."

"Take it anyway you want," Wanda said nonchalantly, and she rose. "Mark my words — those ladies of the Heritage Protection League are involved in this somehow. We've got to keep an eye on them. I've been tracking their whereabouts."

"You have?"

Wanda nodded. "I've been keeping a chart. They tend to congregate in certain places, like the library and the historical society, and the beauty shop."

That perked up Candy's ears. "Freda's place on Main Street? So do you know if they've had appointments there?"

"Sure do. Freda tends to stay open late on Thursday nights, so some of the ladies have appointments at around the same time on Thursday afternoon, generally from three to five. Lydia usually came in right after that."

"At about what time?" Candy asked.

Wanda shrugged. "Five thirty, something like that. Usually the other ladies tried to be gone by the time she arrived, so they didn't run into each other much. But last night they stayed around to see if Lydia showed up."

"And?"

"She never did, of course."

Candy knew why. Lydia had been hiding out somewhere in the woods, waiting for darkness to fall, so she could make her way out to Blueberry Acres without being spotted by the police.

It also meant, Candy realized, that it certainly could have been possible for one of the ladies to hang around until Lydia arrived one Thursday afternoon, wait until she entered the shop, and then take the shovel from the backseat of her BMW convertible.

"I'll let you know if I spot any strange behavior," Wanda said. "By the way, I *have* noticed that Elvira Tremble in particular has been spending a lot of time out at the historical society. I thought it might be because she was sweet on Miles Crawford."

Again, Candy was surprised by this revelation. "Elvira was interested in Miles?"

"From a romantic standpoint, yes, from what I've heard. For a while Miles was spending a lot of time out at the lighthouse, doing some sort of research — something to do with the history of the village, from what I understand. I don't know all the details, but I'm out there quite often myself, as you know, and I do remember seeing him there a number of times, sitting back in some dusty corner upstairs in the archives, going through piles of old ledgers. Anyway, Elvira used to hang around and wait for him to show up. But according to my sources, he never showed the slightest interest in her, and eventually he just stopped coming around. Apparently Elvira was crushed. Maybe she got peeved that he kept ignoring her and swung a shovel at his head."

"Maybe," Candy said with a slight tilt of her head, subtly expressing her skepticism.

"Or maybe it was someone else," Wanda said. "Maybe it was that son of his."

"What son?"

"The oldest one. He's back in town."

"Miles's son is here? How do you know that?"

"Heard it from someone over at the police station," Wanda said. She headed out, pausing in the doorway as she went. "He had to check in with the authorities. Family, you know. And he also made a stop at the funeral parlor. I don't know where he's staying, though. He's a pretty handsome guy, from what I've heard. Backwoods type, bushy red beard, that sort of thing."

"And what's this son's name?" Candy asked, intrigued.

"His name is Neil. Neil Crawford."

Twenty-Seven

Doc had a thousand thoughts going through his mind as he climbed into his truck, cranked up the engine, and backed out of his parking spot on Main Street, headed for home.

He took the old familiar route, south to the red light at the corner and then right on the Coastal Loop, which put the bright ocean to his left. As he drove, he thought about all that had happened over the past twenty-four hours or so, including the most recent news concerning Lydia, and chided himself for starting this whole mess in the first place. If he hadn't left that darned shovel over at Sally Ann's place, he wouldn't have set off this mystifying series of events that resulted in Miles's death, and now Lydia's as well. Yesterday he'd thought he and his daughter had settled the matter, when they'd tracked the shovel from Blueberry Acres back to Lydia and reported their findings to the police. But now, with her dead, the whole thing had gone up in smoke, and new questions emerged.

Had Lydia died because of injuries sustained in the car accident, or had she actually been poisoned, as Finn suggested? And what did that mean? Was the poisoning accidental, or intentional?

Did Lydia murder Miles, or had she been an innocent bystander?

If Lydia *had* clobbered Miles over the head with that shovel, why had she left it at the scene of the crime to incriminate herself? And if she *hadn't* killed Miles, then who had? Had the same person murdered Miles and then poisoned Lydia as well?

That last question was the one that bothered Doc the most, for if someone had murdered Miles and then left that shovel at the scene of the crime to incriminate Lydia, as his daughter had first suggested yesterday, then it meant this whole thing could be premeditated — a murder planned in advance.

And Doc — and his shovel — had been an integral part of the plan.

Of course, there was another possibility. The whole thing didn't necessarily have to be premeditated. The shovel simply could have fallen into someone else's hands by happenstance — been passed around town another time or two. Only later, when it came time to do the deed and the plan was made, had the shovel been worked into the equation.

Either way, the realization that a garden tool from his farm had been used for such a nefarious purpose — as a murder weapon and as a device to incriminate an innocent person in the crime — made him angry in a certain way, but it also made him more determined than ever to get to the bottom of this, and find out who had hauled him and his daughter into the events surrounding the murder of Miles Crawford.

Doc and his buddies had chewed over those events for more than an hour at the diner, and had come up with a number of viable scenarios for the reasons behind the recent deaths. But it had been Artie Groves who had been most adamant about the ultimate motivations behind the two murders. "It's all because of that property of his," Artie had said as he sat in the corner booth at the diner. "Trust me on this. Find out what's going on out at that berry farm, and this whole mystery will start to unravel for you."

He's right, Doc thought as he drove out toward Blueberry Acres. *It all centers on the*

Crawford place.

Then another thought struck him: *Was there a reason Miles had been so unsociable all these years? Maybe he knew something he purposely kept from the rest of us — something about the farm.*

Of course, since Miles ran a you-pick-it operation for several weeks during late spring and early summer, there were people going in and out of his farm all the time. If he was trying to hide something, he wasn't trying very hard.

Besides, what possible secret could have cost him his life?

Still, Doc thought, Artie had been on to something. "That shovel is essentially inconsequential," he had further postulated at the diner. "It was a means to an end, a way for the real murderer to deflect attention by casting blame on Lydia, and it worked perfectly. At this point, *no one* seems to know what really happened out there, since the two key people who might provide some real insight — Miles and Lydia — are both dead. But the most important question we should ask is not *who* murdered Miles, or *how,* but *why?* And that's because of the berry farm. Unfortunately, Lydia was ancillary to the whole thing, a scapegoat — and

278

she died because she probably knew too much."

It was, Doc thought, a compelling argument, and one that got him thinking.

For the past few years, Doc had been working on a number of writing projects, mostly nonfiction historical works. He'd taught ancient history at the University of Maine up in Orono for more than thirty years, but after retiring, he'd turned his interests more toward New England and local history. A few years back, as part of the weekend festivities surrounding the town's annual Winter Moose Fest, he'd delivered a public lecture about the town's founding families. In preparation for the lecture, he'd done quite a bit of research about prominent local families, including the Pruitt and the Sykes families, who had deep roots in the village of Cape Willington and the surrounding region. Both families had arrived in the area in the early to mid-1700s, the Sykeses as seafarers and the Pruitts as landholders and owners of the first mill on the cape. And through the generations, there had been more than a little ill will between the two families, as they clashed at one time or another over the years. On occasion, their disagreements had flared up into actual feuds.

Many of those feuds had been about land, since even the earliest settlers had highly valued the Cape's prime properties, and land speculation had run wild as the village became established during the 1800s. Doc recalled a story he'd read a few years back, recounting a tale in which a male member of the Sykes family had lost a valuable piece of local property to a Pruitt in a poker game. That, in part, had stirred up bad blood between the two families, and it had continued for decades, if not centuries.

Doc had no idea if the animosity between the two families continued today. He knew there had been an issue with a current member of the Sykes family a few years back. Doc suspected his daughter knew more about that episode than she had revealed, but he had never pressed her on the matter. She was a grown woman, on the north side of forty now, as someone had said to him once, and he left her to her own decisions. If she kept some information close to her chest, she must have a good reason for doing so. Still, he worried about her involvement in the rash of murders that had plagued their community over the past four or five years, and was concerned that these two most recent murders, as well as the others, could somehow all be tied together.

That was why he was headed back to Blueberry Acres.

Artie's theories had jogged something in the back of his mind — a memory, something he decided he needed to check on. So he had jumped into his truck and headed home. He wanted to check the notes he'd made for that lecture a few years back, and look through a few historical resources he kept in his office at home.

He took a right on Wicker Road and a few minutes later turned left onto the dirt lane that led back to Blueberry Acres. The summer before, they'd put up a sign out here at the street, with an arrow pointing in their direction. They hadn't yet opened the blueberry fields to the public, since they ran primarily a commercial operation, but they were thinking of changing that. They'd even talked about opening a small farm stand, or perhaps even a garden or craft shop, as a way to make better use of their property and generate some additional income.

As he came up the dirt lane toward the farmhouse, Doc was surprised to see an old red Saab station wagon sitting in the driveway in front of the barn. He didn't recognize the vehicle, which made sense, since he noticed it had out-of-state license plates. Green plates. Vermont.

Who did they know from Vermont?

As his truck came alongside the other vehicle, he glanced in the windows. The second-row seatbacks were folded down, and the rear cargo area behind the front seats was stuffed to the roof with personal belongings and outdoor gear. There was more on top. Attached to the slightly rusting roof rack was an assortment of lumber, canvas, and more gear under a heavy opaque plastic tarp.

Doc pulled to a stop just in front of the Saab and looked out the windshield as he shut off the engine. There was no one around, as far as he could see. The place looked deserted, as it should be, since Candy was at her office in town.

He opened the driver's side door and stepped out, still searching for any sign of a visitor. He took a few steps across the dirt parking area toward the blueberry fields and heard a dog barking somewhere up ahead.

Doc raised a hand, shielding his eyes against the bright June sunlight.

He hadn't been mistaken. There was indeed a dog, fifty or sixty yards away, running lazily along the edge of one of the fields. Doc scanned the landscape, but he could see no one else around.

What was a lone dog doing out here, running through his field? A stray? A neighbor's pet?

He heard something rattle inside the barn.

Abruptly he turned toward the sound, spinning on his heels. He still shaded his eyes, but his pupils were constricted because of the brightness of the day, so all he could see inside the barn were shadows.

"Hello?" he called out. "Someone in there?"

He heard a low, muffled reply and vaguely saw a figure motion toward him.

"What's that again?" Doc asked, taking a few steps closer. The dog had spotted him and was barking again, loping across the field in his direction. It was a big shaggy dog, Doc saw, with a thick coat of white and gray hair, a big muzzle, and big feet.

"Is that your dog?" Doc asked the shadowy figure in the barn, pointing off toward the field at the approaching animal.

Another muffled reply.

Doc had reached the barn door. "What the heck are you doing in there?" he called. "You know this is private property, right?"

This time he heard the reply. "I'm checking your garden tools," the figure said.

Doc squinted into the shadows.

"You're . . . what?"

The dog was sniffing at his heels now. It was a bigger animal than he'd realized. It stood almost waist high. Its long furry coat was speckled in places with bits of leaves and twigs, and its nose held some moist dirt, as if it had been sniffing at the ground. But fortunately the animal looked friendly enough. It gazed up at him with pale eyes.

"Hello, boy," Doc said, and then he turned back to the shadows. "Well, who the heck are you anyway?" he asked the stranger. "Can I help you with something?"

The figure approached him then, and Doc began to make out the details: a man of medium build, a few inches under six feet, wearing faded clothes and worn boots, with a rugged face, sunburned cheekbones, mocha-colored eyes, long brown hair, and a thick reddish-brown beard.

"I didn't mean to intrude," the bearded man said. "I was just looking at your shovels." He stuck out a calloused hand. "My name is Neil Crawford."

TWENTY-EIGHT

The House of Style beauty salon was one of the busiest places on Main Street. It occupied an older storefront a few doors south of the Black Forest Bakery, wedged between a florist shop and an arts and crafts store on the corner. Many of the storefronts along the ritzier Ocean Avenue, anchored by the stately Pruitt Opera House halfway down the block, were newer and more attractive, having been updated or renovated in recent years. But despite its lofty name, the House of Style looked more like a workaday business, with a brick-and-glass facade, a display window with decorations that changed seasonally, and a single glass door that led inside to a large, comfy waiting area in the front, and through an archway into a back area, with three chairs, two sinks, and three hair dryers.

Candy had just spent nearly fifteen minutes talking to the salon's owner, Freda

Winters, an affable woman in her mid-fifties who excelled at hairdressing while making pleasant conversation and ensuring every visitor felt welcome in her shop. She always had the latest story, the silliest joke, or the juiciest piece of gossip, gleaned from her many appointments during the day.

It had taken a little coaxing — and an appeal to her civic pride to help solve this latest murder case as quickly as possible, so they all could get back to village business — but Freda had finally allowed Candy to take a peek at her appointment ledger for the past few months. Candy wanted to get an idea of who might have been at the beauty salon around the same time the shovel had disappeared from Lydia's car six weeks or so ago.

Candy didn't have an exact date for that alleged theft — Lydia had never given her one — but she thought she could narrow it down to a general range of time, taking into account the numerous times the shovel had changed hands after leaving Blueberry Acres. Fortunately, the appointments were fairly well established from week to week, with the same people coming in at the same time. Wanda, for instance, had a standing date at one o'clock on Tuesdays. Cotton Colby came in Thursdays at three, and Mrs.

Fairweather came in Thursday mornings, though once or twice over the past couple of months she'd switched to a midafternoon slot on the same day. Elvira Tremble and Della Swain came in on different days, and at less frequent intervals. Alice Rainesford and Brenda Jenkins apparently visited different salons, or none at all, for their names weren't in the book anywhere, though it was certainly possible one or all of the ladies had stopped by the salon at one time or another simply to visit, say hello, and catch up on the latest news, much as Doc and the boys gathered at the diner.

Candy asked Freda about Lydia's visits and her car. She also asked outright, though in a tactful way, about any animosity between Lydia and some of the other women who had appointments on Thursday afternoons.

"You're talking about the league ladies, right?" Freda said with a roll of her eyes. "Well, so far it's more of a cold war than anything else. I wouldn't say there was open animosity between them and Lydia, but they were definitely wary of each other, mostly because of the whole thing with that berry farm. But there was something else with some of the women, particularly Cotton — possibly because she's their leader, I guess. She and Lydia seemed to have a genuine dislike for each other, for some reason. So I've found the best way to handle the situation is just to keep all of them apart. I've tried moving some of their appointments to different days but they're all stubborn as mules — though don't tell them I said that. They're also pretty good customers!" She laughed easily. "But I try to hustle the league ladies out before Lydia arrives. And it usually works. Of course, it helps that Lydia normally wouldn't stop in until she'd made sure all their cars were gone. I've seen her circle the block half a dozen times or more, waiting for the last of them to leave."

"Have any of your customers had anything stolen from their vehicles while parked in front of your shop?" Candy asked. "Maybe a couple of months ago?"

Freda shook her head. "Other than bored teenagers getting into trouble? We had that rash of robberies from cars a few months back, remember? Turned out to be high school kids having a little fun. But other than that, no, nothing that I can recall."

Now, as Candy stood outside on the sidewalk in front of the salon, she surveyed the street she'd walked up and down dozens, perhaps hundreds, of times over the past few years. But she looked at it with sharper eyes today. She was trying to determine the feasibility of Lydia's claim. Could someone have walked out here on the street in broad daylight and taken a shovel from a parked car without being noticed?

After surveying the scene and giving it some thought, she decided that, yes, it was certainly possible, though it would not have been easy. The street in front of the House of Style was busy, but this was also the lower part of town, away from the more active and tourist-friendly Ocean Avenue. Gumm's Hardware Store, a popular destination throughout the day, was on the opposite side of the street, a couple of doors up, and the deli down on the corner, opposite the arts and crafts store, could be busy around lunchtime. Of course, traffic backed up periodically from the light at the lower intersection. But there were moments when all the activity cleared out, and it was certainly possible someone could have made a quick grab, especially if shielded by other cars and trucks parked along the street.

From Lydia's description, Candy identified the area where the real estate agent had most likely parked her convertible on the day in question, and tried to judge how well someone inside the beauty salon might have seen the vehicle. She also looked at the surrounding storefronts and shops, wondering if someone else coming from a different establishment could have taken the shovel. But after all her efforts, she reached no definitive conclusions. Anything was possible, she decided, if the timing was right. Lydia could have been telling the truth — or not.

Candy checked her watch. It was just past eleven. A good time, she thought, to stop by the Black Forest Bakery. The morning rush would be over, and the lunchtime crush yet to begin.

She wanted to ask Maggie again about the timing of Miles Crawford's visit to the bakery the previous morning. Miles had delivered strawberries around seven thirty or eight, according to Herr Georg. But Lydia said Miles had e-mailed her around eight, allegedly from his home. There could be a simple explanation, such as a smart phone, Candy thought — but it also seemed like a timing conflict to her. She felt she needed better information on where Miles went yesterday morning — and when. He obviously couldn't be in two places at once. It was a loose end she felt she needed to tie up.

She'd hoped Maggie and Herr Georg

could help her with that. But much to her surprise, the bakery was still crowded, even at this hour of the morning. The long line at the counter hadn't dwindled much from the last time she'd stopped by earlier in the day. Maggie looked busy but happy in her element, greeting customers, filling orders, and ringing up sales on the cash register.

Candy waved as she entered, and her friend waved back, then motioned to her. Candy came around the side of the counter and waited as Maggie took an order from a customer, then turned aside and leaned in close to her. "I need to talk to you sometime today," she said. "When can we meet?"

Candy thought about it a moment. "How about four o'clock? The Lightkeeper's Inn?"

Maggie nodded. "That's perfect," she whispered. "I need some of your expert advice."

"About what?"

Before Maggie could answer, she was drawn back to her customers, but she tossed a dreamy glance to the door that led back to the kitchen and smiled wistfully, like a schoolgirl in love.

Momentarily confused, Candy glanced over at the door and then back at Maggie. Her brow furrowed. "Herr Georg?" she mouthed.

Maggie gave her a wink. "Four o'clock," she said before scurrying off to fill an order.

"Okay, I'll meet you there," Candy said, "because I need to talk to you as well." But Maggie was so busy she didn't hear her friend, so Candy gave her a quick wave good-bye and headed back out the door, angling across the street and down Ocean Avenue.

Things were hopping in Town Park, where the ladies of the Cape Willington Heritage Protection League were busy making preparations for the Strawberry Fair, which would take place the following day. Tents, booths, and tables were going up, along with a children's arts and crafts area, a covered stage for performances, a roped-off ring for pony rides, and a food service area. So far the weather had held. The sky was still as blue as the sea, the day was warming, and the smell of salt air rode on the light breeze.

Candy had barely entered the park when she was approached by Wanda Boyle, walking stiffly alongside Cotton Colby, Della Swain, and Elvira Tremble.

"We have a problem," Wanda informed her as they drew near. She indicated the unhappy ladies. "There's been a mix-up. They have no strawberries for the Strawberry Fair."

Candy came to a stop. "I thought that was taken care of days ago."

"We thought so too," Cotton said, her mouth a tight red line. "We were under the impression that Miles Crawford delivered the berries to a warehouse we rented down by the docks, just as a holding place for a few days, until the day of the Fair. But the berries never arrived. Apparently they weren't quite ripe enough, and he wanted to give them another day or two. We've found out" — she raised the back of a hand to her mouth and cleared her throat uncomfortably — "we've found out that he left a message with one of our members a couple of days ago, explaining that the delivery would be delayed. Unfortunately, that message was never communicated to the rest of us. Our member forgot to mention it. So when we got to the warehouse this morning, well, needless to say, we were shocked to find it empty."

"We have no strawberries!" Della Swain said, her face a mask of regret and concern.

"So what are you going to do?" Candy asked.

Elvira gave her a hard look. "Well, we're not going to cancel the event, if that's what you think."

"No, of course not," Candy said, agreeing

293

with her.

"But we have a strawberry shortcake booth to run tomorrow," Della said worriedly. "We *have* to get some berries — and fast."

"Can you get them from somewhere else?" Candy asked. "From another farm?"

"It's possible," Cotton said. "Alice and Brenda are checking on that right now. But why should we do that when we have fields full of them just a few miles from here?"

"We realize there are some complications to overcome," Elvira said. "Naturally, with Miles gone, it makes our task more difficult. We can't just ring him up and ask him to drop them off in the morning, can we?"

Candy wasn't quite sure what she was getting at. "No, of course not. Do you have an alternative plan?"

"As a matter of fact, we do," Cotton said, "and it involves you."

Candy wasn't sure she liked the sound of that. "Me?"

"You're a berry farmer," Cotton pointed out. "You know something about that business. You run your own farm. And you apparently have the ear of the chief of police." Cotton's eyes darted toward Wanda, and Candy realized that she must have told them about the chief's visit to Candy's office earlier that morning.

So that's how news gets around town so fast, Candy thought, casting a furtive glance in Wanda's direction. *I have a spy right in my own office.*

"We need your help," Cotton said pointedly. "We'd like you to talk to Chief Durr for us."

"About what?"

"We'd like permission to take a large group out to the berry farm this afternoon or evening, or even in the morning. We have a long e-mail list Della helped us assemble. We can send out a quick blast and get several dozen people out there on an hour's notice, so we can pick the berries we need."

"We also had an arrangement with Miles about the price of the berries," Elvira added, "which we'd like to remain in place. I'm not sure who we'd talk to about that, but it's rather important. This is not a fundraising event, of course, but we'd prefer not to lose money on it. The strawberry shortcake booth was going to be our main source of revenue."

"We're coming to you because we think you're the right person to help us expedite this," Cotton said with a great deal of forthrightness. "We need those strawberries, and we need them now. This is our league's

295

first major event, and it's designed as a way to promote the village and our local culture. Without strawberries, our Strawberry Fair will be a complete bust. And there are fields of berries just waiting to be picked out at that farm. We have to do this as soon as possible. So will you help us?"

It was, Candy admitted to herself, a viable plan. She took a few moments to think it through, but before she could respond, her phone buzzed in her back pocket.

Well aware there were four pairs of eyes watching her, waiting for a response, Candy reached around, pulled out the phone, and swiped her finger across it, squinting at the dark screen in the bright sunlight.

It was a text from Doc: *Stop by the house as soon as you can. Neil Crawford's here. There's something you need to see.*

Candy read it again, her gaze narrowing in on the words.

Neil Crawford?

Miles Crawford's son?

She glanced up at Wanda, who had mentioned Miles's son just a little while ago, when they were talking up in Candy's office.

What was he doing out at Blueberry Acres?

Candy looked back down at the cryptic message, her head tilted in thought. After a few moments she keyed off the phone and slid it back into her pocket, her eyes lifting toward Cotton and the other ladies, who were still staring at her.

She gave them a smile. "Let me see what I can do."

TWENTY-NINE

The Jeep kicked up a little dust as she drove up the dirt lane toward the farmhouse at Blueberry Acres. Sunlight reflected off the barn's tin roof, and off the hood of an old red Saab wagon parked in the driveway. It didn't look familiar, and the Vermont plates probably explained why. She spotted Doc's truck pulled over in front of the Saab, and off to her right, in an open, level area past the far side of the barn, near a stand of trees, she saw . . . something else.

"What the heck is that?" she said to herself, squinting out through the passenger-side window.

It looked like a round white tent, but unlike any tent she had seen before. There was something rugged yet exotic about it. It had a Marco Polo feel, as if it had been plucked off the plains of Asia from some nomadic tribesman.

And then she saw the dog.

He had apparently heard the Jeep crunching to a stop on the driveway, and he was coming to greet her, loping along the side of the barn in a friendly manner, tongue lolling out one side of his mouth, a great shaggy beast whose whole body seemed to be moving in anticipation of meeting her.

He padded along happily toward her and came around the front of the Jeep just as she shut off the engine, and by the time she opened the door and stepped out, he was waiting for her. He gave her a soulful look and took a few casual steps forward to nuzzle her hand with a cold nose.

"Well, aren't you a friendly one?" Candy said, leaning over to scratch a little behind the dog's ears. "You're a big fellow, too, aren't you? And what might your name be?" She patted him on the side several times, looking up and around. "And where did you come from?"

She heard someone call to her from the house, and looked over to see a bearded man emerge from the back door and cross the porch. He waved as he came down the steps onto the driveway, looking like he'd lived here for years. "He seems to like you," the bearded man called to her, indicating the dog with a flick of his finger.

He was a tall man with an easy gait and

an easy smile, an untamed head of hair that hung over his ears, and loose-fitting clothes that looked well lived in. His weathered face, lightly sunburned on the high cheeks and thin nose, was half hidden by a full beard, and his broad shoulders and sinewy arms, revealed by the rolled-up sleeves of his faded flannel shirt, gave him the appearance of someone who spent a lot of time out of doors splitting wood and pulling out tree stumps.

"He's very friendly," Candy called back, continuing to pet the dog, who had looked over at the sound of his master's voice but remained tight by Candy's side, apparently content with the attention he was receiving. "What's his name?"

"He's called Random," the bearded man said as he approached, "and he usually doesn't take to strangers so easily. He's a bit of a loner, like his master, I'm afraid. But he's obviously very fond of you."

"Well, he has good taste," Candy said with a quick smile, and she affectionately scratched the top of the dog's head.

"I couldn't agree more." The bearded man stopped a couple of steps away and held out a long-fingered hand, with whitish fingernails against his tanned skin. "I'm Neil Crawford."

"Hi, Neil. I'm Candy."

They shook. Candy's small hand seemed to disappear into Neil's, which felt warm and a little callused. With some effort she pulled her gaze away from his and looked back down at the dog. "Random, huh? Why Random?"

Neil looked down at the dog as well. "It's from a book I read ten or twelve years ago, called *Roverandom,* by Tolkien. It's the story of a dog's adventures after he's turned into a toy by a wizard. I'd read all Tolkien's books when I was a kid, of course, and we had a family dog named Rover, so when *Roverandom* came out, I read that, too, and it made me think of that old dog."

Neil flicked a finger at the big shaggy animal still leaning up tightly against Candy's leg. "Then, a few years ago, I got this one as a puppy from a friend of mine, and he reminded me of the dog in the book. I thought about naming him Rover Two or something like that, but I went with Random instead. And he fits his name. He's a wanderer, and tends to roam around looking for adventure. But he always finds his way back home."

As if in response, Random appeared to spy something in the high grass at the edge of the fields to their right, and off he went with a low gruff in the back of his throat to see what he could find.

Candy and Neil stood in silence for a few moments, watching him go, out past the barn and the odd tent behind it. Candy indicated the new addition to the landscape. "I suppose that's yours?"

Neil nodded. "It's my yurt," he said with a smile.

"Your *yurt*?" Candy turned back to him with a quizzical look.

Neil was about to explain when Doc came out of the house and called to them with a wave. "Hey, you two! Come on inside! I've got lunch on the table."

He'd made grilled cheese sandwiches with rye bread and thick slices of sharp cheddar he'd picked up at the deli in town, accompanied by homemade potato salad, thick deli pickles, and iced tea with fresh slices of lemon.

As they ate, Neil filled them in on the past twenty-four hours.

"I was as shocked as anyone by Dad's death," he said, his smile falling away as he addressed the difficult subject. "I have a fifteen-acre homestead in Vermont, west of the Green Mountains near Bristol. I moved there ten years ago with my ex-wife, who was from Montpelier" — here he paused,

302

glancing at the both of them — "but I managed to keep the place when we broke up. Dad wanted me to come back and work the berry farm with him, but I'd more or less established myself over there. The place has a small apple orchard, vegetable gardens, and some good stands of scrub pines and hardwoods I can sell for firewood, plus a pond and some berry fields. I keep sheep as well, though the flock is only a couple dozen at this point. I make a decent living off of it, but it's hard work to do by yourself."

He paused, taking a bite of a crisp pickle, and gazed out the window for a few moments before he continued. "Plus, to be honest, Dad can be — well, could be — a little hard to live with at times. He wasn't the most communicative person, which you probably know if you spent any time with him. He tends to stay to himself, much like Random out there." Neil pointed toward the window with his head. "That's why my mom left, I guess. But Dad and I got along okay. He gave me a lot of advice over the years about farming and running an agricultural business. He knew what he was doing. Well, anyway, as soon as I heard what had happened to him, I drove right over. I got here late last night. I stopped by the police station this morning, and the funeral home.

I'm heading out to the farm this afternoon to check it out."

"Have the police given you any more information about what might have happened?" Doc asked.

Neil shook his head. "I haven't been able to get much out of them. They interviewed me for about an hour, asking about his friends, acquaintances, possible enemies, that sort of thing. But I hadn't seen him in six months or so. Last time we got together was at Christmas. We talked on the phone a few times, but both of us were pretty busy, I guess."

He fell into silence, a hurt look coming into his brown eyes, which were flecked with streaks of yellow, Candy noticed now that she sat close to him. He seemed to be remembering what might have been, running through memories and regrets in his head.

Candy thought it was time to change the subject. "What about the yurt?" she asked, pointing out the window in the direction of the barn.

A casual smile returned to Neil's face, outlined by his beard, which was redder than his hair. "That's my temporary living facility. I lived in that yurt for almost a year while I was remodeling my place in Vermont. It's surprisingly cozy. So I threw it in the car when I came over, along with some other things I thought I might need." He paused again. "I wasn't sure what I'd find when I got here. I'm not even sure I want to sleep in Dad's old house, even though the police have cleared me to enter. And I'm not crazy about hotel rooms. Most of them — well, they're not my style. I'm more comfortable on my own." He nodded toward Doc. "Your father's allowed me to set it up here for a few days, until I can figure out my next move, if that's okay with you."

"Of course," Candy said. "Stay as long as you'd like. It's the least we can do."

"And the yurt's pretty interesting," Doc said, brightening. "It's much studier than a tent, and he set it up in about forty-five minutes. He's even got some furniture in there."

"Furniture?" Candy asked in amusement as she looked over at Neil.

The smile widened just a bit. "Well, it's not like I have a three-piece bedroom set in there — just an airbed, a folding table and chairs, a small shelf, that sort of thing."

"I told him he could use the bathroom, kitchen, and laundry here whenever he wanted, until we get this whole thing at the berry farm sorted out," Doc said. He glanced over at his daughter to make sure she was okay with this arrangement, but Candy had already moved on.

"So, do you have any idea what might have happened to your father?"

Neil shook his head. "I'm as much in the dark as everyone else. That's why I'm headed out there this afternoon — to see if I can figure it out." He paused and looked at them. "And I'd like the two of you to go with me."

THIRTY

They took the Jeep, since Neil's car was filled with his gear and the cab of Doc's truck would have been a tight fit. Candy opened the back hatch so Random could jump up, which took a little coaxing. Then she closed it behind him and moved around to the driver's side door. Doc waved Neil toward the front passenger seat and climbed into the Jeep's second row, pushing aside a folded umbrella, well-used work gloves, a fleece jacket, a box of empty pots, wire flower hangers, and a few small gardening tools.

On the way out to Crawford's Berry Farm, Neil told them why he'd asked them to accompany him. "I'd like you to help me assess the fields," he explained. "Your microclimate is different than ours over in Vermont. I heard at the police station that Dad suspended picking for a couple of days to let the berries ripen, but I'd like to open the fields again as soon as they're ready. I'd hate to let all those berries rot out in the fields. *Dad* would've hated it. Those fields were his life — and I'd like to make sure they're harvested, as he would have wanted."

"I think that's a great idea," Doc said with a bit of emotion in his voice.

"I think so too," Candy said with an approving smile. "Everyone in town will be happy if the fields are opened again — especially the league ladies. They told me they're desperately in need of berries for their event tomorrow."

Neil nodded. "We can take care of that, if you'll help me put it together."

"I'd be glad to," Candy said. "And they'll be thrilled. They wanted to see if they can get out here later today or tomorrow to do some picking."

Neil considered that for a moment. "I don't know about today," he said thoughtfully, "since I want to spend some time at the place myself before I open it up to the public again — just to make sure everything's in order. But tomorrow morning would work."

"Great. I'll let them know. They'll be very happy to hear that."

"And if you and Doc have time in your

schedules, I'd welcome your help with the you-pick-it operation over the next couple of weeks," Neil continued, looking back over his shoulder at Doc in the backseat. "I know you're busy with your own farm, and I have my own place over in Vermont to look after, so I'll be going back and forth a little. But I'm a newbie around here. I don't have the local connections and resources you do — and that Dad did. I'll try to pick up some of his deliveries and outlets, and keep things going as much as possible, so I can make it through the berry season."

"We'd be glad to help you out any way we can," Doc said.

"I'm sure lots of folks around town would be willing to pitch in as well," Candy added. "We just need to put out the word."

"I'd really appreciate that," Neil said sincerely.

"Do you have any idea what you're going to do with the place when the season's over?" Doc asked curiously, and Candy perked up her ears at Neil's response.

"I honestly don't know yet," he said. "My brother's in Singapore on business, and until he gets back, there won't be any decisions."

"When will that be?" Candy asked.

"I don't know. I'm not sure he's going to

make it back for the funeral. He said it could be a few days or it could be a month or two. He's still trying to work things out. So we won't make any immediate decisions. That's why I just want to get through berry season first, and then figure out our next move."

"Any chance you'll take over the place yourself?" Doc asked.

Neil let out a breath and ran a hand through his hair, shuffling it around a bit. "I don't know, Doc. I haven't really thought much about it. At this point anything's possible, I suppose."

"Why was your dad selling the place?" Candy asked.

That stopped the conversation. Silence reigned in the cabin for a few moments. Neil turned toward her as if she'd spoken in a different language. "Say that again."

Candy hesitated, wondering if she'd misspoken. "Your dad was selling the place, right? The berry farm?"

Neil looked mystified. "Not that I'm aware of."

"You didn't know?"

"Know what?" He shook his head. "About him selling the farm? No, nothing. Where'd you hear this?"

Softly, contemplatively, Candy said,

"From Lydia St. Graves, last night. She snuck out to Blueberry Acres after dark and told me her side of the story. She said your father hired her to find a buyer for the place." And Candy recounted her meeting with Lydia, as Doc listened with great interest from the backseat. She explained how Miles had contacted Lydia weeks earlier and surprised her by saying he'd decided to sell the farm. "She'd been pursuing him for years, trying to get him to sell, but he constantly refused," Candy explained. "Then one day out of the blue he changed his mind."

"But that doesn't make any sense," Neil said. "Dad loved this place. Did Lydia say why he decided to sell?"

Candy shook her head. "No, but she said she thought there was something else going on in the background with him — that's how she put it. Something she couldn't identify. She said she thought she wasn't the only one pursuing him."

"You mean someone else wanted to buy the place?"

"That's what it sounded like — but keep in mind, this was just Lydia's speculation."

Again, Neil was silent for a few moments as he looked out the windshield at the road ahead. "I guess I'm not really surprised," he said finally, looking back at Candy. "I felt like something was going on with him for a while. He hadn't talked much about the farm over the past year or so. And when we did talk, he was . . . well, kind of vague. Secretive."

"In what way?" Doc asked.

Neil shrugged. "Nothing I can say for certain. Just a feeling, really. I put it up to the fact that he was living alone and getting older. Normal changes, I thought. These long New England winters have a tendency to harden people a little — physically and emotionally. I figured when he was ready to tell me more, he would. It was always like that with him. He moved at his own pace, and nothing could change him."

"Well, this time something did," Candy pointed out. "Something happened over the past few months that made him decide to sell, and he asked Lydia for her help. She said your father wanted her to find a nice family to take over the place and continue what he'd been doing."

Neil nodded but said nothing. So Doc spoke up from the backseat. "Wouldn't Miles have offered the farm to you if he was thinking of selling it?"

Neil turned toward him. "Not necessarily. Over the years we talked about it. But I always told him I had my own place. I guess he figured I didn't want it."

"But I still don't understand all the secrecy," Candy said. "No advertising, no MLS listing. Lydia was looking around for viable candidates and running them past your father. Apparently he wanted to keep everything off the record."

"Well, he certainly succeeded. He kept it from me," Neil said, and he was silent for the rest of the way out to the farm.

The place was deserted, as before, and eerily silent. Candy pulled to a stop near the barn, shut off the engine, and climbed out of the cabin. The wind had hushed, and high clouds filtered out some of the sunlight. She couldn't help but feel a chill.

The place seems like a graveyard, she thought.

But that changed once they let Random out. His nose went instantly to the ground, and he started roaming through the barn and across the fields, adding at least some sense of life to the place.

Following the dog, they walked together out through the strawberry fields, making frequent stops to check the berries. Doc liked what he saw. "They're ready for picking," he pronounced at the top of one of the fields, and Candy and Neil agreed.

313

"Especially this lower section here," Doc said as he indicated a swath of land with a wave of his arm. "These berries are close to peak. We need to get them picked within the next few days."

"We'll start there tomorrow morning, then," Neil said, his gaze roaming the fields. He looked over at Candy. "Eight A.M. okay?"

She nodded. "I'll make some calls."

"You might want to check the barn," Doc suggested. "See what kind of supplies you can find," and he headed off across the slope to inspect another field.

Candy thought Neil might follow, but instead he stood for the longest time without moving, surveying a nearby hoophouse with a blank expression on his face. Yellow police tape still cordoned off the building's entrances, and some of the plastic siding had been lifted out of place, giving them a peek into the shaded interior.

"You okay?" Candy asked him after a few moments.

He seemed to come suddenly awake, as if he'd been deep in a dream. He looked over at her, blinked several times, and finally nodded. "We'll have to make a few changes out here," he said quietly. "I'm not sure what to do with that hoophouse. I might

314

have to just tear it down."

Candy took him by the arm and led him down toward the barn. "That's a decision for another day. Come on, let's get set up for picking."

Miles had been an incredibly organized man, and it wasn't difficult to find all the supplies they needed, including baskets, tables, a scale, and a metal money box sitting on the spotless workbench. Not a tool, nail, bin, brush, or container was out of place. "When I was a kid, he used to pick up my clothes off the floor in the morning," Neil said as they gathered what they needed. "He was the one who cleaned and vacuumed the house — not my mom. He didn't cook but he kept all the food organized. He had schedules for everything."

They moved the folded tables near the barn entrance, so they'd be easy to set up in the morning, and lined up all the baskets. As they were finishing up, Neil said, "I'm going to check the house."

The way he said it let her know he preferred to do it alone. Without another word, he headed off across the dirt driveway, pulling a ring of keys from his pocket. He stepped up onto the porch and disappeared inside the farmhouse.

Once alone, Candy pulled out her cell

phone and called Wanda. The red-haired woman answered almost immediately. "What's up, Chief?"

"I need to get hold of Cotton Colby and the league ladies. Do you have their numbers? And I need you to post a message on the community blog."

She told Wanda what was going on, and ten minutes later she'd talked to four other people, including Cotton and Mason Flint, the town council chairman, and asked them to pass along the word. "We'd like to get at least a few dozen people out here in the morning," she told those she talked to. "We have a lot of picking to do."

She'd just ended a call to Maggie, pushing back their meeting to five, when Neil reappeared, a mystified look on his face.

"I found something inside," he said. "I'd like you to take a look. It seems like Lydia was right."

THIRTY-ONE

Inside, the house was like a museum, though there was evidence that a forensics team had swept the place. Some of the drawers in the kitchen were still opened, their contents looking as if they'd been riffled through, and in the living room the cushions on the sofa and chair had not been properly replaced.

"They took his computer," Neil said, leading Candy into a small office in the back corner of the first floor, "and some of his papers and documents, but nothing really critical, as far as I can tell."

The room was simply furnished, with an old oak desk in one corner, a wood-slatted office chair that looked like an antique, two wooden filing cabinets, and a bookcase with a few faded volumes that looked decades old. It was all dimly lit, since the shades on the two office windows were pulled down. Candy peeked out first one window, then the other. They offered magnificent views of the ocean to one side and the strawberry fields to the other. In the far distance, at the top of one of the fields, Candy could see her father standing still and straight, peering into the woods beyond.

Neil tugged at her arm. "But that's not what I wanted to show you. This way."

He led her out of the room, into a wood-floored hallway, and up the stairs to the second floor.

"Did they take your father's cell phone as well?" Candy asked as she climbed the stairs behind Neil.

"Good question," he said. "I haven't noticed his phone anywhere, so it's possible they did."

"Did he use a smart phone?"

Neil stopped at the upper landing and looked back at her. "No, why?"

"Lydia said he e-mailed her yesterday morning — early, asking her to meet him out here at the farm. But at the time he supposedly sent that e-mail message to her, someone else saw him making deliveries of strawberries. I'm wondering if he could have e-mailed her using a smart phone."

Neil shook his head. "Dad was low-tech. It took me years just to get him to buy the computer downstairs, and he had that same one for eight or nine years. It still works, so he saw no need to replace it. I showed him how to set up his e-mail account and contact list, so he could send around messages about the farm."

"I noticed a landline in the kitchen," Candy said as she reached the top. "A wall phone."

"That was his primary phone," Neil said, and he started off toward a bedroom at the back of the house. "He had a cell, but it was one of my old ones. It wasn't a smart phone, but I wanted to make sure he had something for emergencies."

"So he couldn't have e-mailed Lydia on the run?"

"His phone didn't have the capability to do that, as far as I know. The only way he could send e-mails was using the computer downstairs in his office." He pointed with a finger. "What I wanted to show you is in here."

The bedroom they entered was somewhat stark, like the office below, but comfortable-looking. It, too, was at the back of the house, looking out over the strawberry fields. The bed was still made, though again it had been ruffled, probably by someone who'd checked underneath it during the house search. The drawers in two bureaus looked as if they'd been opened and their contents examined as well. A few photos in frames, showing the Crawford family during happier times, sat on one of the dark bureaus. But the walls were devoid of decoration, painted an unexciting light green. The wood floor was polished, with a small patterned area rug near the bed. Candy imagined the shirts in the closet were all hung in neat rows, and the socks and underwear smartly folded in the drawers.

"Dad's office was downstairs," Neil said, "and that's where he did all his daily paperwork. But he didn't keep his important papers down there. He kept them up here, hidden away."

Neil pointed to a gray metal security box sitting on the seat of a high-backed cane chair beside the bed. The box, which looked fairly new, was perhaps fifteen inches long, eight inches deep, and six or seven inches high. It had an electronic keypad on the front. The top was open, revealing papers and bundles of cash inside, along with other valuables.

Neil pointed at the keypad. "He used his wedding anniversary as the combination, so we'd all remember it. He told us all years ago that if anything happened to him, we should check the box first. And that's what I did."

Neil lifted it carefully and placed it on the bed. "This is where he kept his emergency money — I think there's probably close to five thousand dollars in here — and all his legal documents, like birth certificates, car titles, the divorce agreement, legal papers, that sort of thing."

Neil picked up a faded, crinkled blue ribbon, lying near the top. "He won this from 4-H when he was about eight years old. He was pretty proud of it."

There were also a few small, monochromatic photographs of people who looked like ancestors, and several pieces of jewelry, including a school ring and a thin gold wedding band.

"And then there's this," Neil said, picking up a sheaf of envelopes that looked fairly new, held together by a rubber band. They'd all been slit neatly along the top, revealing the edges of folded documents inside.

"What are those?" Candy asked curiously.

"Letters. From some firm in New York City." He looked over at Candy. "They're offers on the farm. Someone wanted to buy the place. And they must have wanted it really bad, because they were offering him *lots* of money for it."

He let that hang in the air a moment as he set the envelopes down and picked up something else in the box. It was round, shiny, and yellow. "And maybe this is why," Neil said, holding up the object between his thumb and forefinger. "It's something I've never seen before — at least not in my father's possession. And I have no idea where he got it."

"What is it?" Candy asked, her gaze zeroing in on it.

"It is," Neil said, "an old gold coin."

THIRTY-TWO

Doc stood at the far end of the strawberry fields and gazed into the thick, shadowy woods. He thought he'd heard a muffled sound — a series of sounds, deep thuds that echoed through the trees and underbrush from some indeterminate direction. He looked back and forth along the edge of the woods, seeing nothing, and turned his good ear to the trees.

Low ruffs, growls, the faint sounds of digging.

Doc looked back around him, at the fields that stretched across the slope toward the hoophouses, farmhouse, and barn in the distance.

Where was the dog?

Had he gone inside the house? The barn? One of the hoophouses?

Doc heard the sounds again, from deep in the woods.

It was the dog, he knew.

Probably just found an old bone or something he's digging out, Doc mused.

But that thought suddenly worried him. With all the murders they'd had around town lately, maybe he should investigate, just to make sure.

He noticed a faint trail to his left, with a few shallow footprints locked into the drying earth, leading away from the field and into the woods.

Doc glanced back a final time before following the distant sounds into the shadows of the trees.

They had thinned where they met the field but quickly closed around him as he made his way along the trail. He always carried a compass with him, on his key chain, and he was used to walking in the Maine woods, so he wasn't too worried about getting lost. He only wished he'd brought some insect repellant with him. The bugs were buzzing in the warm air, and there was still some spring pollen hanging suspended in the thin rays of sunshine between the trees, tiny glowing motes that danced around him in slow motion. He sneezed and moved on.

The trail zigzagged around defiles and outcroppings of rock, continued along a narrow stream for a while, and then turned west again, putting the sun slightly in front of him and sometimes to his left.

He moved as quickly as he could with his limp. He had on the light boots he wore around the farm, and they worked fine for this type of terrain. He stopped at one point to pick up a long, straight, dried-out branch that had broken off a tree long ago, and used it as a walking stick after stripping off a few thin, short offshoots that held shriveled brown leaves.

He checked his watch, so he'd have a good gauge of how long he'd been walking, then looked up as he heard the dog's ruffs and growls again. The occasional sounds of digging were more pronounced. They appeared to be coming from his left, and the trail angled off in that direction, so he continued to follow it as best he could.

The terrain steepened and he struggled up the low slope, slowing his gait. He was also treading more carefully now, making sure he didn't slip or lose his balance. The last thing he wanted to do was to fall and break a hip out here in the middle of nowhere.

He lost track of the trail as he came across an area where the ground had hardened and turned rocky, but he knew the dog was close now. He could hear the animal just ahead, through a low screen of shrubbery, in what looked like a clearing of sorts. He could almost feel the dog's movements through the earth as it pawed at the ground.

He whistled softly and called out, since he didn't want to startle the dog. "Hey, Random. It's Doc. Remember me?" he said as he came through the trees. "What are you doing way out here?"

The sounds of the dog's digging and growling continued and grew louder. Doc finally came around a last stand of trees and saw the animal, pawing away at the foot of what looked like an old weed-covered stone foundation, though it was obvious no building had stood here in a long time.

"What'd you find there?" Doc asked, approaching the dog cautiously. Random turned and looked at him with a dirt-covered snout and soulful eyes, then jerked his head around as something popped out of the hole he'd been digging at, darted left and right, and then took a long leap, dashing off into the underbrush to their right.

It was a young rabbit.

The dog snapped his head back, let out a gruff of disbelief, steeled his haunches, and dashed after his prey like a lightning bolt, crashing around the crumbling foundation and into the brush, quickly disappearing from sight.

Doc watched the whole scene with some amusement. The dog had simply cornered a bunny. Even now, he could still hear the two of them in their frenzy, a sonic record of their life-and-death chase resounding through the woods with snaps, rustles, and an occasional playful bark.

Taking a moment to catch his breath, Doc stuck his hands in his back pockets, leaned back, and looked up. There were thickening strings of clouds passing by. He wasn't sure he liked the look of that. He knew there was a front coming through later in the afternoon, but he hoped the worst of the weather would clear out by the morning, so they'd have a good day for picking.

He looked down and surveyed the clearing, focusing in on the foundation around him for the first time.

It looked old, he thought — perhaps a hundred years, perhaps more. He wondered what kind of place had been built out there in the woods, so far from town. A hunter's shed, possibly, or maybe even a maple sugaring shack, something like that. It hadn't been a large place, but there'd been a wing off the back, possibly for a cookhouse or kitchen. There were naked foundations like this all over New England, the remnants of long-abandoned properties.

But when he took a closer look, something odd caught his eye.

He stepped to a nearby section of the foundation and used his walking stick to push away some of the leaves, pine needles, and loamy dirt that clung to the top of the stones. Then he leaned over and brushed away more with the flat of his hand.

Something poked up at him from the foundation. Nothing sharp. He pulled his hand away and looked at it. Part of a wood frame, blackened, as if it were a lump of charcoal.

Bits of charred wood were lodged into the foundation at various places, he noticed. He turned and spotted them in several locations now.

He knew what it meant. The place had burned down.

He paced around it and found a corner-stone at the northwest side. He kicked away a layer of dirt and grime that covered the lower face and bent over to get a look at it. There appeared to be engraving on the stone. But no, not an engraving. Nothing as professional as that. Just a few letters chipped out with a hammer and chisel, now smoothed by age but still clearly legible:

S. SYKES.

THIRTY-THREE

While Neil studied the coin, Candy examined the letters more carefully. There were perhaps two dozen of them, dating back several years. At first they'd come in only once or twice a year, but recently they'd become more frequent, arriving in the mailbox at the berry farm every few months. They were written on expensive watermarked paper in formal legal language, but all said the same thing. The firm — a legal, financial, and real estate investment company based in New York City — represented a client interested in purchasing Crawford's Berry Farm in Cape Willington, Maine. The earliest letters made no specific mention of any financial offering, simply encouraging contact, but later letters referred to a sum "in the seven figures."

"They can't be serious," Neil said at one point as he set the coin aside and read through the letters with Candy. "These sums are outrageous."

"Maybe they know something we don't," she said, and indicated the coin. "Doc will know something about that, but it looks a couple hundred years old. My guess is it's some sort of doubloon — something like that."

"Pirate money?" Neil asked in disbelief.

Candy shook her head, uncertain, and turned back to one of the letters. She pointed with a fingernail at the firm's name, written in black block letters across the top the page:

WYBORNE WHITTLE KINGSBURY LLC.

"Ever hear of these guys?" she asked.

Neil shook his head. "No."

An address line under the name listed a main address on Park Avenue in New York, with branch offices in Philadelphia, Montreal, Chicago, Miami, and London.

"I'll check them out when we get back to Blueberry Acres," Candy said.

Neil nodded, and sat down on the edge of the bed, thinking. "I don't get it," he said finally.

Candy began to fold and bundle up the letters. "Which part?"

"Well, if he was getting offers for that

much money on this place, why not just take the offers? Why hire Lydia to find another buyer for him?"

"Another good question," Candy admitted, "and if we can figure out the answer to *that* one, we might just figure out who killed your father."

"You think it's all tied together?" He held up the coin. "With this?"

"I think it could be, yes. The trickiest part of all these cases is figuring out the motivations behind the actions," Candy said. "Money. The biggest motivator of all. Someone obviously wanted this property pretty bad. They were willing to pay a lot of money for it. And not just for the pretty view."

"What are you saying?"

Candy shook her head. "I'm not sure yet. Just thinking out loud." She ran the rubber band back around the bundle of envelopes and returned it to the metal box. Neil was about to place the gold coin back inside as well, but he changed his mind and slipped it into his pocket. He closed the box's lid and locked it.

"You're not going to leave that here, are you?" Candy asked.

Neil looked down at the box filled with letters and mementos, bundles of cash, and a mysterious gold coin. "No, I guess that wouldn't be a good idea, would it? Especially with all the people we'll have around here tomorrow morning — not that anyone would take anything from the house, of course."

"Of course not," Candy said, "but it's best not to leave temptation sitting around." She glanced at her watch. "The bank is still open. I suggest we get that into a safe-deposit box." She looked out the window, staring off toward the trees in the distance.

"I think it's time we found my dad . . ."

THIRTY-FOUR

Doc straightened and leaned heavily on his walking stick as he stared at the cornerstone for several long moments. His brow furrowed and his mouth tightened to a long, straight line as he considered the implications of what he'd found.

It could be a major discovery, he thought.

S. Sykes.

This cabin must have been built by a member of the Sykes family, who had been in the area for generations. Surely someone must have documented the location of this foundation, especially given the history of the Sykes family in Cape Willington. But he'd dug around the historical society's archives quite a bit over the past few years, and could recall no record that indicated this had ever been Sykes land.

That was what surprised him the most — the fact that this foundation seemed to have been forgotten. He'd never heard anyone talk about it. He'd never seen or read any references to it.

Almost as if it had simply slipped out of the historical record.

Yet here was hard evidence that, indeed, a Sykes had once lived on this property now owned by the late Miles Crawford and his heirs.

Which brought up another somewhat disturbing question: Had Miles known of this foundation's existence, of its link to the Sykes family, and neglected to make it public knowledge?

If so, why had he kept it a secret?

This discovery confirmed an inkling Doc had had earlier in the day, a suspicion, when he'd been at the diner, listening to Artie's theories about the motivations behind the murder of Miles Crawford.

The most important question we should ask, Artie had said, *is not* who *murdered Miles, or* how, *but* why?

And that's because of the berry farm.

That had been Artie's theory, and it made sense. It was why Doc had left the diner when he did, and made his way home to check his resources for the lecture he'd given a couple of years ago about the town's founding families. He was certain he'd remember if he'd seen a reference to this place during his research. But there had been none, as far as he could recall, and he was a fairly thorough researcher. So how had it slipped by him? How had it slipped by all of them? It couldn't have escaped the detection of researchers for all these years, could it?

Unless someone had purposely endeavored to keep it a secret. A cover-up.

But was that even possible? On the surface, it seemed ludicrous.

And again: Why would anyone go to such lengths?

Doc turned back to the foundation, studying the traces of black singes along the stone.

What happened here? he wondered.

He started off again, walking the outline of the foundation, all the way around once, and then twice, studying it with a more discerning eye. He poked at the hole Random had been digging, wondering if it might lead to something deeper. But it simply ended in a small hollow beneath the stones.

He looked up and around. The sounds of the dog-and-hare chase had died away, but he could still hear Random scuffling through the underbrush not too far away, still in frenzied pursuit.

Doc studied the woods around him, and then began a careful, systematic search of the area.

He found the graveyard fairly quickly. It was perhaps thirty paces beyond the house, in an area sheltered by trees, a small cemetery marked off by a black wrought iron fence, now rusted and leaning over in some places, but still standing. A gate remained as well, iron-hinged on a stone pillar, dark chocolate rust stains marking its face.

Doc didn't enter. He didn't have to. He could see everything he needed to from where he stood.

There were five gravestones, some tilted fore or aft, all black and streaked with age. But he could still make out the last names on the stones.

All were members of the Sykes family.

Doc turned and looked toward the foundation, now hidden behind a screen of trees.

Had these people died of natural causes? Or had they been killed by the fire?

As he pondered this question, he noticed something else — something more recent than gravestones that were a hundred and fifty years old.

It looked like another grave, yet this one was freshly dug into the dark, loamy earth, just beyond the back side of the wrought iron fence. It was as if someone else had died and there hadn't been enough room inside the cemetery's iron fence for another grave, so they'd dug it outside in an open patch of land among the trees.

It also looked like it had been a haphazard affair. Doc noticed several other shallower pits in the immediate vicinity, as if someone had started digging those before focusing on the largest one, which looked fairly deep. And the dirt removed from the hole had been flung around all the sides randomly, rather that dumped into a single pile to make infill easier.

But it had never been filled back in.

Doc circled the cemetery and approached the hole with caution. He had no idea what he'd find at the bottom. He only hoped it wouldn't be another body — of either the fresh or the decomposed variety.

He nearly jumped out of his skin when he heard a crash of sound to his left, and a blur of shaggy white and gray fur charged out of the woods toward him. Doc let out a cry of surprise, fell back, and nearly lost his footing. If he hadn't still been holding on to the walking stick, he might have tumbled to the ground.

But he saw almost at once it was only Random, back from his quest, sans rabbit.

Doc gathered his footing and held a hand to his chest. His heart was thumping inside his rib cage.

"Random, goddammit!" he said forcefully. "You nearly scared me to death!"

At the sound of the harsh words the dog slowed, dropped his head, and looked up at Doc with mournful eyes. Slowly the dog paced to him and gave a soft gruff, apparently offering his apologies.

Doc took a moment to calm himself. "It's all right," he said finally in a softer tone. "You just startled me, that's all."

The dog sniffed around Doc's feet, then lifted his head curiously and trotted over to the open pit in the ground, where he continued sniffing around its edges.

"Anything in there?" Doc asked. But he knew he wasn't about to get an answer from the dog. He'd have to go look for himself.

The sides of the pit were fairly steep, and the dirt had dried to a crusty brown. It wasn't as fresh as he had first thought. He guessed it had been dug a couple of weeks, or maybe even a couple of months, ago. There was no way to tell with any certainty.

And, he discovered when he finally sidled up to the edge of the pit and looked down, it was empty.

No bodies down there at the bottom, he

thought, and for a strange moment he wasn't sure whether he was relieved or disappointed.

But something else was odd about the pit. The sides and bottom had been smoothed and weathered a bit, but he could still see *something* down there. If it had been a dark, cloudy day, or if he'd come across the pit at twilight, or if he'd been standing in the thick of shadowy trees, he might not have noticed it. But he stood in a relative clearing with the trees pushed back, allowing in some daylight. He could clearly see a distinct indention at the bottom of the hole. A rectangular carved-out depression, cleanly squared off and deeper than the surrounding earth at the bottom, by about half a dozen inches.

It was as if some object — a box, perhaps — had been plucked from the dense earth at the bottom of the pit, like a tooth from the gum, leaving a cavity behind.

Doc looked at it for quite a while, tilting his head back and forth, muttering to himself under his breath, trying to make sense of it.

Finally it clicked in his brain.

Something had been buried at the bottom of the pit, he realized, and *someone* had gone looking for it, found it, and yanked it out, leaving the indention. The object had been a couple of feet in length and perhaps a foot wide.

About the size of a small wooden box.

Or, Doc thought, a treasure chest.

Possibly a *very old* treasure chest.

Doc's heart thumped inside his rib cage again, but this time it wasn't fright that made it beat so loudly.

It was a spark of recognition.

He suddenly thought he knew what the box was, because he'd seen something like it — another old wooden box of the same general size — before.

"Random!" he called out sharply, and the dog, who had been wandering off again, stopped in his tracks and turned back around with a questioning look.

"We have to go! Now! Come on!"

And as fast as he could move, Doc headed back through the woods toward the berry farm, the dog on his heels.

THIRTY-FIVE

Candy stood at the edge of the woods, her blue eyes searching as she called out for her father. "Hey, Dad, where are you? I have to get back to town!"

"Maybe he's in the hoophouse," Neil said, looking off toward the fields and the farmhouse. They'd searched everywhere else for Doc, but so far they'd had no luck finding him.

They heard a dog bark then, from back among the trees, and the sounds of someone coming through the woods. Half a minute later Doc emerged at the edge of the field, a dozen yards from where they stood. He quickly surveyed the area, spotted them, and started in their direction.

Random appeared a few moments later, bursting out onto the open field with a stick held tightly in his mouth. He turned in a few quick circles before running over to greet his master.

"Where've you been?" Candy asked her father as he approached. "Out for a walk in the woods?"

"You'll never believe what I found," Doc said, looking energized. "We have to get to the historical society before it closes." He checked his watch. "Three thirty. We have half an hour. Let's get rolling." And without another word he started across the sloping field toward the barn and parking area, moving at a good, steady clip.

"Why, what's up?" Candy exchanged a brief, slightly confused look with Neil before hurrying after her father. Random trotted along at her heels, and Neil brought up the rear. He made a quick stop at the farmhouse to grab the metal box and lock up the place, and all four of them climbed back into the Jeep.

Doc provided an explanation on the way back to town.

"I think your father found something out there in the woods," he told Neil, who had insisted Doc ride in the front seat this time. Doc was twisted around as far as the seat belt would allow, so he could address Neil in the second row. "It looks like he was digging around out there in the woods, next to a burned-out foundation and a little cemetery. He pulled something out of the ground."

"Like what?" Candy asked, sounding worried. "Not a body?"

Doc waved a hand. "No, nothing like that."

"Any idea what it was?" Neil asked.

"I have a hunch," Doc said. "That's why we're headed to the historical society."

Neil reached into his pocket and pulled out the gold coin, which he handed to Doc. "Anything to do with that?"

Doc studied the coin for quite a long time before responding. "It might," he said softly. "It might."

The Cape Willington Historical Society was located in the red-roofed Keeper's Quarters at the English Point Lighthouse, which stood on hard black rock near the mouth of the English River, just a stone's throw from downtown Cape Willington, at the foot of Ocean Avenue. Much of the building's lower floor was devoted to the English Point Lighthouse Museum, which was operated and maintained by the historical society. The museum wandered through several rooms of the old lightkeeper's cottage and included exhibits, displays of navigation equipment, clocks, uniforms, and log books, as well as a relatively authentic re-creation of a lightkeeper's family, depicting them as they might have appeared in the late 1800s. The museum's displays continued upstairs, where the archives for the historical society were also located, under the building's sloping eaves.

"The museum received an anonymous donation about a month ago," Doc told them as they pulled into a parking spot at the lighthouse and began to climb out of the Jeep. They had to leave Random in the vehicle, but rolled the windows down so he'd have some air. "It came in by way of a member of the board of directors. She says it was delivered to her house one afternoon by courier, with a note to have it documented and examined by the museum's staff. So she brought it in and we checked it out." He paused. "Well, not me personally, of course, but those who are trained to do those types of things."

"And?" Candy prompted.

"And," Doc said, "I've seen it, and basically it's just a small chest, made of oak about a hundred and fifty years ago, probably European in origin, judging from the wood — we think it's English oak. Steel bands, an old heavy lock, that sort of thing. Typical for the period. But it was quite a find, wherever it came from. It needed some cleaning up — it looked like it'd been in the ground for a while. But the volunteers did a great job with it."

"And you don't know who donated it?" Neil asked, suddenly interested.

Doc shook his head. "It just came out of nowhere."

"You think Miles donated it, right?" Candy guessed.

"That's exactly what I'm thinking."

"He dug it out of the ground at the berry farm?" Neil asked.

"Yup, that's my guess," Doc said.

"Why would he donate it anonymously?"

"That's a great question," Doc said.

"Possibly because he didn't want anyone to know where it came from — or who had found it," Candy surmised.

"Exactly," Doc said, holding up a gnarled index finger.

"Did you open it?" Neil asked.

"Indeed we did."

"And what did you find inside?"

"That's just it," Doc said. "Nothing. It was empty. No treasure. No nothing."

Candy's mind was working quickly now. "You think Miles might have emptied it before he donated it to the historical society?"

"Could be," Doc said vaguely.

"But if that's true," Candy continued,

"then maybe it's connected to the murder somehow."

Doc nodded. "It's possible everything's connected."

"But if it's empty, why are we going to look at it now?" Candy asked as they reached the museum's front door.

Doc stepped up on the stoop and opened the door to the museum for her. "I'll show you," he said with a wave of his hand.

The rooms inside were dark, cool, and quiet. The place had the hushed atmosphere of a typical museum, punctuated by the occasional crash of waves on the rocky shore just outside. Doc greeted a volunteer named Doris Oaks, a silver-haired senior citizen who was working the long counter that served as the museum's front desk. She'd brought along Roy, her pet parrot, who entertained guests from his perch on the top of a straight-backed chair. "Hello, Doris. Hello, Roy," Doc called with a generous wave as they hurried by.

"Ahoy, Matey!" Roy called.

"Hi, Doc, what're you up to today?" Doris asked, looking up from the magazine she was reading. She was dressed brightly today, in yellows and greens, mimicking Roy's colors.

"We're just going to check on something

upstairs. Okay if we go on up to the lab?"

"Sure thing, Doc. Hello, Candy."

"Hi, Doris. How's the toy shopping been going?" Doris had bought Roy on eBay a few months earlier, when winter boredom and cabin fever set in, and she needed some sort of companionship. Now she was continually in search of hard plastic toys for the parrot, since he could gnaw through them in seconds flat.

"I've been scouring the flea markets. And there's a new pet store up off Route 1. I've found a few things up there, so he's been happy enough. Haven't you, Roy?"

"The sun's over the yardarm!" the parrot replied with a click of its beak.

Doris's gaze shifted to the handsome young bearded man walking alongside Doc and Candy. "Who's your friend?"

"Oh, this is Neil," Candy said, pausing for a moment and gesturing toward him.

"Visiting the area?" Doris asked curiously.

"Actually, I grew up around here," Neil said in a conversational manner, "but I've been away for a while."

"Oh!" Doris's head tilted down as she studied him over the top of her reading glasses, her eyes lighting up in recognition. "You're Miles's son, right? I knew your father. I used to see him in here quite often.

He was doing some sort of research upstairs." Her tone softened. "He was a good man."

"Thanks, I appreciate that," Neil said.

"Steer clear of the reefs ahead!" Roy cautioned as Neil nodded toward Doris and her pet parrot, and then followed Candy and Doc out of the room, headed to the second floor.

Upstairs, Doc led them to a small, cramped workspace in one corner of the building, with eaves so low they had to keep their heads bent over. "It's a little tight but it serves its purpose," he said, and he walked to a large gray cabinet in one corner. It stood so tall it nearly touched the low ceiling. It was fairly deep, nearly two feet, so it jutted out into the room. Its metal doors were locked.

"I have a key," Doc said, and he fished out his key chain. He unlocked the doors and swung them open.

Inside were three or four wide shelves on top, and a half-dozen drawers in the bottom half. Some were relatively shallow, but the lower ones were deeper for larger items.

"We keep some of the more valuable items locked up in here," Doc said, "anything with historical significance. But here's what I wanted to show you."

He reached for a sturdy cardboard box on the top shelf and lifted it out. He set it carefully on a nearby folding table and lifted the lid.

Inside was another box, an ancient-looking wooden one.

Doc slipped on a pair of thin white gloves and lifted out the wooden box. "Here it is," he said, settling it gently on the table in front of them. "Isn't she a beaut?"

It was, Candy thought, an attractive piece, built not only for a functional purpose but also with some aesthetics in mind. The slats that made up the box had been carefully hewn and fitted, and the iron straps showed some etchings and fine details at the corners. A craftsman somewhere, long gone, had taken some pride in this piece.

"And look at this," Doc said, tilting the box up on its back edge so Candy and Neil could see one of the bottom corners.

Two initials were etched into the wood, somewhat crudely.

S.S., they read.

"At first," Doc said, "before we were able to date it, we thought the box might have some connection to World War Two. The initials gave us that idea, of course — the *Schutzstaffel,* or SS, Hitler's personal bodyguards and the Nazis' enforcers. But we couldn't find a link anywhere to verify that. So we were at a loss to explain what the initials referred to."

"But you figured it out," Candy said, impressed.

Doc nodded. "I think so. I saw a name with these same two initials just a little while ago, etched into the cornerstone of a burned-down foundation in the woods out at the berry farm. *S. Sykes.*"

"S. Sykes?" Neil's brow furrowed. "Do you have any idea who that was?"

Doc's gaze shifted toward the younger Crawford. "I believe I do. His full name was Silas Sykes, if I'm correct. There are a lot of legends about him in the old history books. He was a scoundrel and, some said, a con artist and thief."

Doc paused to point dramatically toward the old oak box. "I think this was his treasure chest. He buried it out there in the woods, near his old place, where it's been for a hundred and fifty years. And your father found it, dug it up, and took whatever was inside."

THIRTY-SIX

"Buried treasure?" Candy said skeptically. "That sounds a little crazy."

"As trite as it might seem, it makes pretty good sense," Doc responded, his expression clamped down and serious. "I've seen a few references to a treasure supposedly left behind by Silas, though the legends are divergent. But he apparently was quite a character who lived outside the law. He started as a kid working on the steamboats that navigated these coastal waters in the 1800s, and turned that into a lucrative smuggling business by the time he was in his late teens, running contraband from the coast to Canada and back. He ran phony land speculation schemes. He played poker, and usually lost badly. He was married four times and three of his wives died mysteriously. He trusted no one. He liked to carry a long knife at his side. He was, they said, ruthless."

Candy had a sudden ill feeling, and became a little light-headed. She desperately needed to sit down. She settled onto a nearby wooden bench and let out a long breath. "I don't suppose there's any connection between Silas Sykes and the current generation with the same last name?"

"We don't know that for sure, at least at this time," Doc said, "but I'm pretty positive there's a connection somewhere."

"What? Wait a minute." Neil looked with surprise from Doc to Candy and back. "You know these people?"

Candy and Doc exchanged a glance. Then Candy said, "Yes, we do. I've had a few encounters with members of the Sykes family over the past few years, and Dad has given lectures about them, since they were among Cape Willington's founding families. They still own some property around here, although they sold a big spread a few years back after an abandoned mansion located on their land burned down. They still have fingers in the community, and they still show up here every once in a while, for local events and that sort of thing."

"And you think one of them could have murdered my father?" Neil asked, and he pointed at the box incredulously. "Because of this treasure?"

"We don't know that for sure," Doc said in a calming tone, "and we're not accusing anyone of anything at this point."

"We're just collecting facts," Candy agreed, "and we're some making progress. But it also creates a new set of questions."

"Such as?" Neil said.

Candy pursed her lips and let her gaze drop to the old wooden floor as she tried to put all the disparate pieces together in her head. When she spoke, it was almost as if she were talking to herself.

"First, we have to figure out what your dad was up to. I've heard a few people say he was a frequent visitor to the museum over the past few months. Doris just mentioned it downstairs. So what was he doing here? What was he looking for?"

"You think he was researching something?" Doc said, catching her point.

"That's what it sounds like to me. Maybe there's a tie-in to this treasure box. I'll have to check it out. Next, when did he find the box?"

"I can answer that, at least in a general sense," Doc said. "From the condition of the hole he dug, I'd say anywhere from a few weeks to a few months ago."

Candy nodded, and looked back up at her dad. "That fits in with the overall scenario."

"What scenario?" Neil asked, not quite following her.

Candy turned toward him. "Well, look at the timeline. Your father discovers this 'buried treasure,' as Dad calls it, and around the same time he decides to put the farm up for sale, after refusing to sell it for years."

"You think the two are related?"

"Sure, it makes sense," Doc said, nodding. "There were a bunch of holes dug all around that pit out in the woods. Miles was looking for something out there — maybe he'd been looking for it for a while. Maybe that's why he refused to sell all those times Lydia approached him. Maybe that's why he came here to the historical society — he was trying to find out where Silas buried that treasure. And when he finally figured it out and dug it up, well, there wasn't any reason to hold on to the place any longer. He'd found what he was looking for. So he decided to put it up for sale."

"What about those offers from that firm in New York City?" Neil asked. "Why didn't he just sell the place to their client, if he was so eager to get rid of it? Especially since they seemed to want it so badly, and were offering him a lot of money for it."

"That's a great question," Candy said, "and it could be the key to this whole thing.

For whatever reason, it sounds like your father didn't want to sell to them. So instead he hired Lydia to sell the place. Maybe that's why he decided to keep the sale a secret, so this firm — Wyborne, Whittle, and Kingsbury, I think it was — wouldn't find out about it." She paused. "Which brings us to the final point."

"Which is?" Doc asked.

Candy nodded at the box. "What was inside that thing? What were its contents? Why did Silas bury it out there at the berry farm more than a hundred years ago? Why was Miles looking for it? Why did he dig it up?"

She turned back toward Neil. "And most importantly, what did your dad do with whatever he found inside?"

THIRTY-SEVEN

In the silence that followed, as the three of them pondered these latest questions and developments, they could hear Roy chattering away downstairs. "Splice the mainbrace!" the parrot cried, accompanied by a high-pitched squawk. "Who's got the rum? Who's got the rum?"

As he thought through everything he'd just heard, Neil smoothed his beard and turned his gaze toward a small window that looked out over the dark blue ocean just beyond the rocks, while Doc put a hand to his side, scratched the back of his head, and muttered to himself for a while before saying out aloud, "Well, that's a whole lot to process, pumpkin, but I think you're right on the money. We've got a bunch of things to figure out here, that's for sure — and I know a quick way to get an answer to at least one of those questions."

He held up a finger. "I'll be right back."

He ducked out of the room, and they could hear him tromping down the stairs to the first floor. Voices rumbled distantly through the building, intermingled with a few wolf whistles from Roy. Less than a minute later, Doc was back, with Doris in tow. He ushered her into the small, cramped room that served as the museum's lab and workroom, and followed her in.

"Now, Doris," he said to her, "as I mentioned downstairs, we're trying to help Neil here" — Doc flicked a finger in the younger man's direction — "figure out what happened to his father, and we thought you might be able to help us out."

"Sure, Doc, I'd be glad to if I can," Doris said with a little hesitation in her voice. "What do you need to know?"

"Well, when we came in just a little while ago, you said you'd seen Miles here a bunch of times recently. You said he was doing research?"

"That's right," Doris said, nodding. "For a while there he was stopping by pretty often."

"For a while?" Candy said. "So he stopped coming in?"

"He did," Doris confirmed, holding her hands entwined before her, as if she were giving a testimony. "He first started showing up here, oh, sometime last fall, I'd say, and then he was here once a week or so, all through the winter and right into the spring. But his visits tapered off quite a bit over the past month or two, and finally we stopped seeing him altogether. I didn't really realize it, though, until Elvira Tremble pointed it out to me one day."

"Who's Elvira Tremble?" Neil asked.

"One of our local ladies, and a member of the Cape Willington Historical Protection League," Candy explained, not particularly shocked to hear of this latest development. "From what I understand, she had an eye out for Miles." Candy glanced diplomatically at Doris. "If you know what I mean."

The silver-haired volunteer nodded vigorously. "Oh yes, she certainly did. She mentioned it to me a number of times, about how sad it was that Mr. Crawford was all alone out there on that big farm, and how he needed a woman to look after him," Doris said, warming to the story. "She used to ask me all kinds of questions about him — what time of the day he came in, and what days of the week. Where he went, and what he did. And if he ever mentioned her in particular by name. That sort of thing. When she thought no one was looking, she wrote down everything I said in a little notebook. But I saw what she was doing. She started dropping by earlier and earlier, and hanging around the long desk, waiting for him to come in. I think she was sweet on him. Or else she was keeping tabs on him."

"Why would she do that?" Neil asked.

Doris shrugged. "Oh, I don't know. It was just a thought. And, of course, it wasn't really any of my business, whatever she was doing. Still, it was a little odd, and I couldn't help noticing things, could I?"

"Of course not," Doc said reassuringly.

"Did Miles ever say what he was looking for?" Candy asked.

Doris didn't have to ponder that question before answering. "No, and don't think we didn't try to find out. We have quite a few people who come in to dig around and do a little research, and they're usually so excited about whatever they're working on, they can't stop talking about it. But Miles — well, he was different. A little secretive, to be honest. A few of us tried to get him to talk — to say hello, you know, chitchat. But Miles wasn't the talkative type. He wasn't impolite, of course, but he generally avoided us volunteers. We all got the impression he preferred to work on his own. I know where he spent most of his time, though. It was back in this other room here."

Doris pointed out the door and around the corner, indicating the archives room.

"He usually liked to come in early in the day, first thing, when no one else was up here," Doris said, "and since Roy and I are both early birds, and took the morning shifts, we tended to run into him fairly often. But then Elvira started showing up in the mornings, so he started coming in later. He spent hours up here, digging through the archives."

Candy and Doc had both spent time in the archives room themselves, and knew many of its resources and materials. "Any particular section he might have been looking in?" Doc asked.

Again, Doris answered quickly, with some conviction, as if she'd checked up on him. "Local history, nineteenth century — and some of the old volumes on local property and land deeds."

"Land deeds?" Neil said. "Why on earth would he have any interest in those?"

"Maybe it has something to do with that farm of yours," Doc said, "and that box he dug up."

Doris glanced over at the oaken chest on the table. "The treasure chest?" Her eyes widened. "You don't think . . ." But her voice tapered off as they heard the sound of a bell ringing downstairs, and Roy chirping, "Avast, mateys! Shiver me timbers! *Squaw-wwk!*"

Doris's ears perked right up. "Oops, it sounds like we got visitors! Gotta run!"

A moment later she was gone, headed back down the stairs, leaving the three of them arranged in a loose circle around the perimeter of the small room.

"So," Doc said, and he rubbed his hands together in anticipation, "nineteenth-century history and local land deeds. Sounds like a potent topic that's begging for a closer look. It might even yield a few answers. Who's on it with me?"

Neither Candy nor Neil spoke up at once, but finally Candy said with a hint of a smile, "Actually, Dad, I think that's right up your alley, so we'll leave you to it. Besides, I have a few stops to make this afternoon. Elvira Tremble deserves a visit, I believe, so I might start there. And I'm meeting Maggie at five."

"And I'd better get back out to the farm," Neil said thoughtfully, and he pulled the gold coin out of his pocket, holding it up for the others to see. "Maybe this is what he found inside that chest. And if there's one, there might be more hidden around the house. I need to search it more thoroughly."

Candy nodded her approval. "Sounds like a good idea. I'll run you out to Blueberry Acres so you can get your car. But first we'll make a quick swing by the bank, so you can put that money in a safe-deposit box. It should only take a few minutes."

"Right!" Doc clapped his hands together. "Sounds like we have a plan, and I have an enlightening afternoon ahead of me." He glanced at his watch. "It's almost four. Why don't we meet at the diner at six and compare notes? And I can introduce Neil to the boys. They'd sure love to meet you, since they all knew your dad."

"Does that give you enough time to look around?" Candy asked Neil.

He nodded. "I'll get a start on it, at least, and if I don't finish, I'll just go back later on."

"Are you sleeping in the yurt tonight?" Doc asked.

"That was my plan — if it's okay with you two."

"Sure it is," Doc said with a wave of his hand, "but we have a sofa downstairs, too, if you'd like something a little softer. You're welcome to use it."

"I appreciate that," Neil said, his easy smile returning, "but I'll be fine in the yurt for a few days, or at least until we figure this thing out. It's comfortable enough, and I'm used to it."

"Well, it's all settled then," Doc said. "The diner at six. I'll have one of the boys hold the booth for us. And it's Friday. You know what that means?"

"Fish fry night?" Candy asked.

Doc's eyes lit up. "With homemade tartar sauce and their special blueberry coleslaw. Perfect summer meal. And I'm buying!"

His expression turned suddenly serious. "Listen, both of you: Be careful out there, okay? Remember, there's still a killer on the loose, so don't do anything dangerous. And if you see anything suspicious, call the police first, and then me, in that order."

THIRTY-EIGHT

Thirty minutes later, with Random sitting at her feet, Candy watched Neil drive off in his old red Saab, headed back out to Crawford's Berry Farm.

Neil had tried to coax the dog into the car's front passenger seat — one of the few spaces available in the loaded vehicle — but Random had quietly refused, remaining firmly planted at Candy's side.

"I've never seen him do this," Neil said, sounding perplexed after multiple attempts to communicate with his dog. "He usually loves to go for trips, and we're best buddies, but . . . I think he's ignoring me."

It was true. Random refused to even look at him.

"Maybe he's just happy here," Candy said helpfully. She reached down and scratched the top of the dog's head, which made him look up at her with affection. "You like it here, don't you, Random? Tell you what —

you can spend the rest of the afternoon with me, okay?"

This seemed to please Random to no end, and his big tail thumped heavily on the ground, signaling his approval.

"Well, fine, then," Neil said, sounding a little exasperated. "I'll just go by myself." He shut the passenger side door and looked at Candy as he came around the back of the car. "You okay with this?"

"Couldn't be better," Candy said. "Have fun out at the berry farm. See you at the diner."

She waved as Neil drove off, and as dust rose on the dirt lane in the Saab's wake, she walked around to the coop behind the barn and checked on the chickens, with Random on her heels. He was particularly interested in the chickens, but she had a quick talk with him, telling him they were off-limits. "Your job," she said, "is to help protect them from foxes."

The two of them made a quick tour of the property, surveying the blueberry fields and vegetable gardens, which were coming along nicely. She'd have tomatoes to pick shortly, and cucumbers and radishes as well. She was tempted to linger and pull a few weeds, but she knew she had to get going; she had a lot of ground to cover before six.

During their excursion around the farm, Random had made a few detours into the underbrush, so he needed a little cleaning up before she let him into the house. He quickly found a comfortable spot in the kitchen. After putting out a bowl of water for him, Candy grabbed her laptop computer from the desk in a corner of the living room and settled at the kitchen table, where she could look out the side window to the barn and blueberry fields behind the house.

"I just need to research something real quick," she told the dog, "and then we'll head out."

Random's ears stood up and he tilted his head curiously as she started clicking away on her keyboard.

In the search field of her browser window, she typed in the words she remembered seeing on the real estate firm's letterhead out at the berry farm: *Wyborne Whittle Kingsbury LLC.*

She had meant to do this while Neil was still around, but he'd been so anxious to get going she never had a chance to say anything to him about it.

She leaned in to get a better look at the search results.

One of the top links looked promising, so she clicked on it.

It opened a fairly sedate-looking web page with a businesslike design in blues and grays, with simple headlines in block letters and lots of text. Candy skimmed through the copy on the home page. A box of text described the firm's history, properties, and investment strategies in general terms. Across the top of the page were a series of buttons, opening windows that provided more in-depth details about the firm's portfolio, services, partners, and locations, as well as its founders, mission, management, and staff.

Candy clicked through the buttons quickly, scanning the content, searching for anything that might give her some sort of clue as to why this firm had made so many offers for the Crawford place. What was the connection? Why the interest in the berry farm?

Could it have had anything to do with Silas Sykes's treasure chest? Candy wondered.

Nothing caught her eye until she stopped on the management and staff page. Here were typical dry business bios and boring head shots, listing the names of the founders, principals, associates, and other staff members.

Scanning the list of names, one jumped out of her: Morgan S. Kingsbury, Executive

Vice President.

Morgan . . .

A unique name. She'd met a woman named Morgan yesterday morning out at Mrs. Fairweather's place. Her niece, didn't she say? Or grand-niece?

Candy recalled their conversation — in particular, something Morgan had said to her as they'd been walking into the backyard to meet with Mrs. Fairweather: *I'm working in New York City right now. I'm with a financial firm. We're in commercial real estate, property management, investments, that sort of thing. . . .*

New York City.

Morgan S. Kingsbury.

Candy clicked on the name, which took her to another page with a longer bio and a photo.

She felt a sudden chill.

Slim. Dark haired. Dark brown eyes with long eyelashes. Her hair was pinned up. She was dressed in a dark business suit instead of a flowery print dress.

But it was the same woman.

Morgan S. Kingsbury.

Candy focused in on the middle initial.

S.

Her feeling of trepidation grew as she scanned down through the bio copy, looking for a specific fact.

And there it was. Morgan S. Kingsbury's maiden name.

She'd been born Morgan Sykes.

THIRTY-NINE

The full weight of what she'd just learned hit her a moment later.

Mrs. Fairweather's niece is Morgan Sykes Kingsbury, executive vice president of the New York–based Wyborne Whittle Kingsbury LLC — the same firm that was secretly trying to buy Crawford's Berry Farm.

Her eyes opened wide as she let out a long breath. That could mean a thousand things, she thought — or it could mean nothing at all. It could provide an explanation for the murder of Miles Crawford — or it could simply be a coincidence, a strange, unconnected sequence of events and incriminating facts that could be easily explained away once she talked to the right people.

She cautioned herself to think everything through carefully before she proceeded.

And that was exactly what she intended to do.

Morgan Sykes.

In the past few years, Candy had dealt with two other members of the Sykes family — brothers Roger and Porter Sykes, scions of the wealthy Massachusetts-based clan — and those encounters had not been totally pleasant. Were the brothers related to Morgan? Siblings, perhaps? Cousins? Distant relatives?

Certainly there must be some connection.

No matter which way she looked at it, the coincidences were just too obvious to ignore, she decided.

That led to a trickier question:

Could Morgan Sykes Kingsbury have killed Miles Crawford — and then poisoned Lydia St. Graves, leading to her death in a car accident?

She'd certainly had the opportunity. Morgan had been in town yesterday — Doc and Candy had met her at Mrs. Fairweather's place, where she'd seemed pleasant, easygoing, and a somewhat carefree woman — not at all like someone who had just murdered a berry farmer.

But what about the physical reality of it? Could she have surprised Miles in the hoophouse, swung the shovel at his head, dropped the murder weapon beside the body, made her way back to Mrs. Fairweather's house, and casually greeted the Hollidays from her perch on the front porch, looking as if she'd just come from a morning at the spa?

Candy ran over the timeline again in her head. She and Doc had stopped by to see Mrs. Fairweather late in the morning. Miles had died a few hours earlier, sometime between eight and ten A.M., as best she could establish. Could Morgan have killed Miles and made it back to Mrs. Fairweather's in time?

It was certainly within the realm of possibilities, Candy admitted. In fact, Morgan might have had enough time to get a manicure on the way back.

But was she that good an actress? Could she have so easily glossed over a crime like that only a couple hours after committing it?

Candy shook her head. Some people, she knew, were capable of just about anything, as unlikely as it might seem.

More to the point, this latest discovery could provide a reasonable motivation behind Miles's death.

Sometime in the past half year or so, Candy surmised, Miles had learned of the existence of Silas Sykes's buried chest, researched it, located it, and dug it up. And once he'd opened it a month or two ago, he'd apparently taken what was inside.

But did he have a right to the treasure, even though he'd found it on his land? Candy wondered what claim Miles could make to it. More than likely, she guessed, the chest wasn't his. It belonged to Silas Sykes and his heirs. And there was probably some sort of family link between Silas and Morgan. He was, more than likely, an ancestor of hers. It was possible she'd found out about the box, too, and learned Miles had dug it up.

But had that driven her to murder?

It all depended on the contents of that wooden box.

Gold coins? Land deeds?

Candy couldn't quite figure out how those were connected.

Whatever Miles had found in the chest, it all clicked into place a little too easily. And that made her wary.

Too many things in this case seemed all too convenient, like the shovel, left beside Miles's body, which had led back to Lydia St. Graves — only now she knew, almost certainly, that the shovel had been a plant.

But if Morgan had indeed killed Miles, why leave the shovel there? And how had she gotten her hands on it in the first place?

Too many questions, Candy thought, and

too few answers.

And there were other questions rolling around in her mind as well. What about the boots with the star pattern on the bottom? What about the strawberry-picking baskets Chief Durr and his team had found out in the hoophouse — the ones with the initials *M.R.S.* woven into them?

Morgan Sykes?

Again, it fit too easily. Why would Morgan be crazy enough to leave baskets at a crime scene with her initials on them?

The more she thought about it, the more confused she became. When looked at from one direction, all the pieces appeared to fit together. But from another viewpoint, they all seemed scattered.

As Random rose lazily to lap at the bowl of water, Candy gazed out the window thoughtfully, then turned back to her computer. She again moved the cursor to the browser's search window and keyed in the name *Morgan Sykes.*

She spent the next ten minutes clicking through page after page on the Web, looking for the one fact that might tie at least some strands of this mystery together — a middle name, or at least a middle initial, for Morgan Sykes. Her full birth name.

If Candy could identify Morgan as *M.R.S.,*

374

then she could tie the dark-haired woman, at least circumstantially, to the scene of the crime.

But her efforts turned up nothing. All the references and biographical information Candy found online mentioned either Morgan Kingsbury or Morgan S. Kingsbury, though there were a few older references that identified her simply as Morgan Sykes, presumably from a time before she'd married. Nothing Candy could find gave the woman's middle name.

Her search for information on the Internet wasn't working, she finally decided. It was time to go to the source — the one person from whom she believed she could learn the truth behind what was going on.

Random had resettled himself into a corner of the kitchen, but he rose quickly and stretched as Candy powered off her laptop, closed the lid, and placed it back on her desk. She gathered her things, moved the water bowl onto the porch, and ushered Random outside before locking up the house. Then she headed toward the Jeep at a quick pace, but after several steps she realized Random was not at her heels, as he'd been before.

"Random?" She stopped and turned back. The dog was sitting on the porch, watching her expectantly.

She patted her thigh lightly. "Come, Random! Let's go! I have to get back into town."

But the dog did not seem interested in traveling into town. He looked quite content on the porch. In fact, to make his point, he lay down noisily.

Candy stared at him for a few moments, uncertain what to do, but in the end she decided to let him be. "Okay, you can stay here until we get back," she said, "but remember — you're supposed to protect the chickens, not scare them. Just keep the foxes away, okay? And watch the house."

Somewhat reluctantly, she climbed into the Jeep and drove off, leaving the dog behind. In her rearview mirror, she could see him watching her from his vantage point on the porch, until she disappeared down the dirt lane.

She still had about twenty minutes or so until she met with Maggie at five, so she decided to make a quick detour. As she came into town, before she reached the red light at Main Street, she made a left-hand turn onto Shady Lane, headed for Mrs. Fairweather's neat brown bungalow at the corner of Pleasant Avenue. She parked in the gravel driveway, walked up the steps onto the porch, and knocked at the front door.

She waited. She heard nothing from inside. No sense of movement or someone coming to answer the door.

She knocked again, and discreetly peered in through the small etched-glass window in the front door. "Mrs. Fairweather?" she called out. "It's Candy Holliday."

The house looked dark on the inside. In fact, the whole neighborhood had turned a little darker around her, Candy realized. She looked up. A bank of clouds had rolled in, coming from the west. The sun had disappeared behind it. The wind was kicking up. The temperature had already dropped by a few degrees.

She looked back at the house. Inside, she saw only shadows and grays. No lights, no sounds, no indication that anyone was in there.

Maybe she's not home, Candy thought, and she took a few steps to the left so she could peer in through one of the front windows before circling around to the back and taking a quick peek at the gardens behind the house.

But she saw no one. No Mrs. Fairweather. No Morgan Sykes Kingsbury.

She knocked a final time at the back door,

just to make sure, but received the same result. No one was home.

As she turned away, she thought she saw, out of the corner of her eye, a movement inside, the barest shift of light and shadow, a flicker across her corneas. She twisted back around toward the house, certain she had seen someone, or something, move inside.

She returned to the back door and knocked with more urgency. "Mrs. Fairweather! Hello! It's Candy Holliday. Are you in there? Is everything all right?"

But no matter how long or how loudly she knocked, no one came to the door.

She peered in the windows but nothing moved now.

Had she actually seen something? Or had it just been her imagination?

She tried the door handle, wondering if she should enter the house. But the door was locked. She thought of looking around for a key but decided against it. Maybe she'd been mistaken. Maybe it had been a trick of the eye, or simply the shadow of a shifting tree branch cast upon the darker interior. A possible movement inside was no cause to enter someone's house uninvited.

Mystified and a little concerned, she returned to the Jeep. With a final look back at Mrs. Fairweather's house, she backed out of the driveway and drove a few blocks to the Lightkeeper's Inn, trying to figure out her next step.

FORTY

As it turned out, the next step nearly walked right in front of the Jeep.

Still pondering her fruitless search for Mrs. Fairweather, Candy made a right-hand turn onto Ocean Avenue and headed down toward the end of the street. She kept her eyes open for a parking spot, which could be hard to locate at this time of day in this busy area of town, especially during the summer months. She scanned the rows of angled tail lights and trunks first on the right, and then shifted her head left, checking for spaces on the opposite side of the street. She thought she saw a car backing out of a spot farther down the row.

Perfect timing, she thought as she began to apply her brakes — just in time, as it turned out, for only then did she notice that Elvira Tremble had stepped out in front of the Jeep, coming in from the right side, from between two parked cars, waving her down.

Candy reacted in an instant, heavily applying her foot to the brake as she glanced up instinctively to the rearview mirror, checking to see how closely she was being followed by the car behind. But fortunately it was some distance back. The Jeep jerked to a stop, settling on its springs with a few quick wobbles.

Candy's gaze shot to Elvira. The woman was still on her feet, standing just off to the side of the vehicle, staring at her, hard-faced. Candy considered that a good sign. At least she wasn't lying flat on her back with a few broken bones. It didn't look like the Jeep had touched her, though Candy wondered how close it had come. Inches, she guessed.

With an apologetic wave, she allowed the Jeep to drift forward a few feet, so she could address Elvira out the passenger side window, which was rolled halfway down.

"Elvira, I'm so sorry, I didn't see you there. I hope you're okay," Candy said to her, sounding fretful.

But Elvira didn't seem affected — either physically or emotionally. "I was flagging you down," she said in a clipped tone. "The ladies of the league would like to have a word with you."

"A word with me? About what?"

381

Elvira said something but it was drowned out by the toot of a horn coming from behind. Candy glanced up at the rearview mirror again. The car following her was now sitting on her bumper impatiently. She was holding up traffic.

"Could you repeat that?" Candy asked, turning back to Elvira.

"We'd like to meet you in the park. We have a special matter to discuss with you."

Candy scrunched up her face. She was about to decline — she had plenty on her plate as it was — but she decided it was better to stay on the ladies' good side, rather than antagonize them.

"When?" she called out to Elvira.

"Five thirty. We'll be waiting for you."

"Okay, but —" She was about to mention her five o'clock with Maggie and buy a little more time, but Elvira had already turned away. "Is Mrs. Fairweather with you?" she called out, but there were more beeps, and Elvira was back on the sidewalk, out of earshot. Candy had no choice but to move on.

Despite her delay, she managed to snag the recently vacated parking spot, and after grabbing her trusty tote bag from the backseat, she headed down to the Lightkeeper's Inn.

She found a wicker table for two outside on the inn's wraparound porch, where they could look out over the ocean and across to the park. Maggie had just texted her, saying she was on her way. Candy ordered two strawberry wine spritzers from a waiter in a white shirt and black bow tie, and took advantage of a few spare moments to pull out her phone and scroll through her contacts until she found Wanda Boyle's number.

"Where are you?" Wanda asked without preamble when she answered.

Candy was used to Wanda's abruptness and responded in tone. "I'm at the inn. I'm meeting with Maggie for a drink. Why, where are you?"

"In Town Park. Are you going to be here at five thirty?"

"Yes, but . . . why?"

"Just be here," Wanda said.

"Okay, fine, I'll be there. Is Mrs. Fairweather over there?"

"Haven't seen her."

"Do you have her number? I need to give her a call."

Candy memorized the number Wanda told her and repeated it to herself several times as she tapped the digits on the screen. She held the phone back up to her ear but there was no answer. It was still ringing at the other end when Maggie hurried up onto the porch and dropped into the wicker chair opposite Candy, just as their wine spritzers arrived. "Boy, do I ever need that!" Maggie said, setting down her purse and lifting the chilled glass. She took a few quick sips.

"Long day?" Candy asked, keying off the phone and setting it down on the tabletop. She took a sip of her drink as well. It was sparkling pink and garnished with thin slices of fresh strawberries.

"It's been nonstop," Maggie said, brushing a few stray strands of brown hair out of her eyes. Her hair was a little disheveled, Candy noticed, and flat in some places, since she'd been wearing a hair net most of the day. She looked a little frazzled, but there was also an underlying current of excitement about her. "The day has just flown by!" she told her friend. "The cash register was ringing all day. Herr Georg says he's never seen it this busy so early in the season. He's hoping for a blockbuster year."

"Let's hope he gets it. We all could use a good year around here."

"You're right about that. And he's talking about increasing my hours."

"Hey, that's great news! I'm sure you can use the money."

"I sure can. And he wants to start training

me as a baker."

"That's fantastic! Just as you'd hoped. It could be a new career for you!"

"I know, it's very exciting. He says he's going to share some of his old family recipes with me."

"Wow, he doesn't do that with just anyone. He must think you're very special."

"Yes, well, I guess he does," Maggie said evenly, "because he also proposed to me."

FORTY-ONE

"Proposed?" It took a few moments for Candy's brain to absorb what she'd just heard, but then her mouth fell open and she almost rose out of her chair. "You mean *marriage*?"

On that last word her voice became so loud that guests at nearby tables glanced in their direction. "Are you *kidding* me? Herr Georg Wolfsburger *proposed* to you?"

Maggie glanced quickly in either direction. "Well, you don't have to announce it like that to the whole town." She reached out and patted Candy's hand in a comforting manner. "Take a deep breath, honey. It'll be okay. I know you're a little shocked right now but you just need a couple of moments to adjust. I dropped it on you kind of suddenly. I apologize for that."

"You're *serious*?"

Maggie nodded. "Totally. He mentioned it several times just today, as a matter of fact. He wants us to elope. He's talking about Vegas."

"Vegas? You're kidding me!"

"You already said that, and no, I'm not kidding you. I wouldn't do that to you. You're my best friend."

Candy didn't know what to say. Finally, she managed, "So, are you two . . . in love?"

"Well." Maggie pulled her hand back and took a long, long drink of her wine. When she was finished, she wiped the corners of her mouth with her white cloth napkin. "That's where the rubber meets the road, isn't it? That's why I wanted to meet with you. To talk it over."

"Talk what over?"

"You know — what I'm going to say to Herr Georg . . . well, just Georg."

Candy scrunched up her face. "What?"

"Well, that is his first name, you know. He said I should just call him 'Georg.' It sounds funny to call him 'Herr,' don't you think?"

"Yes, but . . . I understand that but . . . you mean you haven't given him an answer yet? You're not getting married?"

"No — not yet, at least. So far I've just been pretending like I'm not taking him seriously. And at first I wasn't. But he keeps giving me this . . . *look*. It's like I'm the only person in the world." Maggie's expression took on a dreamy appearance as her mind started to drift, but then she refocused and leaned forward across the table, her voice lowering. "I don't mind telling you that I haven't had anyone look at me that way in a long, long time. Okay, well, maybe never. Ed certainly never looked at me like that — unless I was cooking his dinner. But the look Georg gives me is just so . . . passionate. I believe he's being completely honest when he says he wants to marry me. So I have to give him some sort of straight answer — you know, because that's the adult thing to do."

"And what are you going to say to him? Are you thinking of marrying him — or are you going to try to let him down easy?" Now that she was over her initial shock, Candy found this whole conversation incredibly intriguing, since she knew both parties so well. And she realized she was suddenly very happy for them.

"Honestly, I don't know." A cloud of uncertainty crossed Maggie's face. "I mean, he certainly *seems* like a nice man, and . . . he's *certainly* successful . . . and he's obviously very talented. I mean, I think he's a good person, but . . . marriage is a big step. Especially with someone I haven't known that well until just recently, when I started working for him at the bakery."

"Well," Candy said, "let me start by saying there's not a better man in Cape Willington, other than my own father, of course. Herr George . . . Georg . . . well, he has a heart of gold. You know that. I worked with him for three years, on and off. He can be temperamental at times and moody in the mornings, especially when he hasn't had his coffee. But he's also one of the warmest, kindest people I've ever known. I think he would make a wonderful husband — if, of course, that's what you decide to do."

"I agree," Maggie said. "And I can add a number of other positive traits as well. He always smells like a freshly baked pie. That's a big point in his favor — especially if you love pie the way I do, and I know you do. His hands are well manicured and amazingly nimble. And his eyebrows are like soft white feathers. But what about the cons?"

"Cons?"

"I need someone to play devil's advocate — to help me look at this from both sides, so I don't make the wrong decision."

"Oh, I see." Candy understood but she had to think a minute. "Well, he's quite a bit older than you, right?"

"Eighteen years," Maggie agreed.

"Not that it's much of a problem these

389

days," Candy added quickly. "Age doesn't make that much difference — at least, I don't think so. But it's something to keep in mind."

"Right," Maggie said. "We've already talked about it. What else?"

"Hmm, well, he only lives in Cape Willington part of the year. He heads south in the winter."

Maggie nodded. "He's addressed that as well. He says he'll live wherever I'm at. If I want to stay here in town all year long, then he'll stay here with me. Or I can go south with him. Either one will work with him."

"Wow." Candy took a moment to shake her head. "That's pretty impressive."

"I know," Maggie said, "which makes me wonder why I haven't said 'yes' yet."

"Maybe you're just not ready."

Now Maggie was silent for a few moments as she took some time to think that over while they both sipped at their wine spritzers. "You could be right," she said finally. "I've only been a single woman for a few years now. And to be honest, I've kind of been enjoying it. It's the first time in my life I've been completely free to do exactly what I what, whatever that might be — as long as I stay within my budget, of course. So I'm relatively happy with the way things

are. But I *do* want to get married again . . .
someday."

"Just not today?"

Maggie nodded. "Exactly."

"Do you want to keep working for him?
And seeing him?"

"Of course!" Maggie said brightly.

"Then tell him that. Tell him you like the
idea of starting a relationship with him but
you need a little more time to see how it
goes before you start thinking seriously
about marriage. If he really loves you, he'll
wait for you to decide what you want to do."

"You think so?" Maggie asked hopefully.

Candy nodded firmly. "I do. He's a good
man, and he'll understand. Talk to him,"
she said as her phone buzzed on the table.

She picked it up and checked the display.
She'd received a text from Wanda, requesting her presence in Town Park.

"I have no idea what's going on over
there," Candy said, shaking her head as she
keyed off the phone, "but I have to get running. Are you okay? Have we solved anything?"

Maggie gave her an honest smile. "I think
so. This has helped a lot. Thanks."

Now it was Candy's turn to place her
hand on Maggie's. "I just want you to know
that whatever you decide to do, I'll always

be there for you. Friends forever, right?"

Maggie's smile broadened. "Friends for-ever."

"And having a wedding like that around here would be absolutely fantastic, whenever it happens," Candy added, her eyes twinkling at the possibilities. "Can you imagine your wedding cake? Herr Georg will make one for you four stories tall!"

"I know," Maggie said happily. "And you'll help me plan it? When I'm ready?"

Candy rose and gave her friend a big hug. "Just try and keep me away."

FORTY-TWO

Five minutes later they parted ways. Maggie headed back up the avenue to the bakery to rendezvous with Herr Georg for a private dinner, while Candy crossed the street to Town Park to meet with the ladies of the Cape Willington Heritage Protection League, quite uncertain of what she was walking into.

There was a small crowd waiting for her as she approached the park's central area, where annual events such as the Winter Moose Fest and the fall Pumpkin Bash were held. Booths and tents were set all around the periphery, the streamers flying from lampposts had multiplied, and the place had a festive feel. A number of people applauded her as she came down the sidewalk, as if she were some sort of celebrity making her way along the red carpet. She spotted Mason Flint, chairman of the town council, standing in a small knot in the midst of the crowd with Cotton Colby, Elvira Tremble, Brenda Jenkins, Alice Rainesford, and Wanda Boyle, who had her camera out.

They were all looking at her.

Candy slowed her pace, suddenly wary at finding herself in the spotlight. "What's this all about?" she asked no one in particular.

It looked like some sort of kickoff event for the Strawberry Fair. And indeed, they had strung a red ribbon between two lampposts along the sidewalk in front of her. Brenda Jenkins stood by with a large scissors.

"It's a small impromptu gathering," Mason told her with a gap-toothed smile, beckoning her forward, "to bring a little recognition to one of our town's most honored citizens."

"And who might that be?" Candy asked, looking around for the guest of honor.

"You!" Cotton Colby cried, and they all gave her a hearty round of applause.

"Me?" Candy was mystified. "What did I do?"

"You just saved the Strawberry Fair, that's all!" Cotton said excitedly.

They'd set up a small PA speaker and microphone at the center of the gathering, and Cotton stepped up to it. She switched on the mic, tapped it a few times, flashed a confident smile, and started in.

"Ladies and gentlemen, I'd like to thank all of you for coming out here today on such short notice. As many of you know, I'm Cotton Colby, president of the Cape Willington Heritage Protection League, and I'd like to welcome everyone to the official ribbon cutting ceremony for our first annual Strawberry Fair!"

The applause started up again, accompanied by several well-rehearsed smiles. Wanda stepped forward to snap a few photos, and Cotton continued.

"As many of you know, we've been planning this particular event for several months now as a way to promote all of our village's many positive aspects. And we've had the support of many wonderful people around town. I'd especially like to thank Chairman Flint, members of the town council, Chief Durr and everyone at the Cape Willington Police Department, all of our volunteers and supporters, and the Pruitt Foundation, which underwrote this event for us this weekend. We're very grateful for their financial support. And now, I'll turn over the festivities to Chairman Flint, who will introduce our guest of honor."

With a final smile Cotton stepped aside, and Mason Flint approached the microphone. Since he was taller than she, he took a moment to adjust the microphone stand, tested it as well, and then gazed out across the crowd with a calm, seasoned demeanor. He began smoothly.

"Thank you, Cotton. I would just like to echo what she said and welcome everyone to our wonderful village. We appreciate everyone's support, and I'd like to give a special thanks to Cotton herself and all the ladies of the Heritage Protection League for their efforts in planning and staging this exciting new event in our community. We're very pleased to add it to our annual town calendar, and I hope we'll be celebrating the Strawberry Fair for many years to come. In just a moment we're going to cut the ribbon and officially declare the event open. But first I would like to recognize someone in our audience here today who was instrumental in ensuring the success of this event. From what I understand, without the assistance of Candy Holliday, the co-owner of Blueberry Acres and interim editor of our local newspaper, the *Cape Crier,* there would probably be no Strawberry Fair, since Candy helped arrange for a community strawberry-picking event tomorrow morning out at Crawford's Berry Farm. I hope to see all of you out there, so we can make sure we have plenty of berries for tomorrow's Fair!"

He paused, and looked in Candy's direction. "Now, if you'd like to join us, we'll cut the ribbon."

Everyone applauded as someone nudged Candy forward, and somewhat hesitantly she joined Mason and the ladies of the Heritage Protection League. They all gathered around her with wide smiles as Wanda snapped more photos. Cotton then announced that Candy had been named the league's first honorary member for her contributions to the community. Brenda Jenkins stepped forward to place the scissors into her hands, and after more carefully staged photos, Candy ceremoniously cut the red ribbon, doing her best to smile broadly and look honored, although she was still flummoxed by the whole thing. Everyone applauded again as Mason announced the first annual Strawberry Fair officially open.

And then it was over. Mason shook her hand quickly, gave her an odd look, and headed back up the avenue toward the opera house, while the crowd began to dissipate, gravitating toward a few of the food booths that had opened for the evening, although the primary events would not take place until the following day.

Candy handed the scissors back to Brenda, and Wanda gave her a big clap on the back. "You handled that beautifully, Chief. I got some great shots!" she said. "I'll get them on the website right away. It'll be great publicity for the Fair — and for the paper."

Candy nodded. "Sounds like a good idea, though I'm not sure what just happened. How long have you known about this?"

Wanda waved a hand. "Cotton texted me an hour ago. They put it together on the fly. Thought it might be good publicity — and they're genuinely happy you set up the berry picking tomorrow."

"Yes, we definitely are," said Cotton, stepping into the conversation. "Thank you for being such a good sport about all this. We didn't really plan to surprise you, but it just turned out that way. You truly saved our event, though, and for that we're grateful. Della's sending out e-mail messages right now, as we speak, to everyone on our list. We hope to have several dozen people out at the berry farm tomorrow. I don't know what we would have done if you hadn't intervened for us and made this happen."

"Well, I guess I was just in the right place at the right time," Candy said honestly.

"Fortunately it all worked out."

"And we're serious about an honorary membership," Elvira Tremble said, joining them. "We talked it over and voted. It was unanimous."

"Unanimous?" Candy looked around. "But your whole group's not here. I don't see Mrs. Fairweather."

"Unfortunately, she isn't feeling well," Cotton said. "She's home. But she gave us her blessing. She said she thought you'd make an excellent honorary member, considering all you've done for the league this week."

"Mrs. Fairweather is home? But I was just over at her place, and she's not there."

"I talked to her on the phone just a little while ago, and that's where she said she was at," Elvira confirmed. "She's been cooped up there all day — which is somewhat unfortunate, since we could have used her help. Fortunately, Alice stepped in and we managed to get everything done."

"But that doesn't make sense," Candy said. "Her place is dark. It's all closed up."

"Maybe she's gone out," Cotton suggested.

"Possibly. But you just said she wasn't feeling well. Why would she go out?"

"Well, I'm sure it's just a mix-up," Elvira

said, her clipped tone returning. "Nothing to worry about."

Candy hesitated. She briefly thought of asking Elvira about her activities at the historical society's museum, and her alleged interest in the comings and goings of Miles Crawford, but her cell phone buzzed, distracting her. The ladies had fallen into a conversation among themselves about last-minute preparations for the Strawberry Fair, so she fished out her phone and checked the display.

It was a message from Neil: *Better get out here right away.*

FORTY-THREE

Neil Crawford stood in his late father's bedroom, staring down with a grave expression at the items arrayed on the top of the bed. They smelled of age and earth and old leather. Neil stroked his beard absently as he studied the items, lost in thought, wondering what his father had gotten himself into.

He'd thought the metal box, which he'd dropped off at the bank, was his father's only hiding place for valuables. But after digging around the house, Neil had found rolls of money stuffed into emptied prescription bottles in the medicine cabinet, and some heirloom jewelry wrapped in a old towel and stashed inside a heating duct that was no longer in use. Neil also seemed to remember his father telling him about a small hiding place behind one of the bricks in the back wall of the fireplace in the living room, though he hadn't been able to locate it yet.

But he had found something else — something much more staggering — at the bottom of an old footlocker pushed into the far corner of his father's bedroom closet. His father had piled old blankets and coats on top of the trunk in an effort to disguise it, and the ploy had almost worked. Neil himself had glossed over it during his initial sweep of the house. Only when he returned to make a more thorough search ofthe bedroom had he taken notice of it. He remembered seeing it when he was younger, and guessed it was from the fifties or sixties, possibly handed down to his father by his grandparents. It had been painted dark green at one time, with brass hardware and a sturdy leather handle, but now it was badly scuffed and tarnished with age, and looked as if it had journeyed to the edge of the earth and back. The clasp was brass as well, and locked, but after some searching, Neil had found the key in a black jewelry box at the back of his father's sock drawer.

Returning to the closet, he had set aside the blankets and clothes, pulled the footlocker out into the room, unlocked it, and opened the lid. Inside he found more or less what he expected — old clothes, keepsakes, and photos from earlier times. Everything smelled old and musty.

Neil had removed the items one at a time, uncovering a few old boxes at the bottom of the trunk, including a small, battered cardboard one labeled *Christmas Ornaments.*

That was where he had found the treasure.

At least, that was what he guessed it was. Taken from the old oaken box his father had dug up, the one that had once allegedly belonged to Silas Sykes.

Those items were now on display on top of the bed. Neil had laid down an old blanket first, and then lined up the items so he could survey them in greater detail.

There were four palm-sized leather drawstring pouches, tightly tied and bulging with what turned out to be a variety of old coins. Some were similar to the one he'd found in the metal box, but others were much older, dating back two hundred years or more, Neil noted in amazement. The pouches were heavy as he weighed them in his hands, each in turn, before investigating their contents.

A smaller leather pouch, which had deteriorated somewhat, held perhaps a dozen large gold nuggets. And a sixth pouch, the smallest of the lot, held a few rough gems — sapphires and rubies, Neil guessed.

And then there was a seventh pouch, the largest of the group. It was document-sized, with a rectangular rather than a round shape. It was leather also, finely tooled. The initials *S.S.* were clearly noticeable, worked into the leather in a neat scrolling design.

There appeared to be small snakeheads at the top of the two *S*'s.

The large document pouch was empty.

Still, it appeared his father had indeed found the buried treasure of Silas Sykes.

Which would perfectly explain the reasons behind his father's murder.

At his initial discovery, Neil had texted Candy. He wasn't quite sure how to proceed, and wanted her opinion, since she was more tapped into the local community and the police than he was. He didn't want to disturb the evidence more than he already had. He had considered calling the police, but had decided to contact Candy first.

That had been — he checked his watch — not quite ten minutes ago.

He thought he heard the sound of a vehicle approaching outside, so he went to a second-floor window on the other side of the house and looked out. He saw nothing, however, other than his old red Saab parked in front of the barn.

He turned away from the window but

thought he heard a muffled *thump* coming from outside. It sounded like a car door closing.

He returned to the window and scanned the driveway and yard again. But clearly there was no other car out there in the driveway, other than his and his father's.

Then he saw a shadow move across the floor of the barn.

Someone *was* out there.

Candy, he thought. She must have pulled up her Jeep on the other side of the barn. *But what was she doing in the barn? Why hadn't she just come into the house?*

He left the pouches of coins, gold nuggets, and jewels on the bed, although he picked up another old blanket he'd dropped on the floor and covered the treasure with it, just in case. Then he went downstairs and headed out toward the barn.

As he walked, he continued to scan the area, searching for the source of that sound he'd heard. But he saw nothing. He walked across the driveway in front of the barn, past his car to the edge of the building, so he could look around the side. "Candy?"

He heard another sound then, a clatter in the barn, as if a couple of tools had clashed together.

He looked curiously back the way he'd

come. "Candy?"

Silence.

He called a third time, but again received no reply. Still, he was certain he'd heard *something.*

He walked back around to the front of the barn, looked into the shadows, and then took a few steps inside. The sun had disappeared half an hour ago, and darker weather was moving in, so the lighting in the barn's interior was muted. Still, Neil didn't need much light to see by. He'd been in here enough times to know his way around.

"Candy, are you in here?"

If she was, there were only a few places she could be. On the other side of the lawn tractor parked along the wall. Behind the pallets of fertilizer. Or in the small tool room in the far corner.

Or, he thought a moment later, she could be behind him, in the small alcove where his father used to do some paperwork.

He heard a footstep and a faint singing sound, felt a shift of air as something behind him moved. He turned.

Just in time to see the flat blade of a shovel coming right toward the side of his head.

FORTY-FOUR

As Candy drove out of Cape Willington, headed toward Crawford's Berry Farm, she wondered what Neil's message could mean.

He said he'd found something, but what?

Probably what he'd gone out to look for, she guessed.

The contents of Silas Sykes's buried treasure.

What had been inside? she wondered again.

She thought of her father's search of the archives at the historical society, and considered calling him. But as it turned out, he beat her to it. The cell phone buzzed in her pocket and she fished it out.

"Where are you?" her father asked.

"I'm headed out to the berry farm. Neil said he's found something."

"I found something as well," Doc said.

"What?"

"The reason nobody knew much about

that property, and the reason the Sykes house and graveyard were never documented. The folios have been removed."

"The what?"

"The folios, the leaves . . . pages of manuscripts. They've all been cut out. It looks like someone purposely went through the historical record and wiped out any reference to that property."

"But how is that possible?" Candy wondered. "Who would do such a thing?"

"That's the million-dollar question, isn't it?" Doc said. He hesitated a moment. "Everything going okay with you?"

"Yeah, why?"

"Just wondering. Listen, if you need me for anything, just give me a holler. I'm going to check through a few more records before I head over to the diner. See you there soon, right?"

She keyed off the phone just as she spotted the turnoff for Crawford's Berry Farm, and the sign with the red arrow pointing toward the barn, farmhouse, and fields off to the right, on the picturesque slope that stretched across the coastal landscape, now under a threatening cloud cover as the ocean to her left began to churn.

She spotted Neil's red Saab right away, and the tail end of another car parked behind the barn. It looked like a tan sedan of some sort, an older car. She studied it for a few moments but didn't recognize it.

Spotting no one, she pulled to a stop in front of the farmhouse, shut off the engine, and stepped out. She scanned the buildings and fields, then crossed the driveway and stepped up onto the porch. She knocked on the door and tried the handle. It opened for her, and she stepped inside.

"Hello? Neil?" she called out. "It's Candy. I'm here."

She listened for a few moments and stepped farther into the kitchen. The room was darkening. No lights had been turned on. She heard nothing. "Neil?"

She checked the lower floor but found him nowhere, so she moved to the bottom of the wooden staircase and, with her hand on the end post, called up the stairs.

"Neil, are you up there?"

The house creaked as the wind rose outside, the only reply she received. She waited, not sure why she was hesitating. Something about this didn't feel right, though she couldn't quite explain why. A warning bell, though still faint, was going off in her head.

There had been two cars outside — Neil's Saab and the tan sedan. At least two people

409

were out here at the farm. So where were they?

She began to climb the stairs slowly, right hand sliding lightly up the banister. A couple of the steps squeaked under her weight. The sounds were like thunderclaps in the silence of the house.

As if reading her thoughts, a low, rolling rumble of thunder echoed in the distance. A weather front was moving through. It would turn cooler and clearer tomorrow, in time for the Strawberry Fair. But first this front would bring unsettled weather tonight.

At the top of the stairs she paused before first turning left and searching the two rooms to the north side of the building, and then the rooms on the south, which overlooked the ocean, though today the blinds were all pulled closed, putting the rooms in shadows. She flicked on lights as she went from room to room, and flicked them off behind her. She moved quickly but cautiously, though she never felt threatened. Only slightly uneasy.

But she found no one. She had, though, found a curious scene in what she guessed was the master bedroom. Someone — Neil, she supposed — had pulled an old beaten-up trunk from the closet. It sat near the bureau, opened, its contents removed.

And there were two old blankets tossed carelessly onto the bed. But other than that she saw nothing of interest.

Back downstairs she did one more sweep before she headed back outside.

She decided to check the barn next.

Thunder rumbled again, closer this time. The clouds had an ominous look. Hot, moist air was being pushed toward them from the west, along the edge of the front. The treetops at the far ends of the strawberry fields were being tossed about by the strengthening gusts, as was Candy's hair. She pushed back at it as she crossed the driveway at a quick pace, head turning back and forth, searching.

Her uneasiness grew. Where was everyone?

At the entrance to the barn she slowed and peered inside. At first she saw nothing out of the ordinary. It was empty and silent. Wide doors on both sides of the barn were opened and hitched back, so she could see straight through and out the other side, to the fields beyond.

"Hello?" she called out, her voice dry and soft. "Neil? Anyone in here?"

Her gaze swept the place. The barn's interior was unlit but she could see the lawn tractor against the far wall, the stacks of fertilizer, the workbenches and tools, a small room in the far corner, and one to her left.

There was something else. A sack of some sort, or a pile of . . . something . . . lying in the middle of the floor, fifteen or twenty feet in front of her. It took her brain a few moments to make sense of it, since it was in an odd position, angled toward the back wall. The boots gave it away, and then she noticed the hands, arms, shoulders.

A body. Not moving.

She scanned the barn a final time and took a few steps forward. She approached the body hesitantly, then more quickly when she realized who it was.

"Neil."

The word came out in a breath as she dropped to her knees beside him. He was lying facedown, unconscious. His hair was askew, and she saw a wound on the side of his head.

She put a hand to his neck, feeling for a pulse. It was there, faintly. She checked the pulse at his wrist as well, just to make sure, but stayed away from the head wound. She wasn't a doctor and didn't want to make a bad situation worse.

As she pulled the cell phone from her back pocket, she turned slightly . . . and that was when she saw someone standing behind her, six or eight feet away.

Candy almost jumped out of her skin. Her hand went to her chest. "Oh my God! You scared me to death. What are you doing here?"

"Is he all right?" a thin, high voice asked. A woman's voice.

Candy couldn't quite make out the face, shadowed against the outside light. She narrowed her gaze. "Who are you?"

"Is he going to be all right?" the voice repeated.

Candy turned back to look at Neil. "I . . . I don't know. He looks like he's hurt pretty badly. We need to get him to the hospital. But he's still alive."

The shadowed figure let out a long, deep breath. The next words, when they came out, were low and menacing.

"Well. That's too bad."

Candy wasn't sure she'd heard that right. "What?"

She sensed the figure taking a few steps toward her, and turned around just in time to see the business end of a shovel headed right in her direction.

FORTY-FIVE

Candy reacted instinctively, turning and ducking out of the way just in time. The tip of the shovel's steel blade swept just past the side of her head, missing her by inches. She could feel the force of air pushing against her as it passed by. It seemed to propel her whole body backward, away from immediate danger, toward the rear wall of the barn.

There was a sound of frustration, as a distressed animal might make, and then the figure came at her, the shovel swinging back and forth, tearing wildly through the air. Candy scrambled back on all fours, the cell phone slipping from her grasp. Everything was moving too fast, and her brain registered only pieces of her attacker — heavy boots, gloved hands, the swish of a polyester knee-length patterned dress. She still couldn't make out the face. It was shadowed and too indistinct for her to tell who it was.

But that didn't matter right now. All that mattered was staying alive. Candy's head twisted left and right, searching for an escape, a weapon, anything. Her gaze alighted on her cell phone, which she'd dropped in her haste to escape. It had fallen to the cement floor several feet away. Again, in an instinctive move, she reached out for it. But the shadowed figure saw what she was doing. A moment later the steel blade came down heavily with great force, smacking into the plastic-and-glass phone just as Candy's fingertips groped for it. The device cracked and splintered apart under the attack.

Candy withdrew her hand just in time as she backed away even farther, until she hit something solid behind her — the far wall.

She was out of room. She had no place to go.

And her attacker seemed to know it.

The shovel paused at the top of its arc. The attacker was breathing heavily, augmented by the sound of the rising wind outside.

"You can't run now, can you?"

"Who are you?" Candy managed to say. "What do you want?"

"You know what I want — I want what was in that chest. All of it."

"I don't know what you mean."

"Oh yes you do. I got the coins and gold and jewels. Took them off the bed upstairs. Now I want the deeds."

"The deeds?" Candy drew herself up as best she could, so she was sitting relatively straight, her back against the wall. She wiped a hand across her face, trying to think clearly. "I don't know what you're talking about."

"They were in that big leather pouch in the chest. The deeds to properties all over Cape Willington. They were part of the deal."

"What deal? I don't know anything about a deal." As she talked, Candy searched surreptitiously for any way of escape. She'd bought herself a few moments. If she could just keep the other woman talking long enough to figure a way out of this . . .

The shovel hovered. "They belonged to Silas Sykes. He got them from some local Indians who claimed to have the rights to this land."

"He . . . he what?" Candy shifted her gaze back to the figure standing in front of her. She studied the facial features. "Morgan? Is that you?"

The shovel teetered again and began to move, swinging in an arc toward her.

But then her attacker howled and stumbled to the side. The shovel shifted in mid-arc and fell away.

An instant later Candy saw why.

Neil had briefly awakened, and with all the effort he had left, he'd kicked out with his heavy boot, striking the dark figure in the back of the knee. It had been a feeble attempt but with enough force to disrupt the trajectory of the shovel and throw the wielder off balance.

Candy knew her moment to act was now. Without thinking about what she was doing, she pushed herself off the wall and sprang forward with every bit of energy and power she had. She made a move for the shovel, but the shadowed figure moved for it as well, angling toward it. Their two hands reached it at the same time.

As the figure bent closer, Candy got her first good look at the other woman's face.

It wasn't Morgan Sykes Kingsbury.

"Della," Candy breathed in surprise.

In that moment, everything shifted.

Knowing she'd been found out, Della Swain backed away from the shovel. She straightened and stared down at Candy, a shocked expression on her face.

"What are you doing?" Candy asked, and suddenly, surprisingly, she found herself growing angry at the woman.

The rain began to fall then, splattering in thick drops to the ground just outside the barn doors.

Candy's fingers firmly clasped the handle of the shovel. She tilted the end of the handle upward, blade on the floor, and used it to push herself to a standing position. She lifted the shovel then, holding it in two hands, one out near the end of the handle and the other up toward the blade, in a defensive posture. "Just what do you think you're doing?" she repeated.

Della looked at a loss for words. "It . . . it wasn't supposed to happen like this," she stammered. "We . . . we had it all figured out. We tried to talk some sense into him but he just wouldn't listen, so we had to do what we did to save the strawberry fields. They're too important to this town. But he said he'd made up his mind. He said Lydia was helping him, so we had no choice but to —"

Then it all clicked into place for Candy. "*You* did it, didn't you? *You* lured Lydia out here. What did you do? Sneak into Miles's house when he was out making deliveries yesterday morning and send that e-mail to Lydia using his computer, telling her to meet him in the hoophouse?" Candy paused a moment, realizing what she'd just said. "That's it, isn't it? You probably received all the e-mails Miles sent out about the farm, telling people when he was making deliveries and when the berries were ready for picking. You *knew* he'd be out." She paused again, her mind working. "That's why you told Lydia not to respond to the e-mail, isn't it? To delete it instead? So Miles wouldn't find out about it, until . . ."

"But we had to," Della said, almost in a pleading voice. "We just wanted to save the farm. But then Lydia figured out . . ."

Her eyes grew wide as she realized what she was saying, and she clamped her mouth shut, pursing her lips tight. To make sure she didn't say anything else, she held a hand up to her face, covering the lower half. She looked like she'd just been discovered robbing a bank. Her gaze shifted wildly from Candy to the shovel to Neil and back.

Then she turned and ran.

She headed out the far door and angled to her right. Moments later, Candy heard a car door slam and an engine start. The tan sedan flashed past the open door on the right, circled around the western side of the barn, and came back around from the other direction, speeding along the driveway. For a moment Candy thought Della might actually drive right into the barn and try to run them both over. But she drove on past, nearly clipping Neil's Saab before her car thumped and roared its way down the dirt lane toward the main road.

Candy's grip on the shovel lightened, and she dropped it to the ground. She let out a long, ragged breath as she ran to Neil's side.

FORTY-SIX

Her phone was busted, broken beyond repair, so she used Neil's to call 9-1-1.

Then she called her father. He arrived ten minutes later in a frenzy, right after an ambulance and a police car came up the dirt lane, sirens blaring.

The next half hour was a blur to her. Neil was awake again, though groggy. "Treasure," he managed to say. "Coins." But no one was listening to him. They told him to stay quiet, stay calm, conserve his energy, and stay awake. Candy took his hand for a few moments, right before they loaded his stretcher into the back of the ambulance.

"Random," was the only other word he was able to speak.

"Don't worry. We'll take care of him," Candy said, feeling herself tearing up. The weight of what had just happened was beginning to sink into her.

But she found she had no time to be

emotional, or contemplative, right now. Chief Darryl Durr had plenty of questions for her. She did her best to answer, telling him about Della Swain, the shovel, the alleged treasure that everyone seemed to be after — though neither she nor Doc really knew what had been inside Silas Sykes's chest, and a search of the house and property turned up no real answers.

"Neil must have found something in the house," Candy said, "but whatever it was, Della took it with her. She mentioned something about gold and coins and jewels."

"We've got an all-alert out," the chief said. "We'll find her. She can't get away. We have the Cape sealed up."

"What about a boat?" Doc asked.

"We've alerted the Maine marine patrol and the Coast Guard. They're keeping an eye out for her." The chief leaned forward then, put a hand on Candy's shoulder, and looked her in the eyes. "Are you sure you're all right, Ms. Holliday?" he asked, the concern evident in his tone.

"I'm taking her to the hospital right now," Doc announced.

But Candy would have none of it. "No, Dad, I'm fine. Just a little shaken up, that's all. What I really need to do is go home, sit down, put my feet up, and have a strong cup of tea." She paused a moment. "Or maybe a shot of bourbon."

"Done and done," Doc said. "We've all had enough excitement for one day, that's for sure." He glanced over at Chief Durr. "I'm not sure my ticker can take much more of this murder stuff, I don't mind telling you."

"That goes for both of us." The chief gave Candy a reassuring clap on the back. "Once again, Ms. Holliday, you got yourself right into the thick of things. Fortunately, again, it worked out okay this time. We appreciate your help, but we'll take it from here."

Outside, the rain had lightened. Her father escorted her out to the Jeep, where he gave her a hug. "Thank goodness you weren't hurt," he said. "Are you sure you're all right?"

"I'm fine, Dad."

"Okay, listen." He held her out at arm's length and studied her face. "You go right home, lock the doors, and settle yourself in. No more adventures today."

"Got it. Right." She nodded. "Wait, where are you going?"

"I'm going to check on Neil. His dad's gone and he has no one else here to help him out, so I just want to let him know he has our support."

That made Candy reconsider. "Maybe I should go with you."

"You're certainly welcome to come along," Doc said. "I'd be glad for your company, and I'd feel much better if we had someone at the hospital check you out. You just nearly got the stuffing beat out of you."

Candy thought about it briefly, but finally shook her head. "I think I'll just go home."

Her father nodded and gave her another hug. "Whatever you think is best. Settle in and have that cup of tea. And be sure to lock all the windows and doors, just in case Della is still hanging around."

Candy smiled weakly. "I'm not worried about her. I have a shotgun, and I know how to use it. And I'm pretty good with a hoe and a shovel too. I don't think she'll give me any more trouble."

Doc smiled as well. "That's my girl. I should be there in an hour or so, once I know if they're going to keep Neil overnight or not. I'll call you if I find out anything important."

Her father watched her drive off, jumped in his truck, and followed her down the dirt lane to the main road. They both turned left toward town, and after a few miles Candy made another left on Wicker Road, which would take her out to Blueberry

Acres. Doc continued on toward town, however, on his way to a small branch hospital on the far side of Fowler's Corner.

Candy watched him pass by in her rear-view mirror. She saw him wave in her direction, and then he disappeared, his old truck following a line of traffic headed east.

She pulled over to the side of the road, shut off the engine, and waited.

She checked her watch. She let a good five minutes go by. Then seven.

Finally, when she decided it was probably okay to move again, she started the engine and made a two-point turn in the middle of the road, heading back to the intersection. She made a left-hand turn and followed the route her father had taken into town a few minutes earlier.

She had every intention of settling in at home with a nice cup of tea. She also knew she had to check on Random and the chickens.

But first she had one last stop she wanted to make.

There were a few questions that still needed answers. And she knew just whom she had to see.

FORTY-SEVEN

Mrs. Fairweather's house was darker than the last time Candy had been there, a couple of hours ago. It was close to seven thirty on one of the longest days of the year, but the lowering sky had pressed down upon them, squeezing out most of the day's light. Some of the streetlights had come on, and a few of the homes along Shady Lane glowed warmly from within. The rain had tapered off, but the evening had a gloomy feel to it.

Candy parked the Jeep where she had before, in the gravel driveway. She switched off the engine and sat in the cabin for a few moments, staring out at the house. There was no light inside. The blinds and curtains were all shut. There was no movement that she could see, no sign of life. The place looked deserted.

She finally climbed out of the Jeep and walked toward the house, keeping her eyes on the front windows. But no curtain moved or blind angled up to indicate someone inside might be watching her.

She climbed the steps to the porch and knocked on the door.

"Mrs. Fairweather," she called in a controlled tone. "It's Candy Holliday again." She paused, then added, "I know you're in there. Are you okay? I need to talk to you."

She waited. Nothing.

She knocked again, louder this time. "Mrs. Fairweather?"

She put her ear close to the front door and listened.

After a few moments she heard a click, as if someone had unlocked the door from the inside. But the door remained shut. Candy rapped tentatively at it with her knuckles. "Mrs. Fairweather?"

This time, when she received no reply, she reached down and jiggled the door handle. To her surprise, it turned easily.

The door slid open a crack, with a low creak.

Candy peeked in hesitantly. "Mrs. Fairweather?"

She placed her hand on the wooden door and pushed it open a little farther, giving her a view of the dim hallway beyond. "Hello?"

The place still looked empty. But a light suddenly popped on in the kitchen at the far end of the hall. "Back here, dear," came a faint voice.

Candy's eyes flicked around, glancing at the dark rooms on either side of the hall. "Um, okay."

She stepped inside and closed the door behind her, moving cautiously. She didn't want a repeat of what she'd just encountered in the barn out at Crawford's Berry Farm.

She started along the hallway, slipping quickly past a couple of dark doorways on the left and right. As she approached the kitchen at the rear, she surveyed it suspiciously, wondering if she was walking into an ambush.

But she needn't have worried. There was no attack this time.

Mrs. Fairweather sat quietly at the kitchen table. Her hands were folded primly in front of her. She wore a dark blue dress with a white frill collar that looked like it might have been reserved for church and special occasions. Her hair was neatly done, though she looked pale, and her eyes were watery as she watched Candy enter the kitchen.

"Hello, dear," Mrs. Fairweather said softly. "Please, have a seat. We have a lot to talk about, and we don't have much time."

"Why not?" Candy asked as she approached the table. Still moving cautiously, she pulled out a chair opposite the elderly woman and settled uneasily on it.

Mrs. Fairweather shrugged rather daintily. She looked over at Candy with a placid expression. "I understand you've had a very busy day. You've been made an honorary member of the Heritage Protection League."

"That's right," Candy said. "It was a surprise, that's for sure. I understand you were aware of the whole thing — though I didn't see you there."

Mrs. Fairweather let out a sigh. "No, I'm afraid I wasn't up to a public appearance today."

"Why not?"

The elderly woman tilted her head. "I had other concerns." She paused. "I suppose you have lots of questions for me."

"I do," Candy said.

"About my family?"

Candy nodded. "Among other things."

"Of course. What would you like to know?"

"Tell me about Morgan. You called her your niece."

Mrs. Fairweather smiled enigmatically, and cast her eyes downward as she considered her response. "Yes, I like to think of her that way sometimes," she mused, "though of course we're distantly related."

"How so?" Candy asked.

"Well, let's see. Gideon Sykes was my cousin. Have you heard of him?"

"I have," Candy said. "He was the patriarch of the Sykes family, based out of Marblehead, Massachusetts, until he apparently took his own life at the Sykes mansion not too far from here."

"Yes, that was back in the eighties," Mrs. Fairweather said with a nod. "A tragic time. His death sent the whole family into disarray."

"It occurred at the same mansion that burned down a few years ago," Candy added.

Mrs. Fairweather gave her a vague look. "Yes, that place had been abandoned for years. The family eventually sold the property."

Candy continued, "Gideon was the husband of Daisy Porter-Sykes, who, I believe, is still alive — although she must be in her nineties by now."

"She'll be ninety-four in a few months," Mrs. Fairweather confirmed, "and still as tough as a New England winter."

"So I've heard." Candy paused a moment.

"I know that Daisy has a couple of grandsons who have made appearances here in Cape Willington. I don't suppose Morgan is related to them?"

"They're siblings, of course," Mrs. Fairweather said.

"Of course."

"They can be nice people when they want to be. Unfortunately, they've been a little . . . misled by their grandmother."

"But there's more to it than that, isn't there?" Candy said, leaning forward in her chair. "They're after something, aren't they — something here in Cape Willington? Morgan works for a New York firm that was trying to secretly buy the berry farm — because, I believe, she and her brothers wanted access to the woods out there, so they could search for the buried treasure of Silas Sykes."

"Ah, yes!" Mrs. Fairweather's eyes lit up briefly. "Buried treasure! How exciting!" But the light died quickly in her eyes. "Funny how those old legends can sometimes come true, isn't it?"

"So you knew about it — about the treasure?"

"I knew it was rumored to be buried around here somewhere," Mrs. Fairweather said, nodding. "But I didn't know it was out at the berry farm, until I saw that old foundation and graveyard with my own two eyes."

"How'd you find it?"

"Well, Miles showed it to me, of course. He stumbled upon it a while back, but I think he only began to guess its significance fairly recently. Strangely enough, he was the one who contacted me. He said he'd found something back in the woods at his farm. He knew I had some knowledge of the history of the village, since I've lived here for so long, so he asked me to take a look at it."

"When was this?"

Mrs. Fairweather pursed her lips, thinking. "A while ago. A year or two, maybe a little more. Time becomes a funny thing when you get older, you know."

"Did you know what it was when you saw it?"

Mrs. Fairweather shook her head. "Not at first. Not until I saw that name engraved into the cornerstone. But then I knew, yes. It was the remains of an old cabin that had once belonged to Silas Sykes."

"And how did Miles know that this legendary treasure was supposedly buried nearby?"

"Well, I told him, of course."

"Of course," Candy said, not quite seeing the connections, "but —"

Mrs. Fairweather interrupted her. "Would you do us a favor, dear?"

Candy stopped abruptly.

"Would you make us both a nice cup of tea?" Mrs. Fairweather continued, without waiting for a response. "And I made some lovely bean soup yesterday. It's there on the stove. Soups are always better on the second day, don't you agree? The flavors have more time to mix. You really must try some — and I'll have a little more, too, if you don't mind fixing two bowls for us." She pointed Candy toward the cupboards that contained the cups and bowls. A large simmering pot on the stove held the bean soup.

Candy did as the elderly woman asked, rising and walking to the counter. She dug into the cupboard for two teacups and looked around for the tea bags.

Mrs. Fairweather noticed her searching, and pointed helpfully. "They're in the basket there on the counter."

Candy looked where the elderly woman had indicated, and saw it then. It was a small white wicker basket with a handle and small pale flowers painted on the sides. It looked quite old and worn, an antique. Woven into the wicker on the front were

433

three capital letters, faintly green:
M.R.S.

Candy pulled her head back as if she'd just been slapped.

"Mrs. Fairweather," she said, wheeling around to face her host. "This basket . . . these initials. *M.R.S.* What do they stand for?"

The elderly woman shifted in her seat, so she could glance over her shoulder. "Oh, that's me, dear," Mrs. Fairweather said cheerily. "I have several baskets like that. They were given to me when I was still a young girl. It's my maiden name, you see. Sykes. Before I married Mr. Fairweather, I was Mary Rachel Sykes."

FORTY-EIGHT

"You're a *Sykes?*" The words came out of Candy in a long shocked breath. "But of course! Gideon was your cousin. Morgan is your relative. It just never occurred to me that . . ." She paused, her mind racing. "But that's it then, isn't it? Your baskets were found in the hoophouse near Miles's body. You were out there yesterday, weren't you? With Della when she . . ."

Candy let her voice trail off as Mrs. Fairweather looked at her sadly.

"Yes, dear, I'm afraid it's true," the elderly woman said, sounding contrite, "and I'm so sorry about what happened to Mr. Crawford. It was never my intention that any harm should come to him. He was a nice man. We just wanted to save the berry farm but, well, things got out of hand."

In a hushed voice, Candy asked, "Did you kill him?"

Mrs. Fairweather held a hand to her chest

and looked offended, as if someone had just cursed in her presence. "Me? Goodness gracious, no. I could never do anything like that. I'm not strong enough to swing a shovel like that, for one thing. Of course, I admit it was very foolish of me to leave my baskets there. I've had them so long! But I panicked, I suppose, and left too swiftly — once I knew Mr. Crawford wasn't going to wake up, of course. Now I'll never get them back."

Candy read the meaning between the words. "So . . . he wasn't supposed to die? It was an accident?"

Mrs. Fairweather was silent for several moments, as if thinking back over the events of the previous day. "I don't know, really. It certainly was never my plan for him to die like that. But I'm afraid I may have been the cause of the whole thing."

"And why is that?" Candy asked.

Mrs. Fairweather took in the deepest breath she could, her chest heaving out. She had a melancholy look on her face. "Because I'm the one who told him that old cabin had once belonged to Silas Sykes. And I told him the treasure might be around there somewhere. That's what caused all this trouble."

"How so?"

The elderly woman looked longingly at the stove. "I don't suppose we could have tea first? And a bit of soup? I'm feeling a bit — tired."

So Candy complied. She heated the water, placed two tea bags in the cups, and ladled warm bean soup into two bowls, which she placed on the table. She found spoons in a drawer, and laid those out as well. And finally she poured boiling water into the teacups, which she also brought to the table. Then she settled back onto her chair, sipping her tea as she studied the elderly woman.

"Should I call a doctor?" Candy asked, watching her carefully. "Or the police?"

Mrs. Fairweather waved a casual hand. "There's no time for that now. We should continue."

Candy hesitated, and then nodded once. "Okay. So you told Miles about the treasure — and then what?"

"Well, others found out about it, too, of course. That's when things began to get out of hand."

Candy thought about that for a moment. "Morgan," she said finally. "You told Morgan about it also, didn't you?"

Mrs. Fairweather nodded gravely. "I had to. It was my obligation. The family has been searching for that place for years — decades. Generations. It's an old family legend, part of our history. We'd heard it might be around there somewhere but we never knew for sure — until Mr. Crawford showed me that old foundation and grave-yard. I suspected it might have been what we'd been looking for all those years, so I did some research at the historical society, and found a few old sources that confirmed my suspicions. When I told Morgan about it during one of her visits, she went back to the city and began making offers on the place. Of course, Mr. Crawford refused to sell. And it made him suspicious of all of us."

"When did he realize you and Morgan were related?"

Mrs. Fairweather shook her head. "Not at first. Not until he started digging into the archives himself. I realized what he was do-ing. He was researching the place, trying to find out its history, and looking for informa-tion about where the treasure might be buried, so he could dig it up for himself. But I'd already taken measures to prevent that from happening."

She picked up her spoon and dipped it into the bowl of bean soup. She blew on it to cool it, raised it to her lips, and savored the flavor for a few moments. "This is wonderful," she said. "It's from an old family recipe. You should try it."

"I will, in a moment," Candy said, not wanting to get distracted. "So what kind of measures did you take?"

In response, the elderly woman pointed with her spoon to an antique credenza pushed up against the wall behind Candy. "You can look over there," she said.

Candy turned and studied the credenza. The upper shelves held fine china and pottery, as well as keepsakes and photos. There were several drawers in the lower half. She rose from her chair, walked over to it, and pulled open the top drawer.

"Next one, dear," Mrs. Fairweather said helpfully.

In the second drawer Candy found a faded manila folder, worn at the corners and held together by a thinly stretched brown rubber band. It appeared to contain a number of old, faded documents. "What's this?" she asked, pulling out the folder.

At first she thought they might be the missing deeds, but when she removed the rubber band and opened the folder, she saw they were pages torn from old historical books and records.

"I'll leave those with you," Mrs. Fairweather said. "They should be returned to the archives at the historical society. I apologize for the damage to the books, but at the time I thought I was doing the right thing."

Candy realized what they were — the missing folios Doc had mentioned. Pages ripped or snipped from books and historical records her father had checked.

"Why?" Candy asked, looking over at the elderly woman.

Mrs. Fairweather tilted her head again as she gave the question some thought. "Family loyalty, I suppose. I was trying to keep information about the treasure — and that property — a secret. But I must have missed something somewhere. I only knew later on, when I saw that treasure chest anonymously donated to the museum, that Mr. Crawford had actually found it — the treasure that had once belonged to Silas Sykes." She paused to eat another spoonful of the soup. "I think he did that on purpose, by the way, to send us a message — to let us know he'd found the treasure himself. But it was a foolish thing to do."

Candy closed the folder. "What was in the chest?" she asked.

"No one really knew for sure," Mrs. Fairweather said. "Gold, jewels, that sort of thing. The family could only speculate until we actually found it."

"But there was something else inside, wasn't there? Deeds?"

"Oh yes, those famous deeds. Those are part of the legend as well."

"Deeds to what?" Candy asked.

"Property. Here in Cape Willington."

"What properties?"

Mrs. Fairweather straightened in her chair and waved her arm around her. "All of them."

"*All* of them?"

Candy remembered now, something Della Swain had said to her in the barn at the berry farm a little while ago:

They were in that big leather pouch in the chest . . . deeds to properties all over Cape Willington. . . .

Candy felt a jolt go through her. "That's what they've been looking for all along, isn't it? The Sykes family? They didn't care about the gold. They wanted the deeds!"

"Apparently they're quite valuable," Mrs. Fairweather said. "I don't know the whole story, or the legalities of it all, but I've heard they could supersede all existing deeds for properties in the village and throughout the Cape."

Candy was stunned. "But that means

whoever has those deeds —"

"Could reclaim all of Cape Willington for themselves," Mrs. Fairweather said. Her demeanor lightened, and she smiled mischievously. "Think about it. All the businesses, all the properties — including Blueberry Acres and Pruitt Manor. All this land belonging to someone else." She chuckled softly to herself. "Of course, that would cause quite an uproar around here."

"Yes, I'm sure it would," Candy said, still trying to digest all she'd just heard. "And Miles had them?"

The amusement died in Mrs. Fairweather's eyes, and she shook her head. "We don't know. It's certainly possible. But he knew about them. That's what he was doing up in the archives — researching them. Of course, since he was suspicious of me, I couldn't spy on him myself. So I asked Elvira to monitor his activities when he was out at the museum. I told her it was for the good of the league, and for the community. Naturally, she willingly agreed, since she was sweet on him."

"Does she know about any of this?"

"Oh no." Mrs. Fairweather shook her head. "None of the ladies were aware of what was going on. Only myself . . . and

442

Della." This last word she said rather harshly.

Candy caught the nuance. "She said something to me out at the barn . . . something about a deal." Candy paused, thinking it through a little more. "She's the one who did it, right? She killed Miles? Hit him over the head with that shovel — just like she did to Neil a little while ago, and like she tried to do to me."

Mrs. Fairweather didn't appear surprised by this revelation, but it seemed to sadden her. "Unfortunately I misjudged that woman. I didn't realize the level of her . . . desperation. She's fled, of course, but she wanted the money first — the treasure. That's why she went out to the Crawford place this afternoon. She wanted to search it before she left town. She thought she might encounter someone out there, but she also knew we were out of time. The police interviewed both of us today, and you and your father were out here yesterday as well, asking about that old shovel of yours. We both knew it was only a matter of time before the authorities closed in on us. That put her in a bit of a tizzy."

"That was her motivation — the treasure?"

Mrs. Fairweather nodded. "Greed can be

an awful thing, can't it?" The elderly woman paused, and swallowed hard. "We had a general agreement — she could have the money, since I didn't care about it, and I would get the deeds." Mrs. Fairweather pushed away her bowl of soup. She suddenly looked exhausted. "Everything escalated when that wooden box showed up at the museum. Elvira told us about it, and Della began to put all the pieces together. She did her own research and realized what was going on. She found out about my involvement, so she came to me with a plan. She wanted to search the house out at the berry farm herself, and talked me into going along. We decided to pretend like we were picking berries. That's why I took my baskets along. Of course, as I said, I now realize how foolish that was."

"And you took our old shovel too," Candy said.

"Yes, and it almost worked. It was all part of Della's plan. She knew Miles would be furious if someone took the treasure from him, so she wanted to pin the whole thing on someone else — to cause a diversion. That's why she lured Lydia out there. Her plan was to hit him over the head with the shovel, knocking him out, and then leave the shovel there. We both thought they'd trace it back to Lydia — or to you. Either way, it would point the finger at someone else. But it all went wrong. Mr. Crawford showed up too early and surprised us. He knew what we were looking for. Della panicked —"

"And hit Miles too hard."

Mrs. Fairweather nodded. Her chin was low to her chest now. "As I said, I misjudged her. She was too strong. And when she saw what she'd done, she decided to finish the job. It was . . . quite awful to witness. But when it was done . . . well, there was nothing we could do to bring him back, was there?"

"How did you get the shovel?" Candy asked.

A small breath escaped from Mrs. Fairweather, but she pressed on. "I saw it in the backseat of Lydia's car a while ago, when I had a late appointment at the beauty parlor. I noticed the initials on it, and remembered seeing Doc with it when he came out to knock the icicles off my house. I couldn't figure out why Lydia had it. To be honest, I thought she was trying to steal it from you, and I wanted to make sure it got back to Blueberry Acres. So I took it from her car and put it in mine."

She managed to raise her head, looking

up at Candy. "I want you to know that I had every intention of returning it to you. But I forgot about it, until Della started putting together her plan." She sighed deeply. "I've made a mess of things, haven't I? But I'm trying to make things right now."

Candy had only a few more questions for her. "What about Morgan's role in this?" she asked. "Did she know about your plan?"

"Oh, no," Mrs. Fairweather said. "She tried to get me to do the opposite. She told me to stay out of it. She said she and her brother would take care of everything. But Miles was about to sell the place to someone else. Who knew what would happen then? So we decided to act while we could."

"And what about Della? Do you know where she's at now?"

"Oh, I'm sure she'll turn up soon enough," Mrs. Fairweather said vaguely.

Candy nodded. "I think that explains just about everything," she said, "but I have one final question. Last night, when I saw Lydia out at Blueberry Acres, she said she had one more stop to make before she left town. She didn't happen to stop by your house, did she?"

For the longest time Mrs. Fairweather studied Candy with her tired eyes. "You're very perceptive," she said finally. "It's no

446

wonder you have a reputation around town as a great detective. Della and I should have known better."

Candy pressed on. "Lydia knew — or suspected — that you took that shovel from her car, right?"

The elderly woman nodded. "We saw each other on the street outside the beauty parlor that day. She must have realized I took it." Her voice was becoming strained now, after all the talking she'd done. "You should eat your soup, dear. It's getting cold."

Candy looked down at the bowl in front of her. "What's in it?"

"As I said, it's an old family recipe." Her eyes had become unfocused, as if she were gazing into the distance — or remembering a much earlier, happier time. "I used to make it with my mother. We used brown sugar and molasses, plus I added a little mustard, which is my own secret ingredient, and sautéed onions. And there are a few other things in there as well."

"Well," Candy said, "it certainly looks delicious. And you're right — it is getting cold."

She took up her spoon, scooped some of the soup into it, and raised it to her nose so she could sniff it. She noticed Mrs. Fairweather watching her every movement with great interest. "And it smells wonderful," Candy said.

She began to move the spoon to her open mouth. She opened her lips.

"Wait," Mrs. Fairweather said.

The spoon hesitated in midair. Candy gave the elderly woman a questioning look.

Mrs. Fairweather looked like she was about to faint. "I made a mistake. Don't eat it."

"Why not? What's in it?"

She never received an answer.

A short time later, when the ambulance arrived, Mrs. Fairweather was dead.

FORTY-NINE

"Well, that should just about do it," Doc said, wiping his hands together. He surveyed his handiwork with a satisfied expression.

He'd removed the sign that read, NO BERRY PICKING TODAY and replaced it with another: OPEN FOR BERRY PICKING.

The unsettled weather of the previous evening had cleared out. They'd had a few overnight sprinkles but the dark clouds were gone, and the sun had returned. The ground was still damp throughout the strawberry fields, but it wouldn't hinder the morning's picking operations.

"Well, would you look at that," Doc said, shading his eyes against the sunlight as he gazed out over the surrounding fields. "Practically the whole town's turned out this morning."

"They sure have," Candy said. She stood beside her father, looking out over the fields as well.

The first pickers had arrived right at eight that morning, and their numbers had increased steadily over the next hour. There were fifty or sixty people out there now, walking the fields, searching the low bushes for ripe red berries.

Crates of them were now being loaded onto trucks and making their way to Town Park. Some of the league ladies were already back in town, overseeing last-minute preparations for the event, but Alice Rainesford was still here. She'd stationed herself at the tables just outside the barn at the berry farm, where she kept a close eye on who picked what, and how much, so she could make an accounting of everything for financial purposes. She and Candy had agreed to settle up at the end of the morning.

But not all the berries were going to the Fair. Other villagers had turned out, couples and families and senior citizens, filling up baskets with the fresh berries, before the picking season was gone for another year.

Candy heard a dog bark and glanced to her left. Random was playing fetch with a couple of kids, who were tossing a stick for him. He looked as happy as she'd ever seen him.

"That dog is going to love it out here," Doc said.

Candy nodded her agreement. "Depending on what Neil decides to do. But he says he's thinking of keeping the place and running it himself for a while."

As if on cue, Neil Crawford emerged from the farmhouse and walked over to where they stood at the edge of the fields. He had a bandage wrapped around his head, and one of his eyes was blackened, but he looked surprisingly upbeat. "I couldn't have done any of this without your help," he said to them as he approached. "And the villagers are wonderful. I can see why Dad loved this place, and stayed on here for so long."

"It's a good community," Candy agreed.

Doc had picked Neil up at the hospital that morning. The medical staff had wanted him to stay longer for observation, but he had insisted on being here when the picking started. He wanted to see the operation for himself, and he'd had a chance to meet many of the villagers.

Maggie and Herr Georg were out there in the fields somewhere, filling a few baskets with berries before they opened the bakery for the day. Candy had spotted them holding hands just a little while ago. Judicious F. P. Bosworth had caught a ride out with Sally Ann Longfellow, who had wanted to bring along her goats but had trouble

451

getting them into her car. Doris Oaks had showed up with Roy perched on her shoulder. Cotton Colby, Elvira Tremble, and Brenda Jenkins had all showed up as well, though none of them had much to say about the loss of two of their members. They seemed determined to get through today and then assess the damage to their organization and its reputation.

Despite all that had happened over the past few days, the morning had a festive feel to it. But everyone involved with those recent events knew they had barely averted disaster.

"I just want to say again how much I appreciate everything you've done, for me and my father," Neil said, looking over at Candy and Doc. "Without your help, none of this would have been possible. And, well, I'm sure Dad's happy with the way things turned out — wherever he is."

"It's the least we could do," Doc said. "You're part of the community now, Neil. You're one of us — if you want to be, that is."

Neil let out a big breath as he studied the buildings and the fields. "It's a lot of work, that's for sure. But this is where I grew up. I have a history here. It would be a shame to sell it — especially after all that's happened." He turned back to Candy, his brown eyes focusing on her. "And, of course, there's no way I can possibly thank *you* for all you've done.

Candy waved a hand casually, downplaying her role. "Oh, it was nothing, really," she told him. "Like my dad said — it was the least I could do."

"No, it's more than that." Neil looked at her with great sincerity. "You saved my life last night."

Candy smiled. "I seem to remember it was the other way around."

A moment passed between them, as they stood looking at each other. But oblivious to that fact, Doc spoke up.

"Well, it's all behind us now." He slipped his hands into the back pockets of his chinos and leaned his head back so he could look up at the bright blue sky. "And my, what a beautiful day it is."

They heard the toot of a horn behind them then, and turned to see Chief Durr pull up in his police cruiser. He spotted them, climbed out of the car, and walked over to join them.

"Morning, everyone," he said with a tip of his hat. "How's everyone doing today?"

"Just fine," Doc said. "Taking in some sun, and about ready to go pick some more berries."

"I have instructions to pick up a few baskets myself," the chief said, looking out over the fields. "Wendy's going to make strawberry jam this weekend. She usually puts up a couple dozen jars. Lasts us most of the year."

Neil made a move toward a table that held baskets of berries. "I'll put some in the car for you," he said.

"Hey, wait a minute. You're injured," Doc said. "I'll help with that." And together the two walked off, leaving Candy standing next to the chief.

He was silent for a few moments, as he surveyed the activity around them, until he said, "Well, once again, Ms. Holliday, you've solved one of our local mysteries." He turned to look at her with a tight expression on his weathered face. "You know you should have contacted us last night before you went over to Mrs. Fairweather's place. You put yourself in danger — again."

Candy shrugged. "I know that, Chief, but it was just a hunch."

"It was a good one," he said honestly.

"Any idea what was in that soup of hers?"

The chief nodded. "Hemlock, they think — lots of it, although we're still running tests to verify that. Nasty stuff. Apparently it's just some type of weed. They say it looks like parsnip, so it can be tricky to identify. And all parts of the plant are poisonous."

"Where'd she get it?" Candy asked.

"We think she grew it somewhere in her garden. We have someone over at her place checking on it right now. Good thing you didn't eat any of that soup yourself."

Candy nodded in agreement. "Good thing," she said, and wondered why, at the last moment, Mrs. Fairweather had a change of heart and stopped her from eating that spoonful of soup — though Candy had never intended to eat it. She'd suspected it was poisoned. But she'd wanted to see if the elderly woman would actually let her.

In the end, Mrs. Fairweather had done the right thing.

Of course, Candy remembered, *I did eat a slice of her strawberry pie yesterday. . . .*

Breaking into her thoughts, Chief Durr said, "Well, we'll need you over at the station later on today so we can do a few interviews and close the book on this thing. And as I've said before, if you ever need a job, just let me know."

Candy gave him a warm smile. "I appreciate that, Chief. But I think I'll stick to farming. It's safer."

"I hear that." He nodded firmly. "Well, I

suppose I should get a move on. See you over at the Fair?"

"I'll see you there."

"I'm looking forward to having some strawberry shortcake," he said with a grin, and he started off toward the table to pay for his berries.

But Candy stopped him. "Hey, Chief!" she called.

Chief Durr stopped and turned back toward her with a questioning look. "Yeah?"

"Any word about Della Swain?"

"Oh, that." He nodded. "I meant to tell you. I heard just a little while ago. They found her car in an abandoned barn up on the north side of the Cape. She was still inside it."

"Did she have the coins and gold?"

"She did," the chief said. "We've recovered just about everything."

"Did she have any deeds with her?"

"Deeds?" The chief gave her a quizzical look. "Don't know anything about any deeds."

He turned and started away again, but Candy had a final question for him.

"So was she alive when they found her?"

The chief stopped and turned back, shaking his head. "No, unfortunately she was dead. There was an opened plastic container on the seat beside her. It looked like she'd been ill. It was the same thing we suspect happened to Lydia St. Graves. Apparently they both ate some bad soup."

EPILOGUE

Morgan Sykes Kingsbury stood at her office window on the seventh floor overlooking Park Avenue in Manhattan and frowned. "Of course I had no idea about this," she said into the phone cupped to her ear. "I told her repeatedly to stay out of it. But she grew too stubborn in her old age. She wouldn't listen to reason."

"She was loyal to the family," said the male voice at the other end of the line. "Perhaps she thought she was helping us."

"Of course that's what she thought," Morgan replied somewhat testily, "but she was in way over her head. And look where it led her."

"Yes, her passing is unfortunate. But she helped us locate that treasure box. We're one step closer to our goal. Let's at least give her credit for that."

Morgan let out a sigh. Sometimes she thought her brother was an idiot. "How do you see that? The last time I checked, none of us have access to that treasure. It's locked up in a police vault somewhere. We'll never get our hands on it now. It was a wasted effort."

"Not necessarily so," Porter Sykes told her calmly. "It's out in the open now. We know where it's at. The rest is just a matter of logistics."

"How do you see that?" Morgan was losing her patience. She'd worked for the better part of two years trying to get Miles Crawford to sell his farm. Now it seemed all her efforts were in vain.

"You forget who we're dealing with. A small-town police force. Backwoods folks. We'll just spread a little money around. Bribes can make people extremely cooperative, I've found — even those in the law enforcement business."

Morgan's bad mood eased just a bit. "You know someone in the police department up there?"

"I have my sources," her brother replied. "This is not over yet — not by a long shot. As I said, the hard part is done."

"So you think you can get your hands on that treasure?"

"The gold?" Porter laughed softly. "Who cares about that?"

"What about the deeds?"

"Ahh, yes, the deeds. The Holy Grail for the Sykes family."

There was silence for a few moments on the other end of the phone, prompting Morgan to say in an exasperated tone, "Well?"

"They were in the box, obviously, just as we suspected. But they seem to have disappeared."

"Disappeared? To where?"

"No one knows, but my guess is that Crawford hid them somewhere before he died. Or maybe he just destroyed them. That's what we — you and I — have to figure out."

"How are we going to do that?"

"I have a few ideas."

Morgan wondered what he meant, but put that aside for the moment. "How's Grandmother?"

"Daisy? Ornery as ever. She wants this over."

"As do we all," Morgan said. "So what's our next step?"

"I'm putting out some feelers now," Porter said, "but I suggest you lie low for a while. You were at Aunt Rachel's house while all this was going on. You don't want to get on their radar up there."

Morgan didn't want to tell her brother

that she feared she already was. That local blueberry farmer, Candy Holliday, and her father had come snooping around her aunt's house just at the wrong time. Morgan had barely had enough time to get herself and her aunt situated at the house before they'd shown up looking for that damned shovel.

Morgan's gaze drifted across the floor of her office, to where a pair of black rubber boots sat in the corner. She'd bought them in Europe, on a spending spree six months earlier. She'd liked their design, but they had a distinctive star pattern on the heels, and she was concerned she'd left footprints when she'd gone out to the berry farm that morning to try to prevent her aunt from doing something stupid. But she'd been too late. The other woman, Della, had already fled, and Morgan had found her aunt hovering near the body of the dead man, frozen with fear and regret. It was all she could do to get the woman back home and safely seated in her garden in an effort to calm her down. Fortunately, they'd both been good actresses when the Hollidays had showed up unexpectedly.

Now she'd have to get rid of the boots. Too bad. She liked them a lot.

And she had a feeling this was just the beginning of the sacrifices she'd have to make for her family's schemes. She wasn't sure she liked where all this was headed.

"It's getting too dangerous," Morgan said into the phone. "Maybe we should back off — just let it go."

Porter laughed again, his voice sounding harsh and mocking over the phone. "Losing your nerve, little sister? Just when it's getting good? Well, you'd better steel yourself, because the ride's going to get a lot rougher before it's done. But look on the bright side — we have a front-row seat for all the fun. The villagers of Cape Willington, Maine, have no idea what's about to happen. For them, the worst is yet to come."

RECIPES

HERR GEORG'S *OBSTKUCHEN*
German Strawberry Torte

Cake/Crust

3 eggs
3/8 cup sugar
3 tablespoons cinnamon sugar*
3/8 cup butter, softened
pinch of salt
1 1/3 cups flour
1 teaspoon baking powder
Fine bread crumbs

Filling

2 pints strawberries
3 tablespoons strawberry jam

For The Cake/Crust:

In a large bowl and using a hand mixer on high speed, blend the eggs, sugar, butter, and salt.

Mix until the mixture is foamy.

Add the flour and baking powder. Mix until blended.

Grease a flat baking pan, sprinkling the bottom with fine bread crumbs.

Pour the dough into the pan, spreading it to the edges.

Bake at 400 degrees for 12 to 15 minutes or until golden brown.

Remove the cake and cool.

For The Filling:

Hull the strawberries and place the whole fruits on the cake top.

In a small pot, heat the strawberry jam.

Using a pastry brush, spread the warm jam over the strawberries. This makes a glaze.

* To make cinnamon sugar, add 1 teaspoon of cinnamon powder to 3 tablespoons of sugar and mix together.

Guten appetit!

MAGGIE TREMONT'S GERMAN STRAWBERRY APPLE PANCAKES

1 cup milk
3 eggs
3/4 cup flour
3 tablespoons sugar
2 tablespoons butter

1 medium-to-large apple, peeled and
   chopped
6 to 8 medium-size strawberries, hulled and
   chopped
1/4 teaspoon cinnamon

Preheat the oven to 375 degrees.

In a bowl, whisk together the milk, eggs,
flour, and 2 tablespoons of the sugar.

In a large ovenproof skillet, melt the butter at medium-high heat.

Add the apple, strawberries, and cinnamon, and the remaining 1 tablespoon of
sugar.

Reduce the heat to medium and cook, stirring often, for 2 to 3 minutes, until the fruit
is soft.

Remove the pan from the heat.

Pour the batter from the bowl over the
fruit mixture in the pan.

Place the pan in the oven.

Bake for 30 minutes or until the pancake
is light brown and fluffy.

Cut the pancake into wedges and serve.

If you do not have an ovenproof pan, put
the cooked fruit into a casserole dish or pie
pan, pour the batter over the fruit, and bake
the same as above.

This is a wonderful recipe for brunch!

PASTA WITH STRAWBERRY, LEEK, AND FENNEL

fennel, one half of a bulb, cut into small pieces, about 1 cup
1 leek
1 dozen strawberries
2 tablespoons olive oil
2 tablespoons butter
angel hair pasta, 8 ounces
parmesan cheese, grated, 1/2 cup

Chop the fennel and leek into small cubes or strips.

Hull and chop the strawberries.

In a skillet, melt the olive oil and the butter.

Sauté the leek and fennel for 10 minutes on medium heat.

Add the strawberries to the pan, sauté for an additional 2 to 3 minutes or until they are soft.

While the leek and fennel are in the pan, fill a pot with water and boil it for the pasta.

Add the pasta to the boiling water and cook for the time listed on the box.

Drain the pasta.

Add the leek, fennel, and strawberry to the pasta and mix.

Serve with grated parmesan cheese sprinkled on the top.

*This is a favorite dish
at the Lightkeeper's Inn!*

KEY LIME STRAWBERRY
WHIPPED TOPPING PIE

Pie

1 can sweetened condensed milk
4 egg yolks
4 ounces key lime juice
1 9-inch graham pie shell

Topping

1 cup strawberries blended in a blender
1 cup whipping cream
1 teaspoon vanilla

For The Pie:

In a mixing bowl on low speed, blend the condensed milk and egg yolks.

Add the key lime juice and continue mixing.

Mix until blended smoothly.

Pour into the pie shell.

Bake at 350 degrees for 20 minutes.

Chill until cool enough to cover with the topping.

For the Topping:

Mix the blended strawberries, whipping cream, and vanilla with a mixer on Whip for approximately 8 minutes or until peaks form.

Drop by large spoonfuls on top of the pie and smooth out with a knife.

Refrigerate.

The strawberry offsets the strong key lime flavor and makes for a fruity deliciousness!

THE PROS AND CONS OF RAISED GARDEN BEDS

by Candy Holliday
Interim Managing Editor, the *Cape Crier*

It may be the end of June, but it's never too late to start a new garden — or two or twenty! One of the first choices to make when starting your garden is whether to till into the ground for your garden, or build raised garden beds. I have both at Holliday's Blueberry Acres, so I've learned the ins and outs of both over the past few years. Time, money, and space are all involved in the decision, so let's get started.

If you want to build raised beds, first decide how big and how many. A perfect size is eight by four feet. This allows plenty of room to grow vegetables, and you'll be able to garden up and down both sides of the bed without having to step inside it, or requiring a path down the middle. A foot deep is a good depth, leaving plenty of room for healthy roots to grow.

Next, decide which type of wood you want to use for the framing of your bed. Cedar is popular because it's a hardwood, and repels insects. Pine is also fine to use, but it won't last as many years.

Measure your yard space so you can figure out how many beds you can fit in. Once you've done that, you can purchase the wood. Many garden centers sell the easily attachable corners for the beds, or you can nail or screw them together.

Deciding what to fill them with is the next step. I prefer a compost mix. Garden centers will deliver this to your home. Then get out the wheelbarrows and shovels, and fill the beds to the top with compost. This can be costly at the start, but once the raised beds are set up, they don't need much more work. You'll also want to add compost to a dug garden to improve the soil, especially in the first year.

One of the biggest differences between the two types of beds is the weeds. I've found that raised beds have very few weeds, while dug beds can be endlessly weedy, especially by August. Pulling out weeds is an activity that needs to be kept up all summer. However, raised beds tend to dry out faster than dug beds, so they need to be watered frequently.

Dug beds are ideal for certain types of crops, especially pumpkins, squashes, and large vegetables. I like giving them plenty of room to spread out and grow.

So, the pluses for raised beds: They're neat, easy to care for, and they last for years, but they do dry out faster, needing more water, and they don't offer as much room for larger squashes and melons.

The pluses for dug beds: They provide more room for larger vegetables, and require less watering, but they have way more weeds than raised beds, and need to be tilled every year.

Whichever you choose, your work will be well worth the effort when harvest time arrives!

CPSIA information can be obtained
at www.ICGtesting.com
Printed in the USA
FFOW05n1045130914

9 781410 468987